WITHDRAWN
UTSA LIBRARIES

WITHDRAWN
UTSA LIBRARIES

THE MASTERS AFFAIR

Also by Burt Hirschfeld

FIRE ISLAND

THE MASTERS AFFAIR

―――――― ★ ――――――

BURT HIRSCHFELD

ARBOR HOUSE

NEW YORK

Copyright © 1971 by Burt Hirschfeld and Irwin Touster

All rights reserved, including the right of reproduction
in whole or in part in any form. Published in the United
States by Arbor House Publishing Co., Inc., New York,
and simultaneously in Canada by Nelson, Foster &
Scott, Ltd.

First Edition
SBN: 0-87795
Library of Congress Catalog Card Number: 70-139296
Manufactured in the United States of America

LIBRARY
The University of Texas
At San Antonio

Some kinds of wrong there are,
which flesh and blood
cannot endure.
—Francis Beaumont and John Fletcher

THE MASTERS AFFAIR

I

By NOW his eyes were accustomed to the darkened office. He went into the adjoining room, past some metal desks, and examined the street below through a window streaked and stained and neatly lettered in black and gold:

GERBER, LITTLE & KINDERMAN
THEATRICAL ACCOUNTANTS

He raised the window eight inches and lowered the frayed green shade, considered the result. Perfect for what he was going to do. He rolled a typist's chair into place and sat down. He lifted the guitar case onto his lap and opened it.

Everything was still secure. Working with controlled speed, he peeled away the tape and wiped each metal part with a dry, clean cloth. Next he fitted the barrel into the stock and inserted the trigger mechanism, then locked it all together.

The rifle felt good in his hands, reassuring. It was a pleasurable sensation. In a swift practiced move, he snapped the butt up against his shoulder, sighted down through the window opening at the Hotel Americana, almost two blocks away. His finger squeezed the trigger. *Clunk.* Satisfied, he leaned the weapon against the wall.

He adjusted the watch on his wrist to a more comfortable position and sat back to wait, hands limp in his lap, face turned toward the window.

The summer air was charged with Manhattan night sounds. Hoarse cries and forced laughter, the screech of brakes and the impatient honking of horns. He heard it all through an invisible baffle and was unmoved. He listened again to a private, interior summons, a jangling systole that demanded his attention.

Who called?

Why an unknown voice? A voice beaded with . . . with mockery, conveying a soft authority, an implicit threat. A cunning voice that seemed to know it all, to understand everything. It was as if his so carefully hoarded secret had been exposed, as if once more he had been placed on display and commanded to perform to the will of an unseen and unnamed master.

Why a stranger?

Always this way. This renewal of disappointment and despair. The awful fear. He made a great effort to evict those serrated echoes from his head, to concentrate exclusively on what he was going to do.

Must do . . .

Increased activity along the street drew his attention. The theaters were emptying now and everywhere there was the flow of people and cars, an intensification of noise. He blinked and raised his eyes. Taking up positions on the steps of the hotel were reporters, photographers, the television crews. Uniformed policemen had set up wooden restraining barriers to hold back the crowds and between them doormen whistled for taxis and ushered sleek men and women into limousines. How credulous they were! Every one of them oblivious to the danger. They must learn the truth, be made to *understand . . .*

He fingered the thick, drooping mustache. It felt strange, an unnatural attachment. He looked again at his watch. The subject was late—why?

He set himself against a growing uncertainty and kneeled, peered through the window opening. He reached for the rifle. The texture of the wooden stock, the cool steel, the neatly tooled bolt handle; it felt *right.* He drew a .30 caliber cartridge from his pocket and wiped it clean, dropped it into the chamber. He shot the bolt and brought the rifle to bear on the steps of the hotel.

Under the entrance canopy, five steps led to a broad terrace and to the double glass doors that opened into the ornate lobby. He had a clear field of fire.

Sweat gleamed on his brow and his eyes blurred. He imagined he could already see that familiar face floating on the front sight. *Not yet* . . . He blinked and lowered the rifle, wiped his eyes. He became aware of his watch, heavy and oppressive, the band constricting. He took it off, put it down on the nearest desk.

He lifted the rifle and planted his left elbow on his knee in the accepted form, holding steady, ready to do the correct thing.

II

"HIS EMINENCE the Cardinal extends his profound gratitude to all of his dear good friends for helping him to celebrate his seventieth birthday and wishes each and everyone of you a very good night."

That final message delivered, the distinguished Catholic layman stepped away from the microphone, hoping to kiss again the ring of Henry Cardinal McCoy. He was too late. Cardinal McCoy had already left the dais, was engulfed by well-wishers. The distinguished Catholic layman thought about pursuing His Eminence, but gave it up as a bad idea.

As for the Cardinal, he shed celebrants with a cool social dexterity acquired over half a century as a priest of Rome, smiling at this one, speaking a few words to someone else, nodding with benevolent but brief concern. He made his way to the public lobby behind the ballroom, where he knew Father Perez would be waiting.

Father Nestor Perez was a slender man with moist eyes and the patient expression of a man used to waiting. He watched with interest while the Cardinal bid good night to his many attractive, successful, and influential friends. On such occasions, Father Perez frequently passed the time attempting to identify the various important people. Tonight, the Governor and the Mayor; but of course they had been easy, their faces so well known. Four or five television performers, two movie actors, some diplomats, three newspaper publishers, the president of the Patrolmen's Benevolent Associations, and W. W. Masters.

It pleased Father Perez to be able to see W. W. Masters.

That elegant face and physique had seldom been displayed in public, nad seldom been reproduced in the newspapers or on television. Had not Cardinal McCoy pointed out Masters earlier, Father Perez might not have recognized the Director of the Internal Investigative Agency. The Agency, as it was referred to by those who knew of its existence, was one of those rare and very worthy government bureaus that labored with quiet effectiveness, seldom calling attention to itself. Father Perez supposed such planned obscurity aided IIA agents in the performance of their delicate and sometimes dangerous tasks.

He watched Masters closely, viewing him as one of God's blessed personages, a good and perhaps even a holy man. That finely boned face, the erect, graceful posture, the tastefully graying hair and neatly trimmed mustache to match. Perez saw Masters and Cardinal McCoy come together, speaking and laughing in the subdued, intimate way of the truly powerful.

Too soon their talk was ended. They shook hands and parted and Father Perez felt some regret; for him, a special moment was over. His eyes trailed after Masters and he spied the cane, the perceptible limp, and the priest felt sadness that such a fine man should be afflicted in any way. But God's ways, he reminded himself, were not man's ways.

Masters paused on his way out, turned back to greet another man, a man equally tall, equally graceful. Father Perez identified him as Charles Reese, the United States Senator from Connecticut. There were some priests at the archdiocese who insisted that Senator Reese would win the Presidential nomination of the Democratic Party at the convention later in the summer. Some even went so far as to claim that he was the only man who could reconcile the differences that divided the country, pull the disparate elements together, and make America more truly a nation indivisible. But those who said so, Father Perez remembered with some distaste, were almost always Jesuits, and they were much too cerebral.

Nevertheless, Father Perez could not deny that Charles Reese had the manner of a leader, perhaps even a President. He was handsome in that special way that academic men were often handsome, the individual features strong and cleanly sculpted but the overall result slightly delicate, perhaps, Father Perez thought, even decadent. He possessed the casual, confident air that Father Perez had often detected in men educated in the exclusive schools of the Northeast, those who had become accustomed early in life to the fine things rich and indulgent parents could supply.

Unlike his Jesuit friends, Father Perez viewed Senator Reese as a man false to his background, his training, his traditions. The Senator, for example, had been a vocal and effective spokesman in the fight to abolish the abortion laws and he had campaigned vigorously against direct Federal aid to parochial schools. At the very least, the man was misguided and Father Perez couldn't help wondering what Mr. Masters could find to say to him.

The priest's ruminations ended when he saw Cardinal McCoy coming toward him, ready to depart. With a fixed smile on his thin brown face, Father Perez led the way to a side entrance, where a policeman stood guard over the Cardinal's Cadillac.

W. W. Masters watched the departure with no change of expression. "A beautiful person, His Eminence," he remarked to Charles Reese.

The Senator answered without emphasis. "A man of considerable authority and diverse interests. He makes a formidable political enemy, I suspect."

Masters brought his eyes back to Reese. "To measure all men as political friends or enemies, Charles—that way lies paranoia."

Reese laughed easily. "An occupational disease. It's hard not to view men—even like McCoy—in terms of votes, blocs of votes, campaign workers, funds. Politics tends to dehumanize the best of us."

Nodding amiably, Masters reached for Reese's arm, started him across the foyer toward the stairway leading down to the main lobby. "Why do you suppose it is, Charles, that we see so little of each other in Washington? You are almost never at those receptions I manage to attend."

"Politics again, and the discretion of Washington's hostesses.

They see us as political opposites, often enemies, I imagine, and want to keep peace at their dinner parties."

"Aren't we both loyal Americans, Charles?"

Reese grinned briefly. "I've certainly never heard your patriotism questioned in public . . ."

Masters nodded his approval. "Very good," he said. "But then you've always been good with words. Your speech this evening, very polished. To the point, carefully nonpolitical, and therefore triply effective."

Reese felt a vague discomfort, as if he were being manipulated, as if Masters were probing, trying to locate some exploitable flaw. He glanced at the other man and saw nothing remotely sinister on that fine face.

"Our being seen together," he said, "may be the most significant event of the evening."

"Why should that be, Charles?"

"Here we have the discreet, the nonpolitical director of the IIA with what some consider the very liberal Senator from Connecticut. One published photograph may very well swing a substantial segment of middle America into my camp."

"Or turn them against me," Masters replied softly.

"There we have the instinct of a natural politician. Or is it simply the quality that makes for a good policeman?"

"Don't judge us too harshly. At the Agency we look for the truth and try to dispense justice equally for everybody. This is, after all, a nation of laws."

"I'd never admit it in public, but we both know better. Men run this government, all governments. Men and power. Money. Pressure."

"As long as the right men use power rightly," Masters said. "Don't you agree, Charles?"

"Why is it," Reese said, annoyed by the possessive touch of Masters' hand on his elbow, "that I get the impression you're behaving like everybody's political guide?"

Masters smiled and said nothing. Ahead of them, the glass entrance doors that led to Seventh Avenue. Masters stopped, pivoting on the cane so that he faced Reese. "Charles," he said quietly, "my career has been built on the proposition that the most effective public servant stays outside the political sector. Elective politics lessen a man's independence, make him susceptible to lobbying, to powers other than his own conscience. I've played several roles, but I have shown no partisanship."

It was true, Reese told himself. Masters was one of those almost silent, almost invisible men in government who owned a growing power, yet were carefully nonpolitical. Somehow he managed to find admirers among different political groups, becoming all things to all men. Or nothing to any single man, Reese corrected wryly. Yet Masters had managed to maintain a kind of private integrity that made him admired, gave him an apparently unsolicited reservoir of powerful support.

Reese reminded himself that he really knew very little about the man and even less about his work, and that troubled him as a United States Senator. For some time Reese had felt uneasy about the rising power of the IIA: there was its invisible funding, done through the Treasury Department budget, with its own allocations and specific activities never fully revealed even to those elected officials who were entitled to pass on them. Masters and his IIA were indeed in a unique position. The man was better known nationally than the truly anonymous head of the supersecret CIA, yet far less public in his pronouncements than J. Edgar Hoover of the more publicized and prominent FBI. And his agency was neither associated with intelligence (as the CIA) nor with interstate police duties (as the FBI). Yet by his association with Treasury, his access to tax records, for example, his vague and, thereby, flexible jurisdiction of troubleshooting for *all* the Department's bureaus, he emerged as a man of great but not defined powers, with relatively few enemies, and enormous influence. Quite a challenge and opportunity for any man, Senator Reese reflected.

Perhaps soon, Reese thought, after the convention, after the election, he might be in a position to change all that. With hard work, planning, and a great deal of luck, he might end up in the oval office in the White House, in a position to demand more information about the activities of the Internal Investigative Agency and W. W. Masters.

"After you, Charles," Masters said, opening one of the glass doors. He indicated that Reese was to precede him.

Outside, Reese turned back, waiting for the other man to catch up. It seemed to him that Masters somehow managed to make every pronouncement sound like a threat, all done in very circumspect language with no change of tone. Reese also conceded grudgingly that the threat might be one of his own making, all in his own mind.

The Senator looked out at the photographers and reporters as they advanced up the hotel steps. A picture with Masters would undoubtedly influence some people to vote for him in November. Politics, he reminded himself ruefully, was indeed the art of practical men.

Masters took Reese's arm. "The press," he said. "Let's not keep them waiting."

"It seems to me," Reese said, continuing their exchange, "that your hand has been evident in congressional committees, on the floor of the Senate, even in the White House."

"Really, Charles, you disappoint me. You know people frequently see that which exists only in their minds. A dangerous indulgence for a public man, don't you agree?"

"As director of the IIA, I suggest your influence is subtle, more wide-ranging than your congressional mandate intended."

"If so, it's because I've always tried to act only in the best interests of my country."

"*Our* country," Reese corrected mildly.

"Our country," Masters conceded. They were at the top of the steps now, the photographers ranged below, snapping away. Masters arranged himself so that the cane was concealed.

Reese wondered about that; Masters seldom allowed himself to be photographed, with or without the cane. He could have easily avoided the photographers, yet had made no effort to do so. Why? And why did he want to be seen with Charles Reese?

"Our country," Masters said again. "Let us wish it well."

Reporters were shouting questions and television interviewers with microphones extended came up the steps.

"Mr. Masters, Senator Reese," one of them asked. "Seeing you two gentlemen together—should we infer some sort of political support is indicated? After all—"

"Neither Senator Reese nor I," Masters said, producing a good-natured chuckle, "questions the right of the media to assume anything it wants to assume. All of us have the privilege of being wrong." The reporters laughed and Masters went on more soberly. "The Senator and I are just a couple of workers in the Washington vineyards visiting the big city to help our good friend, Cardinal McCoy, celebrate his birthday. His Eminence is a fine man, a great American."

"Senator," a reporter called. "Do you agree with Mr. Masters that nothing political is involved here?"

"Mr. Masters said it very well," Reese answered. "Let's not make a Federal case out of it . . ."

The reporters laughed again. Masters leaned closer to Reese. "Your jokes are much better than mine, Charles. Your laughs are bigger."

The two men started down the steps, the newsmen giving way before them. On the third step, Masters paused, searched the crowded street.

"My car isn't here . . ."

"Can I give you a lift?" Reese said.

In the cacophony of city noise, the babble of voices, the blaring of horns, the shriek of brakes, the distant report of the assassin's shot went almost unheard . . .

III

EIGHT THOUSAND btu's of conditioned air circulated around the bedroom, drying the thin coat of perspiration on Hellman's naked skin. He focused hard, trying to perceive the precise instant the moisture evaporated, drawing the heat from his body. A stiff, odd sensation, it made the hairs on his body and arms tremble faintly. Hellman lifted himself into a sitting position, adjusting the extra pillow at the small of his back. He reached for the remote control unit and switched on the television set.

The picture faded into view. As usual, too much yellow in the flesh tones. Hellman swore silently at the contrived incompetence of industry and changed channels. Soon the eleven o'clock news. He turned up the sound.

The girl next to him made a protesting sound and punched the mattress to signify her annoyance. She rolled onto her back, pale breasts flattening, the nipple areas small and iceberg pink. She flung an arm across her eyes.

"The TV woke me," she complained.

"You're too young to sleep so much."

She looked up at him and approved of what she saw. A thick, hairy chest, square shoulders, the almost complete absence of a neck. His black hair was shaggy and unkempt and his dark eyes were lidded, as if he remained on the near edge of sleep. A splendid animal, she told herself; getting him had been a coup. She had gone to bed with older men before, but Hellman was the first lover of consequence she had ever had. A smug warmth filtered through her young body; every one of the girls at Hiram Concord College had been turned on to Dan Hellman, even before this afternoon. Before any of them had actually seen him. Well, why not? His reputation was increasing all over the campuses of the northeast and she was sure, *absolutely sure*, that one day soon he would rank with contemporary heroes like Ralph Nader and Marcuse and Eldridge Cleaver. Admittedly he had yet to attain that level, but he was on his way, a man who knew how to beat the system. A man who stood up to authority, who confronted and confounded the Establishment. What was the subject of his lecture that afternoon? Oh, yes—"A System in Decay, U.S.A."

Beautiful!

"You'll want to shower," he said. His voice was a rough growl, triggered good vibes in her. She inched closer. "I dig the way you smell," she murmured. "Everywhere is good."

"Get dressed."

"Not yet." She touched his thigh. "If you want, I can stay all night. It's all right, is what I mean. Since the big sit-in last semester, no more curfew in the girls' dorm."

Hellman kept his gaze fastened to the TV screen. The announcer was reporting on the most recent happenings in the Middle East. Hellman's concentration faltered; there was nothing for him to use in that situation.

"Anytime you want," the girl was saying. "Just call the dorm. Leave a message, if I'm not there."

Hellman looked at her. She had the kind of prettiness you saw frequently in sleepy Southern towns or on Midwestern campuses. The short nose, the shiny cheeks, the light-colored eyes and freckles; such girls were among the fringe benefits of Hellman's work. Hellman could claim a modest celebrity as a leader in the struggle for people's rights. He liked to call himself a member of the People's Lobby, to say he was out front in the Citizens' Revolution. To this end, Hellman wrote and lectured, lobbied journalists and congressmen, trying to build up his effectiveness, to enlarge his reputation. He spoke occasionally to consumer groups and students, to housewives and senior citizens, to garden clubs and union conventions. But mostly he made the rounds of small colleges for small fees, unable to insinuate himself into those lecture halls that paid big money, unable to attract important press notices. As compensation, there were always beautiful young girls willing to climb into his bed. Hellman understood that he was a minor Everest on which nubile students could practice until bigger challenges appeared. Hellman didn't mind—as long as they were young and pretty and made only small demands of him.

Yet it seemed to add up to less and less each time. The same sophomoric idealism, the same bleating about utopia on earth, the same desperate fantasizing. And between the sheets, the same anxious scrambling for orgasm. The American university system had failed, he decided, producing a race of women who confused jerking hips with sensuality and mistook lust for love.

"I've got an early morning," Hellman said.

"There isn't anything I wouldn't do . . ."

"Take a shower," he urged.

"You're obsessed with cleanliness. Freud says . . ."

"Did you know that in ancient Aramaic, Freud meant flabby penis?"

"Really? I didn't know you knew Aramaic."

He stared at her.

"Oh!" she said. "You're putting me on."

He turned back to the TV set. The newscaster had been replaced by an airline commercial. They were, Hellman conceded, the most artistic of all the commercials and therefore the most insidious. Traps designed to lure people to travel who couldn't afford it. Creating desire where there was no need, seducing the consumer. There might be an article in it, Hellman remarked to himself. Hellman had never been able to break into high-paying markets such as *Playboy* or *Life* or *Look,* and for a while that made him resentful. In time, however he had convinced himself that it didn't matter. Such journals appealed to the banal in the American character, catered to whatever was in vogue.

Hellman yearned for more satisfying achievements. He walked another path, would find success in his own way. Nor had he done too badly so far. Success and fame, the inevitable material rewards, were at least within sight. He stood poised on the launching pad and one spectacular idea would send him out into orbit. The kind of thing Nader had done so effectively with the automobile industry.

"For you," the girl was saying between gritted teeth, "I would be a beast, an absolute beast." She lowered her face between his legs, reached for his slack member with her lips.

He admired the curve of her bottom, the fall of her breasts. She had an excellent body, firm and strong, the body of a trained athlete. He supposed she swam well and skied, maybe even sky-dived. Jocks, he had long ago decided, were out of a singular mold—all flesh and bone and little else.

"Watch the news," he commanded. "A little knowledge may be dangerous, but it certainly won't hurt you."

She failed to recognize the annoyance and irony in his voice, and applied herself to his flesh with increased diligence.

He reached for her hair and yanked. Her head came up and she let out a protesting yelp.

"You hurt me!"

"Watch the news," he said.

She sat back and examined him. In profile, there was an aggressive thrust to his face, a half-done, primitive cast. A real beast . . .

"Why bother?" she said. "Television's so much crap."

"Do me a favor."

"Anything."

"Get dressed. Go home."

She folded her arms and sulked.

The announcer reappeared on the TV screen, began his lead-in remarks to the birthday dinner for Cardinal McCoy. McCoy, Hellman considered idly. McCoy and the Catholic Church. The Church and God. One way or another, people were hooked on religion. The idea was to come up with a different angle, create a stir. Religion, sex, money. Those were subjects that attracted attention, sold magazines and books. Discover the right proportions, mix and stir, serve while hot . . .

"And now," the announcer was saying, "we take you to the Hotel Americana and Mark Trotter . . ."

". . . The celebration has ended," came Mark Trotter's familiar voice, as the Seventh Avenue entrance to the hotel flashed into view. "The guests are departing and we're waiting for—Oh, there's . . . Senator Charles Reese, Democrat of Connecticut. Some political pundits expect Senator Reese to be the leading candidate for the Presidential nomination when his party meets in convention later this summer. With the Senator is . . . oh, yes, W. W. Masters, the somewhat mysterious Director of the Internal Investigative . . ."

"IIA, CIA, FBI," the girl muttered. "What's the difference?"

Hellman kept his eyes on the TV screen. "You're wrong, they're not the same. Masters runs a different kind of outfit. The IIA seldom breaks into print. They do their thing on the quiet."

"Like what, for example?"

"Like they pull together and oversee all the different functions of the Treasury Department's criminal branches. What the other branches can't do, the IIA does for them. Their people are supposed to be first-rate investigators."

"Superfuzz, you mean. I bet they hassle a lot of poor kids burning pot. That's how they get their kicks."

"Oh, they're into drugs. Trying to stop the bootlegging of drug products, as well as dangerous drugs. Every kind of junk is dumped onto the open market. Half the time when you read about a junkie dying of an overdose it's just that he got more than he bargained for from the pusher. Junkies never do know what they're shooting."

The girl shrugged. "Oh, Masters is probably just another square Establishment type . . ."

"I hear he's very smooth, very hip. Cultured and smart. Not that I'd call him a liberal, he's not. But years ago he cut a pretty good record on protecting individual rights when he was a Special Prosecutor . . ."

"That's irrelevant now."

"You mean what's he done lately?" Hellman mocked her.

"Okay. What *has* he done?"

Hellman grinned. "I bet Senator Reese turns you on!"

She hugged her knees. "He's fantastic. He's for the right things.

2 5

But they won't ever let him be nominated. They'll screw him, those pig politicians, the way they did McCarthy in 1968."

"A gentle reminder, Reese is also a politician."

"But different."

"Put them all into the same power bag and shake well. There are no nuggets at the bottom."

The girl made a face and turned back to the television. "Hey! Your friend Masters has a gimpy leg."

The TV camera closed in on the two men as they came out of the hotel, the newsmen pressing forward, shouting questions. Watching, Hellman reached into his memory. Somewhere he had read that as a child Masters had polio. The doctors had insisted that he would never use the leg again. But his mother had refused to accept that prognosis; she had massaged the leg every day, forced him to use it until some strength returned, until he learned to walk.

Mark Trotter's heavy voice could be heard. "Mr. Masters, Senator Reese. Seeing you two gentlemen together—should we infer some sort of political support is indicated? After all—"

"I think Reese is groovy," the girl said.

Hellman laughed openly. "Most women find Masters extremely attractive."

"Why don't you expose Masters?" the girl said.

"There may be not be anything to expose. Besides, Masters looks like a man who doesn't lose many fights."

On the screen, reporters were laughing at something said by Senator Reese, falling back as he and Masters started down the hotel steps. They paused and at once the crowd noise was perceptibly altered.

"What is it?" the girl said.

Hellman blinked his eyes back into focus. People moved with sudden urgency, their backs obscuring the view. There was the shrill, plaintive sound of confusion and fear. The camera seemed to jerk around, searching for a line of sight and the voice of Mark Trotter pierced the furor.

". . . Ladies and gentlemen, something terrible . . . absolutely awful . . . *again* an assassin in America? . . . I don't know . . .

please let us through, please . . . I can't be sure. There's confusion everywhere . . . why doesn't somebody get a doctor? It's terrible. The police have their guns out but they don't seem to know. . . . Ladies and gentlemen, it's awful. Where does this stop? I'm trying to get closer, trying to see. Please let me through, please. Coming through. Please open up, let the camera through. Who is it? Who's been shot? Who—"

"Oh, my God!" the girl shrilled, voice lined with horror. "They're shooting *everybody!*"

"There's blood on the steps," Mark Trotter said. "And I can't see . . . oh, oh, it's Mr. Masters. Director of the IIA. I don't know if he's alive or dead . . ."

"Jesus," Hellman said.

"Senator Reese," Mark Trotter called hoarsely. "Will you speak to the television audience?"

"Jesus," Hellman said again.

The girl hid her face in her hands, began to cry. "I don't want anybody to die, I don't, I don't, I don't . . ."

IV

A NICE day for a funeral, shining, cloudless. The warm, green scent of fresh-cut grass made Arlington seem like a good place to be. A procession of mourners advanced up the long incline toward the flag-draped coffin that contained W. W. Masters, and arranged themselves around the grave in order of official importance.

The President stood beside the Bishop of the Cathedral Church of St. Peter and St. Paul, his tired face gray and sober. Next to him, the First Lady. Then the Cabinet officers, the leaders of the Senate and the House of Representatives, foreign diplomats, a few of ambassadorial rank, the chiefs of various government agencies, a number of business executives and industrialists, the Joint Chiefs of Staff, honored guests and friends. Standing at attention, and facing into the sun, a Marine rifle squad.

When all the mourners were in place, the Bishop raised his face upward and brought his soft hands together, began to pray.

Behind the assembly, higher on the gentle hill, in the shadow of a large plane tree where he would attract no special attention, Malone stood alone. To stand apart was an inevitable choice for him. Even in a crowd, Malone was aware of the solitariness of his condition.

Malone closed out the pious droning of the Bishop, allowed himself to tune in on the conflicting emotions of the official mourners. Among those important men and women were some for whom Masters' death was an occasion of great bitterness; others would surely greet his removal from the public scene with relief and even joy. Malone had understood for a long time that depending on private and political tastes, W. W. Masters could be either a hero or a villain.

Soon all the words had been spoken, a bugler blew taps, and the Marine honor guard fired a rifle salute. The smell of burnt cordite drifted up to Malone; the pungent odor pleased him. It had bite and strength.

The ceremony was over, the mourners went back down the hill, got into their limousines and drove away. Only then did Malone go down to the open grave. He stood without moving, a deceptively slender man in a gray suit and a Brooks Brothers blue shirt, a closed expression on his vaguely Oriental face. His arms hung loose and his shoulders were slightly slumped, his wide mouth was at rest. His eyes, the color of rainwater, stared at the coffin as if trying to penetrate the covering flag and the polished mahogany to the remains of the man inside.

The silence was broken by the scrape of a shoe on the gravel walk, but Malone didn't turn. A figure appeared on the other side of the grave.

Malone looked up and saw Shipley. He was a large man with a large head and he sweated a great deal. To Malone, he looked like the owner of a workingman's bar or a cop on the beat, with a dozen boring years behind him. In fact, Shipley was Associate Director of the IIA, currently ranking officer of the Agency. Shipley frowned and mopped the back of his thick neck.

"I'd like to talk to you, Malone."

Malone gave no indication that he'd heard.

Shipley grimaced. There was *that* about Malone, that remoteness, never speaking unless he had to. Shipley preferred people who talked easily. Extended quiet lapses had always disturbed him.

"We're all very shocked about Masters," he began. He hadn't intended to extend condolences; after all, the entire Agency was affected by the loss. "I've talked to the President," Shipley added. His mind reached back. That morning had marked the first time Shipley had entered the oval office without the Director, the first time he had spoken for the Agency. Always it was Masters who did that. *Always.* And Shipley had functioned as nothing more than a clerical adjunct, present to supply reports or to make statistical presentations.

Malone continued to stare at Shipley.

Shipley's irritation grew. There was a suggestion of arrogance about Malone, arrogance and something more. At once he seemed in harmony with himself and whole, yet unfinished, a discordant note threatening to destroy the entire mechanism. In some odd, unidentifiable way he reminded Shipley of Masters. Shipley had decided years earlier that he didn't like Malone. But he respected him. And envied him.

"The President wants this mess cleared up at once," he declared. "He doesn't want another Kennedy affair. He was very clear about that."

Malone looked at the coffin again. In profile, his features were matched, perfected, fitted, with a soft, almost feline cast. But straight on there was only the wintry set of those eyes, the persona of purpose and private power.

"New York is on the case," Shipley offered. "And the FBI will cooperate."

Malone could almost hear W. W. Masters speaking, directing that the FBI must not be allowed to intrude on the authority of the Agency in any matter.

"The Director belongs to us," Malone said. "The Agency has to do the job." The words were neatly spaced, as if each one had been subjected to careful scrutiny.

"Exactly what I told the President." Malone turned away and Shipley spoke quickly, trying to pull him back. "I was at the White House. The President called me in. The Secretary of the Treasury was there . . . Mr. Fuller, he's a very political man. He's concerned that this will hurt the Party in the next election."

"The President? What does he think?"

"He wants the case solved and right away. He says he is President of all the people and doesn't care who is hurt politically. The President is concerned that we might have another Warren Commission fiasco."

Malone raised his eyes. "Who is going to replace Mr. Masters?"

"I will. Temporarily, at least. The final decision isn't made."

Malone gave no sign that he'd heard. Shipley was not the man for the job, never had been. "Masters always kept the Agency out of politics."

"Yes, yes. But there's an election upcoming and everybody is jittery. I know what Masters meant to you, Malone. He meant just as much to the rest of us. Well, maybe you were closer to him than most."

"He brought me into the Agency," Malone said absently, thinking back to the final month of his time at law school. Law graduates were in demand that year, appraised and solicited with the kind of fervor usually lavished only on football players. Malone, ranking high in his class, had been sought out by representatives of the big corporate law firms. But he had exhibited no interest in their offers. He had promised to consider a job with a criminal lawyer on the West coast and there had been feelers from district attorneys in four major cities; and a pleasant man from the Federal Bureau of Investigation had interviewed him.

But it was W. W. Masters who made up his mind. The IIA was new, organized by Masters only a few years before, and it had yet to do anything spectacular enough to capture the public's imagination. Few of the new lawyers had even heard of the Agency and even fewer considered enlisting in its ranks.

Malone had just finished listening to the FBI agent catalogue the benefits of joining the Bureau and was picking his way across the varsity gymnasium past the interviewers' tables, past knots of students, when he heard his name spoken.

He turned and saw a tall man advancing. There was a penetrating clarity to his eyes, as if they possessed a special vision, and the bristling mustache on that elegant face seemed to be worn as an act of defiance. Malone didn't notice the cane that first time, didn't notice the limp, and later when he did, he was shocked; it was wrong for a man so perfectly detailed to be flawed in any way.

The tall man offered his hand and smiled and Malone, who almost never smiled, was forced to smile in return. "I'm Masters of the IIA. Let's talk, shall we?"

Malone had wanted to respond, to please the other man, an alien impulse which puzzled him.

Masters had tilted his head, as if he were selecting his words with great care. "You were with Hoover's man. Are you going with the Bureau?"

"No," Malone said, his decision coming as a surprise.

Masters nodded solemnly. "They're an excellent group. But we'll be better. Qualitatively, of course—Civil Service is both impartial and niggardly with money."

"Money isn't a primary concern . . ."

"I know that about you," Masters said. "I know a great deal about you now."

They moved along the corridor outside the gymnasium, Masters setting the pace. Malone felt as though he had been stripped down, probed and investigated until all his secrets had become known to this stranger. Yet he didn't mind, was in fact complimented that Masters was interested in him.

"I am going to fashion the IIA into the most efficient anti-crime agency in the world. To that end, I require committed personnel. Commitment, Malone, is like sand in an hour glass; ride it hard before it runs out. Can you commit, Malone?"

Malone had never before been forced to consider the question. His brain turned over sluggishly, seeking an answer.

Masters didn't wait. "I'm recruiting the best law students in the country. Not the most academic. Not the most spectacular. Not the sleekest, or the most ambitious. The *best*. Judged from a strict and demanding perspective. The men I want would find the memorizing of precedents a bore. They will be men who don't measure success in dollar signs. They will be men who won't look at life through the narrow end of the telescope. The Agency offers the unusual, the exciting, an opportunity to make the United States of America your life and to make a better life for the United States. The nation will become your family, Malone, and the Agency your wife. This requires a special kind of man. Are you one of them? Will you enlist?". . .

"He brought me into the Agency," Malone said again.

The words, spoken without emphasis, embarrassed Shipley; they seemed to reveal too much about Malone.

"That's why I was certain you'd want to head up the investigation. Crack this thing. I know you can. Find the killer, put the blame where it belongs, Malone."

"Find another man," Malone said, after an interval.

Shipley glanced over his shoulder. Most of the mourners had departed and only a few limousines remained in the access road. He felt a growing urgency. This was taking too long and the Senator was waiting. . . .

He spoke in a commanding voice. "What's your problem, Malone? I was sure you'd want the job." Shipley decided that Malone disliked him. Strike that! Malone simply didn't care, one way or another. He was a man worth knowing, Shipley told himself, but not somebody you could call a friend. Malone didn't make friends. "I was sure you'd want the job," Shipley repeated.

"I don't deserve the case."

Deserve . . . Tension drained out of Shipley. He wanted Malone to accept the assignment. More than any other agent, Malone would do a proper job, without mistakes or omissions. That was vital, to allow no opportunities for future criticism.

"I don't agree," Shipley said.

"I drove Mr. Masters to New York that night. I should have stayed with him. If I had, he might still be alive."

To discover that Malone was capable of feeling remorse, even some guilt, pleased Shipley. He filed the knowledge away.

"No one could have stopped it," he said solemnly. "A sniper from a window, it's an impossible situation. Oswald got Kennedy that way; every public official is vulnerable. Besides, Masters told you to pass up the dinner." Shipley thought he detected a small change in Malone's expression, a softening, a flicker of gratitude perhaps.

"Mr. Masters said, 'Take a few hours off, Peter. Entertain yourself.' There was a movie. While they were waiting to murder him, Peter Malone was looking at a movie! And then was twenty minutes late getting back with the car . . ."

"New York traffic," Shipley said.

"Faulty planning."

"No one blames you, don't blame yourself. Face it, a determined assassin can succeed almost every time." Shipley looked down the slope. "We have to get the people who did this, Malone. The President said I was to put my best people on the case. That means you and Herman Flood."

"Not Flood," Malone said flatly.

Shipley almost smiled. Flood and Malone, they had always competed for Masters' approval, the Director's two fair-haired boys. "Take the job, Malone."

"It's impossible to believe anyone went after Masters deliberately. He was a wonderful man. Decent, generous, a good friend, a sincere public servant. It had to be a mistake."

"What kind of a mistake?"

"The man on the rifle, I believe he was after Senator Reese. For political reasons maybe—he's a major Presidential candidate. He missed the shot. It had to be that way."

"Some of us think that's a possibility. I suggested it and the President seemed to go with it. . . ."

"And the Secretary?" Malone said thinly.

"Fuller," Shipley said at the weak end of a breath. "Fuller's trying to make political capital out of this. He insists the gunman was after Masters, that it was some radical leftist."

"No. Killing Masters would make things more difficult for the Left, turn people against them. Reverse Fuller's logic."

"You think some wild kook on the Right tried to knock Reese off, to keep a liberal from becoming President?"

"Yes."

"That makes sense, Malone. I want you to follow through."

"Find the man who wanted Reese dead and we'll find the man who killed Masters. . . . Secretary Fuller might not approve of an investigation that goes that route."

Shipley drew himself up. "I'm running the Agency, not Fuller.

34

Do it your way and I'll give you all the help you want. Anyone you want."

Malone considered it, nodded once.

"Good! I knew I could depend on you. Do whatever's necessary. But be careful," he added. "There are some tender toes around. Try not to walk on any of them." He took two or three steps down the slope. "Stay in close touch, will you?"

Malone watched him hurry down the incline toward the last limousine.

V

THE CADILLAC rolled smoothly along in the stream of Washington-bound traffic. Behind tinted glass, in dim and air-cooled comfort, deep in tufted black leather, Shipley tried to wipe away the lingering tension, the anxiety. With Masters gone, his life had changed radically, and would continue to. He was acutely aware of the increasing pressures and longed desperately to measure up, to be all that Masters had been. And more . . .

As if able to penetrate into the dark areas of Shipley's brain, the man next to him spoke. "You want help," he said. It was not a question.

Shipley tried not to look directly at the other man. Senator Leland Fitch Abernathy was a man of immense proportions, his boneless face a succession of pouches and jowls, of sagging flesh and fatty dimples. Tiny black eyes peered out of milk-white skin and his small features were set far apart, all framed by a cap of electric-red curls. For Shipley, it was an intimidating amalgam of color and texture and size.

"Well, Senator—"

"Hah! I have been thirty-odd years in the Senate," he drawled. "A state assemblyman before then and six years a mayor and a two-term governor of Alabama. I know when a man's rootin' around and lookin' for favors. Good Lord, yes, I do."

Shipley managed a smile. "There is something."

"Something indeed." Abernathy touched a silver button on the leather arm rest and a panel slid open in the back of the chauffeur's seat, revealing a compactly designed bar. He filled a silver tumbler with bourbon, offered it to Shipley.

"Steady your nerves."

"I'm fine, Senator."

Abernathy raised his brows slightly. "Well, of course you are!" He swallowed the bourbon. "You don't drink, do you, Shipley? Or smoke?"

"Is that of consequence, Senator?"

"Tells me something about you, is all. Just information. You and Masters, a tandem of Puritans. Purity is all things, that was Masters' rule of thumb. Leastways, that was the impression he managed to convey."

"I've never known a man quite like the Director."

"Hah! Well, I agree. Neither have I, neither have I. And his untimely demise has left me grievously agitated. Grievously agitated," he repeated, as if pleased with the phrase.

Shipley made an effort to arrange his thoughts in orderly fashion, to express them in suitable language. When dealing with someone like Senator Abernathy, language was crucial. A complicated and confusing man, Abernathy could be a stump-standing backwoods politician dealing in the clichés and customs of the deep South and moments later a cultivated sophisticate intent on finding *le mot juste,* as he liked to say. He made Shipley uneasy, but he was right—Shipley had come for help. The kind of help only the majority leader of the Senate could provide. Abernathy possessed as much power as any man in Washington, short of the President himself, and he reveled in its exercise.

"You're after Masters' job," Abernathy grunted, staring at the silver tumbler. "You and a dozen other men." The tiny black eyes examined Shipley carefully and the small pink mouth lifted at the corners. "We are all political creatures, wheeling and dealing for our own reasons. Not one of us should be trusted. Old Sam Clemens said it best—'It could probably be shown by facts and figures that there is no distinctly native American criminal class except Congress.' Hah!" He sobered rapidly. "You believed your ambition to be a concealed and unknown factor, Shipley? It surprises you that you've been found out. Director of the IIA. One of the most desired positions in the land. There is so much power to be wielded. What great pressures can be brought by the man in that job! Subtle and forcible pressures both. My mind comes back to the national sport, the evasion of income-tax payments. Which of us has not cheated a little? Which of us is not vulnerable to a close examination? The IIA has the power to go beyond anything Internal Revenue can do, it has the manpower, the authority, the investigative skills. The Director has infinite personal power, the iron fist in the velvet glove. Enormous influence and therefore the opportunity to have lasting satisfaction. Masters performed like some Oriental potentate at times, full of his own self, putting lesser folks through a fiery hoop."

"Mr. Masters was widely esteemed."

"Good Lord, yes. And see what's become of him. Shot in the head, took from us before his time was up." The milky skin seemed to blotch with emotion; the dark eyes were shiny slits. "Interfered with matters that were near to completion, they did. I say to you, Shipley, that this shocking affair has cut through to the marrow of things, upset me greatly. I tell you true, in striking down Mr. Masters, they have done me dirt."

"We all feel the loss greatly."

"Spare me unprofitable sentiments. The public ceremonies are concluded, the funeral is done. I am telling you facts, mister."

Shipley started to respond, but Abernathy cut him off with a wave of his great white hand. "We Southerners are weary of being treated like stepchildren who have committed some irreparable breach of etiquette and so have been designated to remain in the back rooms of polite society. We have not forgotten the slurs and insults we have suffered. Nor have we failed to comprehend such humiliations as the rejection of certain nominees for the high court. Nor shall we forget. I look upon the death of W. W. Masters in the same light, as an insidious piece of violence against the South and its good people."

Shipley stole a look at the Senator. The fleshy face was set, the black eyes hard and cold. Shipley thought about making a display of understanding and sympathy, chose instead to say nothing. Silence seemed the best tactic.

Abernathy went on. "Mine is the bitterness of my state, of my region, of an entire people. The philosophies and attitudes of my constituency are taking hold across these United States and they will prevail . . ."

"The silent majority," Shipley put in.

"The *American* majority."

The limousine was speeding across the Arlington Memorial Bridge, a graceful structure with nine low arches. "See those monumental statues at the Washington end of the bridge," Abernathy said quietly. "Muscular men on muscular horses. Symbols of the arts of war—Valor and Sacrifice. These are noble concepts, Mr. Shipley."

Shipley struggled to make sense of this meeting. What was Abernathy working toward? Was this a test to evaluate his fitness for the directorship? If so, Shipley meant to get a passing grade.

"It's my job," he said solemnly, "to make sure the nation gets justice in this matter."

The small, pink mouth pursed and Abernathy heaved his great bulk around. "Yes. Justice. And quickly."

"Only a few minutes ago, Senator, I named my best agent to head up the investigation."

Abernathy peered through the tinted side window. "Mr. Masters and I, we talked many times. Privately. Masters agreed with me that the affairs of state were in a sinfully bad and precarious position, worsening every minute. He understood, as do all clear-thinking men, that the country is swinging dangerously toward rebellion, even anarchy. People are frightened and with cause. Our cities are cesspools of crime and degeneracy. Our resources are being depleted, our wealth wasted, our energies drained away."

"Mr. Masters was concerned, I know that."

"Yes. He understood that a firm hand was required, a captain not afraid to establish a direct course to a safe harbor."

Shipley felt his heart speed up and he willed himself to remain calm, to say no more than was necessary.

Abernathy began to speak again. "Few men are equipped by experience, temperament and stature to get the job done. I indicated as much to Masters. But of course that was a conclusion he had long ago reached on his own."

Shipley held himself still.

"I am about to take you into my confidence," Abernathy said, making it sound like a threat.

"I appreciate that."

A Turk's-moon smile came onto Abernathy's mouth, faded quickly. "I won't waste words, Shipley." He spoke now in a low, rumbling voice. "Masters and I agreed that he would be the candidate of the Republican party for President. He was to be nominated by acclamation on the first ballot in a full-blown draft."

Shipley's surprise was complete, and it showed. "I always understood that a draft was impossible, that it had to be managed beforehand."

Abernathy regarded Shipley balefully. "Correct. That is a job I would have performed for Mr. Masters. The machinery had already been put into operation. Key people who think properly —party leaders, publishers of certain newspapers, the owners of radio and television stations, sympathetic businessmen, military men—all were contacted by me, and many have enlisted in our crusade. There has been a glorious rallying around. Funds have been raised in impressive amounts, cadres formed that can swiftly transform themselves into efficient political organizations, pressure groups. Skilled writers and political theoreticians had begun preparing releases, feature stories, position papers.

"People have come to realize that there is an implicit danger in too much freedom without control, in the continued corruption of our Constitution and in the legal misinterpretation of it. There must be an end to trouble, to student strife, to racial unrest, to the repeated flaunting of legitimate authority. The country must soon return to fundamentals, those concepts of freedom and justice that made the United States of America the great and formidable country it is. Masters' election would have been a signal to the world that America has once more chosen to walk the path of its true heritage."

Shipley was afraid to answer, afraid not to. "I never knew the Director had political ambitions."

Abernathy grunted. "Masters was no ordinary man. He had been aware of the disintegrating state of the union for a long time,

40

had wanted to put matters right. But his authority was limited and his influence had only a minor effect on the larger issues. He was forced to operate within a prescribed framework and that, for a man like Masters, was a painful exercise.

"After much soul-searching and many, many extensive discussions with certain men, myself included, Masters decided. He would become President and as President he would be able to do what so badly needed doing. He was a sound man—courageous, intelligent, imaginative.

"He commanded our little group with a firm hand, reined us in when our impatience grew, directed those of us in the Congress to enact certain legislation and defeat other bills. He made contacts with the governors of the more important states, sought and created support wherever possible. He established a wide base including industry and labor, the media, politicians of several stripes."

"I never heard a word," Shipley said.

"Masters did a *discreet* and proper job. Thorough. He worked, we worked, for years toward our goal with a single-mindedness, sparked and fueled by his vision, waiting for the time to be right. That time is now, Shipley. People cry out for strong leaders, for a return to the old, trusted ways. Less than two months ago, Masters gave us the word. He was ready at last to surface, to put himself before the American people, to lead them. Years of preparation and planning, but finally we were going to make our move."

"How can you be sure Mr. Masters would've been elected?"

The small black eyes stared at Shipley. "The time was right, I said. Not for a flannel-mouthed fool. Not for some redneck racist or a star-spangled Hitler. No. Our people won't accept such men. The American voter demands sophistication in his leaders. He wants to believe that those who govern are bigger men than he is himself, more honest, smarter in every way. Masters represented all of that and at the same time he was a self-made man. He had labored hard to achieve his success and he obviously operated within the rules, respected the foundations on which this nation was built.

"Could he have been elected? I'm certain of it. During the last ten years he had cultivated the right people, made the right friends. He was equally careful not to make enemies who could damage him. His friends were in every walk of life, of all political persuasions. That was his special gift, to allow people to believe that they knew his innermost thoughts while revealing very little of himself. Many liberals fancied Masters as one of their own because he spoke their language, had gone to the right schools, wore properly tailored suits. As for the conservatives—they worshiped Masters, and why not? He spoke of law and order, freedom of choice, gave them what they wanted.

"I'll tell you this, Shipley, whatever Masters truly believed, he was always a one-hundred-and-fifty percent genuine American patriot . . . like myself, he understood that the march of anarchy had to be halted and turned back, defeated. But they got to him first, the agents of the radical conspiracy. They understood that by removing this splendid man they dealt a heavy blow to all true Americans. And they did. This assassination was a personal attack on every one of us, Shipley, on you and on me."

"The President said—"

"This President, though a member of my own party, and a man of decent instincts, is not a creative force in the nation. He is inclined to look too often at the different sides of an argument. The time for such indulgence is past. This President, and men like him, uncommitted men, are a luxury we can no longer afford. In these dangerous days we require a strict constitutional constructionist in the White House, a blood-red patriot, a leader who knows his duty and will do it." The huge head swiveled around, the pale skin shimmering, the tiny eyes lost in folds of flesh. "I intend for the United States of America to get the leader it deserves . . ."

Without thinking, Shipley spoke. "You could be that man, Senator."

"A generous thought, Shipley. Ordinarily one hesitates to consider one's self for such high office, even when duty becomes evident. Your support is reassuring."

"Thank you, Senator."

"But I am not Masters, Shipley. Unlike him, I do have enemies, political liabilities and limitations. My main power is within the Senate and in some segments of the Party. To run for the Presidency cannot be done without tremendous backing from people, and without funds."

Shipley spoke quickly. "I'll contribute, of course . . ."

"Don't be a fool!" Abernathy said, the great head swinging to one side. "Do you think I'm talking about some hundred-dollar donation? Millions are necessary to launch a campaign and sustain it, to buy advertising, television time, to hire the professionals needed."

"If there is any way I can help . . ."

Abernathy nodded. "Not long ago Masters mentioned that he had unloosed his agents onto some domestic drug companies. A handful of the largest and most important firms."

"Yes, sir," Shipley said excitedly. "We've turned up some interesting information. Three companies are producing amphetamines and barbiturates in tremendous amounts. In such quantities that the domestic market—the legal market, that is—cannot absorb them. What these producers have done is to set up dummy corporations in foreign countries. In Mexico, for one, and Canada, and they ship these pills by the millions out of the country. Once there it is impossible to keep track of them and they are smuggled back across the border and sold on the black market. . . ."

"Consider, Shipley, what might happen if the investigations are called off. The danger of criminal action against these firms is terminated. The managers are no longer haunted by the specter of prison terms. They would be most grateful, I should think."

Shipley hesitated and wet his lips.

Abernathy went on. "Consider that Masters understood such matters. Consider too that whatever you believe he would have done, Masters is gone. I have replaced him, will pursue his important ends, faithfully adhere to his beliefs. I need your assistance in this matter, Shipley, and in other situations that may arise, that will surely arise."

"I'm not sure I understand, Senator."

"There will be some who do not look upon me favorably, who

would prefer that I not be elected President. They would withhold their campaign contributions. You might be able to influence them to change their minds."

"How?"

"I leave that in your very capable hands, Shipley."

Shipley made up his mind. The beefy face broke into a grin. "There are occasions when the Agency assumes certain responsibilities from Internal Revenue. The investigatory and enforcement duties. We analyze and investigate the tax declarations of certain individuals and corporations. We check *all* channels of income, declared and otherwise. We have the authority to look into bank records, to check out relatives, friends, and we often get to look at numbered overseas bank accounts. If there is fraudulent activity . . . Well, there are persons and firms currently under investigation. I could supply you with a list of names that your representatives might contact . . ."

"Ah, Shipley, not for a moment did I doubt your ability to adapt, to operate in the Director's chair. Oh, yes, there is one more thing. If it should become possible for me to go to the convention knowing who murdered Mr. Masters, if I could tell the delegates in the bluntest of words where the threat to the nation lies, if I could name names and be supported by facts . . ."

"I wish I could guarantee . . ."

"You said your best agent was on the case. Give him every assistance, but make sure he understands the delicate facts of life."

"What facts are those, Senator?"

"The agent?"

"Malone. He was Masters' protégé, you might say."

"Hah! Malone. I've heard Masters speak of him. A good man. Perhaps too good," the words trailing off in a low grumble. His head lifted after a moment. "Understand where lies the political power I seek to marshal. These are the solid folk, the folk who believe in the verities. Such people are the heart and the soul of our system, of our national destiny. I refer to the doers, the kind of men who created America out of a wilderness. A dramatic

44

solution to the killing would do much to establish my credit with them, could bring me their total support."

Shipley suddenly felt himself threatened.

Abernathy went on. "These men tend in their fervor to involve themselves in a variety of activities and organizations that do not always make their purposes clear to the casual observer. I say this—should either blame or stain in this affair attach itself to my friends I would be displeased."

A spasm gripped Shipley's guts. "Malone," he offered. "He's a trained agent. Persistent, intensely dedicated, difficult to control."

"No mention was made of controlling any man. I simply point out to you the delicate intricacies of an evolving situation. Let me tell you, boy, my friends could be your friends and that would be a very good thing."

Shipley recognized the invitation. "I'd like to be able to consider you a friend, Senator."

Abernathy sat back in the soft leather seat. "As Malone's superior, you will take an active and constant interest in the investigation. Make yourself aware of his every step, his every thought, especially his suspicions. Under your guidance, Malone should find himself traveling a proper course so as to arrive at a suitable conclusion. He should not be misdirected by emotion, by false clues, or by the machinations of those who do not want the truth to come out."

"I'll try."

"Succeed, Shipley. When this is over, when matters have developed as I anticipate they will, you will have a very appreciative friend in the highest office in the land. That friend only will decide who shall be named permanent director of the Internal Investigative Agency." He refilled the silver tumbler and lifted it in a silent toast.

For the first time in his life Shipley wished he had learned to drink, wished he could celebrate this special moment appropriately.

VI

"You won't go for it?" Hellman said sullenly.

"The story doesn't work," Wayne Murdoch said. He spoke with all the bright, comradely authority that befitted his position as editor-in-chief of *Masses & Progress,* the weekly political journal. *M & P* had a limited but influential subscription list in the intellectual, liberal, and academic communities. It carried no advertising and was supported mainly by an annual grant from a philanthropic fund.

Wayne Murdoch had created *M & P,* kept it alive for nearly a dozen years, provided its energy, its taste and its purpose. A tall, craggy man with mutton-chop sideburns and a wide, wet mouth, he sat behind a desk littered with manuscripts, bills, and scraps of paper containing notes to himself.

"I would like for us to collaborate, Dan. I really would. Your name is becoming known to more of the right people every day and you've done some good work. The story about the migrant farm-workers upstate was a gem, a real gem, and I wish you'd let us have it. We'd have gone higher than *Exposé* by at least twenty-five dollars."

"You turned the idea down."

"In outline, yes. In outline, a story must display something special, generate in me a kind of inner excitement, anticipation."

"You responded to the Masters piece when we talked," Hellman said, his resentment showing. Murdoch had encouraged him to write the story, had urged him to complete it swiftly so as to make the next issue; and now he rejected it, as if Hellman were some journalism major trying to break into the field.

46

"It *sounded* better than it reads, Dan. I'm sorry. A biographical sketch of Masters—well, it simply doesn't cut."

"It's a good story—I've done my homework."

"Well, sure. But *M & P* is an enlightened journal. Politically hip and progressive."

"That's why I came to you first. That's why this should be published by *M & P*. Frankly, I'm disappointed. You don't understand what I was reaching for. Seems like I made a mistake. . . ."

Murdoch spread his hands. "I'm an honest editor, Dan. Always have been. I have to say what I think. The article, the way it stands, isn't for us. Yet I think *we* are for *you*. Oh, I know we don't pay much. But there are many good reasons why people want publication in *M & P*. For one thing, we're often reprinted in mass-circulation magazines and many of our writers have been able to use their articles as a foundation for full-length books. And our stories attract a great deal of attention; hardly a week goes by without the *Times* commenting editorially on something I've printed. *M & P* can mean a great deal to a man trying to establish a national reputation."

"The Masters piece—"

"Consider the people who read us. Political scientists, sociologists, teachers, lawyers, professionals, authors, politicians, you name it. Informed types, very in. They often know as much about a given subject as our authors do. Our mail says so. That's why I can say that a biographical outline of Masters' life won't do for us. It won't tell our readers a thing they don't already know."

Hellman recognized the accuracy of Murdoch's words and he wanted, *needed,* publication in *M & P*. It might project him onto an entirely different level of operation, a level where the rewards were greater. At this moment, he hated Murdoch for rejecting the story, for rejecting him; but it would be self-defeating to allow his true feelings to show.

"Allow me to disagree," he said mildly. "But I won't argue the point. Will you give me your reaction to a couple of other ideas I have on the subject?"

"Try me."

"I submit that it was Senator Reese the killer was really after. How about a think piece exploring the reasons why the political Neanderthals would want him dead?"

"Good try, Dan, but no good. Dr. Sudeck, up at Columbia, is covering that for me."

Hellman became aware of the stiffening in his cheeks. With status publication, with the right topic, a profitable lecture tour could be arranged, his fees increased. "Assassination as a political weapon?" he said. "Assassination has become a major element on the American political scene."

Murdoch gazed off at an angle. "Try *Ramparts*. It's more their style." Murdoch placed his hands flat on the desk, as if to push himself erect.

Hellman realized he was about to be dismissed and the need to conclude some sort of an agreement with Murdoch became stronger. He explored his memory.

"Okay," he said gravely. "I wasn't going to talk about this yet, but I'll level with you."

Murdoch settled back in his chair.

Hellman inched forward, the swart face intense. "I had my doubts about *M & P* being the right forum for what I've got in mind."

"Come on. If it's good, it belongs in *M & P*."

"Maybe. I'm willing to risk talking about it with you."

"What are you onto?"

Hellman explored that craggy face as if making a final assessment. He grunted affirmatively. "Given, most of your readers *want* to believe that bullet was intended for Reese. It fits their notions that the far-out Right wanted the most progressive candidate for President dead."

Murdoch frowned and spoke defensively. "There's something of a pattern. Look at the people who have been killed."

"My point exactly. It seems logical to believe that this time was more of the same."

"You're saying it wasn't?"

"I'm saying the gunman was after W. W. Masters. That the

snot was no accident. It was on target, a clean hit. The killer wanted Masters dead."

"Why?"

"For political motives."

Murdoch tugged at his sideburns. "That would suggest somebody on the Left pulled the trigger."

"Why not? Look at the guerrillas in Brazil, Uruguay. Didn't Trotsky take a pickax in the brain, courtesy of Joe Stalin? There are varieties of Left, and an extreme version can turn assassin for its beliefs."

Murdoch scowled and shook his head.

"Of course," Hellman said, "you may not want to risk offending some of your readers."

Murdoch stared at him.

"There is a risk . . ." Hellman went on.

"I'm not afraid," Murdoch said, adding quickly, "if it makes sense. What you've said, pure conjecture. What about proof? Can you put it all together?"

"I think so. Oh, it'll take some doing. Some real digging."

"Are you prepared to—"

"Yes."

"If you're right, we may have to re-evaluate the radical scene— the revolutionaries, the militant blacks . . ."

"The only honest way to go! What do you say, Murdoch?"

"I don't know. No offense meant—but are you really equipped to pull off something like this? It's provocative to some very volatile people who can get freaked out . . ."

"I rate with those people. Doors are open to me."

"It could be dangerous."

"I can take care of myself."

But that night when he was alone, Hellman was less confident. He had no idea of where to begin, no clear vision of where he was headed. He was, he finally admitted to himself, worried. And frightened.

VII

THE NEW YORK bureau of the Internal Investigative Agency was situated on two high floors of an old but still desirable apartment building on Central Park West. Three years earlier the building had gone cooperative and the two apartments had been purchased in the name of Herman Flood. Other than Flood's name on the mailbox and on the doorbell, no legend announced the presence of the IIA, no insignia declared its existence, no guard protected its portals. As with every other Agency office, its telephone was unlisted and its employees came to work in staggered shifts so as to arouse no suspicion on the part of the neighbors. All official correspondence went through a post-office box and was picked up each day by a different courier.

The two apartments had been divided into small, rectangular offices enclosed by beige plywood partitions, and a black iron staircase connected the two levels. Malone stood at the window of Herman Flood's office and looked down at the city below.

"Central Park looks good from here," he said.

Herman Flood, from his place behind his neat, beige, metal desk, laughed. It occurred to Malone that Flood's laugh was like his desk—carefully tooled, hard, without humor or interest. "I checked it out my first day on the job."

"And never again?"

"Something like that," Flood said dryly.

Malone blinked and in that instant saw himself sitting behind that uncluttered desk. His vision cleared and a suite of related images flashed through his mind, moments when he had perceived

Herman Flood as a facsimile of himself. They were of an age, with similar physiques and faces structured almost alike, though their coloring was different. Flood had yellowish hair and smooth, white skin and his eyes seemed to change color with his moods. But Malone had never been able to rid himself of the haunting sense of sameness and he was disturbed by it. He had never learned to appreciate Flood.

Once he had made the mistake of expressing this feeling to Masters and the Director had laughed at him. "You are a matched pair," Masters had said. "A show team. I trained you both and directed your careers and you have progressed equally. One day one of you may replace me." He had laughed again, as if the idea were beyond serious consideration. "But which? Which one?"

Malone recalled his resentment. Resentment at being laughed at; and envy of Flood's parallel position. Afterward, there was a stronger reaction, anger, the desire to eliminate Flood as a competitor. Malone had vowed to work harder, to become a more efficient agent, exactly the kind of agent Masters wanted him to be.

Malone had labored to perfect his work methods, demanding a high degree of excellence from himself, hoping to satisfy the Director. But he had been unable to outdistance Herman Flood. With methodical diligence, Flood had advanced himself, matching Malone step for step.

Malone glanced at Flood now; the pale face was watchful and faintly amused, as if Flood were aware of some joke Malone knew nothing about.

"Shipley spoke to you?" Malone said.

"He called. He's going to get Masters' job. I'm sure of it. He isn't half the man Masters was, not as good as I am. Nor you, Malone," he added, an ironic edge in his voice. "Shipley was never a good agent."

"Masters chose him."

"Masters did things for his own reasons. He wanted a desk-man at his back, an administrator, someone dependable but not strong, not too ambitious. That was Shipley."

Malone had never thought of it that way before. He had accepted Shipley's appointment as Associate Director years before as logical, sensible, the best man for the job, else Masters would not have chosen him. Now he wasn't sure.

"Shipley's smart," Flood said. "He's made political connections. That's the way to make it, Malone."

Malone stared at the other man without speaking.

"That's what we should've been doing," Flood went on. "It's what I intend to do from now on. Shipley's not going to last, he hasn't got the brains, he hasn't got the belly for the job. But I do and I want to be Director. Three or four years ought to swing it for me." He laughed and leaned back. "Don't worry, Malone. When it happens, I'll see that you get a good desk somewhere."

"Let's talk about the case," Malone said.

Flood nodded. "How can I help?"

"There have been conversations with Hoover's people and the printouts from the information banks have been studied. The probable assassin profiles . . ."

Flood made a disparaging sound. "They won't get us a thing, you know that."

Malone agreed but didn't say so. "The prime numbers have been isolated and people are out after them now. We may turn up something."

Flood said, "I make it out to be somebody who's never made it into the computer. Some political freak, maybe."

Malone waited for him to go on.

"Well, you'll cover all the angles, Malone. You're good at that."

Malone had the feeling that everything Flood said was designed to provoke, to taunt, to elicit a response in kind. Malone spoke deliberately.

"What came out of the Reese hate mail?"

Flood showed surprise; he leaned forward. "As a matter of fact, my people haven't gone that route. You see—"

Malone was pleased to catch Flood in a fundamental omission. But nothing changed on his face or in his voice.

"Time is vital, Herman. It works against us. You should have talked to Reese, broken the mail down, matched it against the memory banks."

"Shipley said it was your baby. I figured I'd let you lead the parade."

Malone stared.

Flood shifted around. "You'll get full cooperation from this bureau, Malone. Whatever you need. I'll send a man out today."

"Don't," Malone said. He wanted to speak to Senator Reese, to look into his face, to discover for himself the kind of man he was. At the door, Malone turned back. "Make sure your people know who is in charge," he said.

"Well, *sure,* Peter. Anything you say."

Malone was particularly fond of police station houses, especially those scattered around New York City. Ancient and deteriorating, they smelled of urine and sweat; yet they possessed an air of dignity and authority, an imposing tradition of men who enforced the law and kept the peace. He asked the desk sergeant for Captain Capolino and was directed to the second floor.

Capolino greeted Malone in a small, airless office off the squad room. He was a squat man with gray in his stiff black hair and thick-lensed glasses that made his eyes look like raw eggs. Corded wrists bulged out of his rolled shirt-sleeves. His collar was open, revealing a powerful neck. He waited for Malone to sit down in an unsteady oak chair, mopping his brow with a handkerchief already damp and gray.

"This city treats cops like they aren't human. Look at this crummy place. Looks like a zoo, smells like a zoo. No wonder people act like animals." He rocked his head in disbelief. "Can you imagine, no air conditioning!" He peered critically at Malone. "Don't you ever perspire?"

"I'm going to see Reese," Malone said.

Capolino sniffed. "This city is killing me. Too hot, too cold, and always the damned pollution. My sinuses are blacker than the subways. You won't get anything from Reese. We interviewed him. It's on tape, if you want to hear it. Nothing."

Malone nodded. "I'll talk to him."

"Pick 'em up, put 'em down. That's what being a cop is anyway.

Twenty years of asking questions and every case turns out to be like every other case. Interview the principals, check out alibis, read the lab reports, talk to informers in cruddy bars. Very ordinary stuff."

"Homicides must be different."

"Junk stuff. Hatchet murders. Last week a guy got his ass shot off. His ass shot off! The poor sonuvabitch bled to death. Ah, junkies and jealous husbands, madmen. That's all I get."

"How do you make the Masters' shooting?"

"I don't know. The boys from downtown, they do a lot of heavy thinking. They like it to be complicated, like some kind of a Paul Newman movie. But it's not that way. Nothing ever is. You get hold of people who are connected and put them against each other, compare their stories, pressure them. That way it opens up finally. Ah, maybe it's a psycho. I don't know. Anyway, this character we've got might amount to something. Then again he might not. That's why I called you."

"Name?"

"Jethro Stark. The sunuvabitch is from Oklahoma. A goddamned cowboy."

"How'd you find him?"

"We got undercover people too. In all those extremist groups. The boys who know they're right and the rest of us are wrong. The ones who think justice comes out of the barrel of a gun."

"Is that what Stark's into?"

"He belongs to an outfit called Continental American Patriots, maybe you know them."

Malone lowered his chin in assent.

"Well, this Stark showed up in New York about ten days ago. He set himself up in a midtown hotel and began contacting some of the crazies on the right wing. He talked at meetings, distributed literature—y'know, Jews, niggers, Commies are ruining America and we hundred-per-centers have to purify the blood by shedding blood. A few days ago he started going around loaded."

"A pistol?"

"And a rifle. Waving them around. Recommending that everyone get a gun and begin using it. He kept talking about getting

54

the leaders of what he calls the liberal conspiracy and he named names, including Reese. Said he'd enjoy putting a bullet in his head personally."

"What else?"

"That was on the afternoon Masters was killed. Our undercover guy got jumpy and called it in and we decided to pick Stark up. That room of his, filled with hate stuff, also a few pictures of naked girls, and those loaded pieces. He tried to get to a gun when my men showed up but they put a stop to that."

"What's he said so far?"

"Crazy talk. The sonuvubitch called me a wop traitor." For the first time, Capolino smiled, showing a lot of large white teeth. "He better be careful, I'll put the Mafia onto him. You want to talk to the guy?"

Malone nodded.

The detention cells were in the basement. The air was thick, musty, untouched by sunlight. In the corner cell, a man lay on the bunk, hands folded under his head, staring unblinkingly at the light in the ceiling. He made no move when Capolino and Malone appeared.

"Get up, Stark," Capolino said. "We're gonna talk again."

Stark gave no sign that he'd heard. His gibbous eyes, hard and intense in a wide, heavy face, swung toward Malone. His brass-colored hair was neatly cut behind his ears and along his neck.

"Get up," Capolino said again.

"I've been treated like a criminal," Stark said, still studying Malone. "Like a damned pervert. A real American shouldn't be treated this way."

Malone almost smiled. He'd had other experiences with men like Stark. When Stark found out that Malone was with the Agency his manner would change. He was the sort to be impressed by the presence of a Federal agent and he'd feel more secure, certain he'd receive a more sympathetic response from the IIA. It was, Malone told himself wryly, a conclusion often justified. He displayed his ID card and, after reading it carefully, Stark came to his feet, hand outstretched.

"Well, that's more like it." He pumped Malone's hand. "I figured

55

some good American eventually would be around to straighten this out."

"What can the Agency do for you, Mr. Stark?" Malone said politely.

"These monkeys," Stark said, "have pushed me around, deprived me of my constitutional rights."

Capolino sighed. "Nobody's touched you, Stark. You've been told about your rights and you refused legal representation."

"I have done nothing wrong!" Stark shouted. "I'm a loyal American citizen trying to work for law and order, to eliminate corruption, to turn the nation back on the path the Founding Fathers set us upon. Who has defamed the flag? Who has prevented good Christian children from acknowledging their Creator every morning in the classrooms? Who has forced the mixing of the races upon us? I ask *you*, Mr. Malone, as a servant of the people . . ."

"Oh, Jesus!" Capolino muttered.

"Mr. Stark," Malone said without expression. "Captain Capolino is investigating the death of Mr. Masters. The IIA is doing the same. Of course you want to cooperate."

Stark's manner softened. "Well, sure. But you can't suspect me. One of us trying to kill Mr. Masters!"

"You mean," Capolino said softly, "one of you Continental American Patriots?"

Stark's face closed up. He spoke in a voice thin and querulous. "I should not have been pulled in. Cops ought to be out protecting property instead of hassling patriots. I mean, what about your oath, your duty, the country comes first?" He glanced sidelong at Malone, a sly smile lifting the corners of his mouth. "Isn't that right, Mr. Malone?" He sat back down. "But I was confident that someone would be along to see to my interests . . ."

Capolino looked at Malone, then back at Stark. "What is that supposed to mean?"

Stark set his mouth.

"What are you trying to say, Mr. Stark?" Malone said.

Stark lowered his voice. "The bastards are moving against us. You can see that. They got Mr. Masters and who can say who will be next? Something has to be done. The enemy is out there. That's why we—" He broke off and looked away. "An IIA agent should understand these things."

"Stark," Capolino said. "You were carrying weapons, loaded and concealed, which at the very least is a violation of the Sullivan Law in this state. More, you made threats. We might even be able to make a case of sedition against you. I have a witness."

"An informer," Stark said.

"Did you shoot Mr. Masters?" Malone said.

Stark jerked around, eyes going. "That's crazy! I loved him. We all loved him. If I was going to kill anybody . . ."

"That's it, isn't it?" Capolino said. "You were aiming for Reese and you missed."

"Let me get a traitor in my sights and I won't miss."

"You were trying to shoot Reese," Capolino said.

Stark folded his big hands in his lap, stared at the wall. "You're wasting your time. I won't be intimidated. I won't say anything I don't want to say. You won't be able to keep me here. I have friends. Powerful friends. You'll see." He swung around to Malone. "You disappoint me. You should know better."

Stark lay back down, cradled his head in his hands and peered into the ceiling light again.

Capolino walked out of the cell and Malone followed him back to the second floor office.

"The bastard did it," Capolino said, settling behind his desk.

"You want him to be the one."

"Yeah, I guess so. I don't like his kind. I wish I had enough to charge him, then we'd see how tough he is."

"Are you going to hold him?"

"Yeah," Capolino said after a moment. "For another twenty-four hours, maybe thirty-six. That's the best I can do."

"What about the gun charge?"

"I could lay that on him. Maybe I will."

"We'll run a bureau check on him."

Capolino scribbled something on a piece of paper. "He's from nearby Oklahoma City. Recruiting for the CAP. That should be enough for your people."

57

Malone accepted the note.

"Stay in touch," Capolino added.

Malone made a noncommittal sound and left.

It took less than an hour for the seaplane to reach Senator Reese's Connecticut home on the edge of Long Island Sound. From the air, the complex of buildings appeared neatly geometric, modest. The main house was red brick, encircled by a screened porch, a carefully tended lawn sloping gently down to the sea wall. In the most westerly corner, there was a swimming pool and beyond it a red-clay tennis court. Two diminutive figures in white swatted a ball back and forth.

The landing was rough, the tiny plane bouncing from wave to wave, finally settling down and taxiing into shore. On a planked pier, two men were waiting. One, clearly an employee, tied the plane securely in place.

Malone climbed out of the plane and as he did the second man came forward. There was the hunched thrust of a sprinter about him, the distrustful look of a man who didn't know what to do with his hands.

"I'm Martin Williams, Malone, the Senator's executive assistant." Williams withdrew his hand and hurried along the dock, Malone following. "This won't take long, I hope. The Senator needs his holidays. Washington drains a man, and the events of the last few days . . ."

"Surely the Senator wants this affair settled quickly," Malone said.

"Naturally," Williams said, not looking back. "All of us do."

Naturally . . . The word was repeated in Malone's brain. It came so easily, not only to Williams, but to everybody connected with the case. That glib assurance left Malone wondering whether anyone really cared if the murderer were caught. Had it been a mistake to accept the assignment? He had wanted the job very much, more than any other. But the doubts continued. Pressures were building and he was being drawn into sensitive areas, faced with powerful forces and ambitious people, people who could do him damage should he make even a single mistake. He allowed his eyes to rest on the quick-striding man in front of him. Martin Williams gave off that scent of danger, of threat. And Charles Reese . . .

They swung onto a rock path that carried them past the red-brick house. Now Malone was able to see its impressive proportions, one of those houses that had mushroomed as additional rooms and wings were needed. They went past the house toward the tennis court.

Williams pulled up in the shade of a green, canvas awning. "The Senator's in the far court. He plays an excellent game, almost at a professional level."

Malone watched. Tennis had never been his game. He preferred the intimacy and contact of rougher sports. There had been a deep satisfaction in pitting himself against another man, the close competition of sweating flesh and muscle and bone. That way it was all guts and strength, man against man. And nothing matched that instant when an opponent gave way—the stench of his fear a palpable thing.

Seeing Charles Reese play made tennis seem less effete to Malone. The Senator was a large, wide-shouldered man with strong legs and an aggressive style of play. He attacked the ball, moving forward swiftly, his shots low, skidding, never giving up. Malone imagined Masters would have played tennis the same way, and he judged Reese to be a tough opponent in any endeavor, someone who never quit. There was, Malone told himself admiringly, something eminently correct about a man in his middle years who kept himself in competitive condition.

After a few minutes, Malone's attention was drawn to the other side of the court. Two women in tennis whites waited their turn to play. The taller of them was Reese's wife, Dorothy, and Martin Williams' first cousin, Malone knew. There was a faintly reminiscent quality about her, but Malone was sure they'd never met. She was a tall woman with a glowing skin and her brown hair pulled straight back off her smooth brow, making her seem much younger than her years.

All at once Malone remembered—and remembering, a vision

of Helen Wilson drifted into view. Another agent had introduced them during Malone's third year with the IIA. The daughter of an Army colonel, Helen Wilson had been very much like the other girls he had met in Washington. Sweet-faced girls in McMullen blouses and Shetland sweaters, with the shining veneer of carefully scrubbed choirboys. She was slender, pretty, with brown hair that was always combed and barretted. A conscientious girl, she had a minor talent for the kind of simple cooking Malone had always enjoyed. She kept her apartment immaculate, everything in its own place, and Malone's extended silent periods didn't offend her.

They saw each other twice a week, having quiet dinners at inexpensive restaurants, going to movies mostly, and seeing an occasional touring Broadway musical at the National Theatre. After a year, Malone decided that he was unlikely to find a girl who would make him a better wife. His mind made up, he requested an interview with the Director. Three days later, he was summoned into Masters' private office.

"There's a girl," Malone had begun. "She would make a good wife . . ."

"Helen Wilson," Masters said flatly.

Malone wasn't surprised that Masters knew about Helen Wilson. He nodded.

"Have you proposed to the young lady?"

"Not yet."

Masters looked past Malone for a long silent time and Malone began to feel uneasy in his skin. "Ask yourself," Masters said finally, "if marriage is a correct step for you, Malone. At this time. If the answer is yes, then by all means get married. But examine your motives. Are you being entirely fair to Miss Wilson? Your life is uncertain. There will be abrupt changes of assignment, shifts of station, personal danger. Is marriage now in her or your best interest, in the best interest of the Agency?"

Malone made no reply.

Masters smiled. "I am not opposed to marriage. I have a lovely and dear wife. But I did not marry in haste, nor too young. I was well established in every way before making that commitment."

Malone went away and considered what Masters had said and

decided that if marriage to Helen Wilson was meant to be it would eventually happen. But not yet. Not now. His work and the Agency came first.

Twenty-two days later he was transferred to San Diego. After six months, he was sent to Laredo, Texas, where he worked with the border patrols. Next, Minneapolis for eight months, then Detroit. While in Detroit, he learned that Helen Wilson had married a dentist and settled in Boston. Malone was going to send a congratulatory note, but decided against it; a clean break was always best.

Malone had never regretted the loss; at least, not for very long. The nature of an agent's life prevented him from being a normal husband and father. Masters, able to see ahead with an objective view, had understood that. He was a man who dealt realistically with every sort of problem, a man whose judgment could always be trusted.

A high lob sent Senator Reese back to the baseline, and pulled Malone's attention back to the court. He watched as the Senator twisted and came up on his toes, smashed the ball back across the net. It went skipping past his opponent, untouched. The women clapped enthusiastically. The match was over; Reese had won. A few minutes later, Charles Reese came over to where Malone was waiting with Martin Williams.

"Sorry to have kept you waiting," he said. "Ralph and I always seem to get involved in these extended matches. Ralph is a first-rate player. Shall we go up to the big house, have a drink?"

"I'm taking you away from Mrs. Reese," Malone said.

The Senator shook his head. "Dorothy won't mind. Having me around puts a competitive strain on her game."

Malone looked out at the court. Dorothy Reese moved with the easy grace of a woman who functioned well under pressure. Not that Malone particularly wanted to watch; women rarely did these things as well as men.

On the wide back porch of the main house, the three men settled into painted wicker chairs and looked out at the Sound. A servant brought gin and tonic for Malone, iced tea for Reese, and nothing for Martin Williams. In Reese's presence, Williams appeared to fade into the background, a man who would say little and remember everything.

"Malone," Senator Reese began. "I appreciate your coming out here to see me. I try to spend as much time as I can with Dorothy."

Malone respected Reese's affection and concern for his wife. He had never enjoyed that kind of relationship with a woman, concluded finally that men's lives led them in separate directions. His life had been shaped by the Agency, given depth and meaning by his associations in the IIA and the community of concern that the Director always insisted upon.

"Politics makes stringent demands on people," Reese was saying. "Families often are separated and Washington can be a stultifying city for a woman of Dorothy's temperament and intellectual interests. She prefers it here among the things she loves, near her old friends. I suppose your work takes you away from home often, Malone."

"My home is wherever the Agency sends me, Senator. I never married."

"I see. That may be the best way for men in demanding careers. It simplifies life." He smiled wistfully. "But you're here to talk about other matters."

"Yes sir," Malone said.

Martin Williams shifted around in his chair. "What have you got, Malone?"

"The investigation is moving ahead—"

"Oh, hell," Williams said. "People are shooting at Senator Reese and nothing's being done."

Malone turned to face Williams.

"Wait long enough," Williams continued, "and someone will try again. Whoever did this, they must be exposed, brought to trial, punished."

Reese looked into his glass. "Easy, Martin. Mr. Malone wants the same results we do."

"Yes, but all this dawdling. What if they try again?"

Malone said, "The President ordered the Secret Service to provide . . ."

"Six men," Williams said, voice climbing. "In shifts. They didn't even show themselves when your plane landed."

"They were watching."

"I'm not so sure. Not of the competence of the police or of the IIA. Except for a single interview the day after the shooting, not one police officer has been near us. It's as if the Senator was on the moon when this happened."

"The New York police are holding a man," Malone said, voice dropping.

"You see, Martin," Reese said. "Things are happening. I don't imagine it would be sound police work to announce everything in the press. Isn't that right, Malone?"

Malone appreciated the Senator's attempt to ease the tension. It was the kind of thing Masters did so well, to exclude emotion from their work, to keep every man's attention firmly on target.

"This fellow the police are holding?" Reese went on.

"He's being checked out," Malone said. "He might've done it, he might not."

"Oh, that's great!" Williams said. "The very efficient IIA operating behind the scenes like some domestic version of the CIA. I thought it knew everything, could do anything. At least J. Edgar Hoover gives us those yearly reports of his, lets us know what the FBI is doing. Well, running down some small-time gamblers or hauling in a handful of Mexican wetbacks isn't enough. This is murder we're dealing with and the public is entitled to some action."

Resentment gathered in Malone and he set himself against it, spoke in a low, measured tone. "There's something you should know, Mr. Williams . . ."

"Martin," Reese said quietly. "Remember, it was Mr. Masters who was killed."

"An accident," Williams said with contempt in his voice. "I want you to know, Malone. We've been getting a succession of scurrilous phone calls, anonymous letters, threats . . ."

Reese exhaled audibly. "In light of the kind of hate mail that's come in, Malone, I too feel that perhaps the bullet that killed Mr.

Masters was meant for me. My public image doesn't please all Americans."

Malone said, "It's possible the assassin was after you."

"Well, surprise!" Williams said. "A policeman with an imagination."

Reese raised a hand. "The political polarization in the country seems to have spilled over, Malone. No matter what your attitudes are these days, your enemies place you on one extreme or the other. Even the middle is dangerous ground."

"The Agency wants the man who pulled the trigger, Senator, and anyone else who may be involved. Beyond that—well, politics is not my business."

Williams hunched forward. "Then you admit there's a conspiracy?"

"It's possible."

Williams snorted disparagingly.

"We don't have information that tells us it was a conspiracy."

Reese said, "The nation is mobilized. There are subgroups armed for confrontation, ready to kill and destroy in the name of freedom. But the freedom they talk about so readily they deny to everyone else. For them, political assassination is, I'm afraid, the inevitable weapon."

"This guy you're holding . . . ?" Williams said.

"The New York police," Malone corrected. "His name is Jethro Stark."

"What about him?" Williams said.

"He hasn't been charged," Malone said. "There's nothing to say until we get something one way or another."

"Fair enough," Reese said. "Our concern, Martin's and my own, is that this matter be thoroughly investigated. A prompt solution is vital, not only for my peace of mind, Malone, but to help calm the entire country. The people are unsettled, suspicious of each other . . ."

"When there's something definite," Malone said, "you'll be told. Meanwhile, we want your cooperation."

"Of course," Reese answered promptly.

"The night it happened, did you see anything prior to the shot?"

64

Reese shook his head. "I never actually heard the shot. We had started down the steps, there were the reporters, the TV. Masters said something about his car not being there, he seemed to stumble, go down. I tried to help him up, I saw the blood. It was all very fast, stunning . . ."

"You left the hotel with Mr. Masters. Was there any indication that someone had alerted the gunmen to your appearance?"

"You mean a signal?"

"Yes."

"Nothing that I noticed. Masters seemed anxious to talk, though we were never friends, hardly knew each other. I had the feeling he was after something."

"What did you talk about?"

Reese considered. "Nothing really. Only a few words about politics, patriotism, on the facetious side. Just some words."

"We'd like to examine the mail you've received."

Williams stood up. "You won't find anything there. The usual crank stuff. Bigots and racists, the radical militants, gun-lobby types, and a passel of retired Army colonels."

Malone agreed with Williams' description. For the most part, it would be accurate. Few of the letters would be signed and many of those would have false names on them. Still, there was always a chance . . . Malone would have the technicians in the Agency lab go over each piece. They would match handwriting and frequency of word-usage to the printouts from the National Crime Information Center. They would discard crank material and turn over to psychologists the remaining letters. There might be a fingerprint to trace, or an identifying watermark, or a postmark that would lead to a post office that would lead to . . . In any case, with typical Agency thoroughness, the margin for error would be cut down. False trails would be eliminated, leads that went nowhere. The procedures had long ago been standardized, according to Masters' directives. Nothing would be left to chance.

Williams led the way into Senator Reese's study. He handed Malone a large brown envelope. "I hope your people know their business," he said.

Malone swallowed. "We do our best."

"Is there anything else, Malone?" Reese said.

"Not now. But I may have to get back to you."

"Of course. Here or in Washington, or at my New York office. Just call, someone will always know where I am. I'll go out to the plane with you."

They were on the narrow wooden pier when Reese cleared his throat. "Have you been with the Agency for very long?"

"Almost twenty years."

"You look too young to have done anything for two decades." Before Malone could reply, he hurried on. "I suppose you spent a great deal of time with Masters?"

A succession of blurred images faded onto the screen of his mind. Masters . . . there was a fine angle to that sensitive mouth, an amused tilt to the aristocratic mustache, and as always the cool, gray eyes were remote, all-seeing.

"I owe everything to Mr. Masters."

"You liked him?"

"He was the greatest man I ever met. Perfect."

"Sometime perhaps we can sit down and talk, over dinner one night, or drinks. I'd like to hear all about him. He was a fascinating figure—rather mysterious, remote."

"A very special man."

"I confess, Malone, I was never one of his admirers. Not that I really knew him. Until that night, I'd spoken to him only across committee tables. He always seemed withdrawn, almost"—he shrugged—"as if he was above the rest of us."

"He was actually a warm man, devoted to his work, loyal to his staff. The men at the Agency trusted him with their lives—all of us."

Reese nodded thoughtfully. "That night, for the first time, I was allowed to see his charm. He was affable, easy. I was impressed by his personal force, a kind of magnetism. I distinctly felt he was exercising some kind of control over me, manipulating me for some purpose only he knew." Reese laughed shortly. "Do I sound confused? It's because I am. Masters had quite an effect on me, one I've not yet figured out."

Malone thought he understood. To be in Masters' company was

to discover yourself placed in a secondary position, made somehow passive and powerless, conscious of weaknesses formerly unrecognized, of inadequacies, even guilt. Not that Masters visibly imposed his will or his desires. Yet just by the impact of his personality, a defined hierarchy was established and there was no doubt in anyone's mind as to who stood first and on top.

"There was real greatness in Mr. Masters," Malone murmured.

Reese responded without haste. "I'll always be curious about that night, about why Masters sought me out. He seemed to want us to leave together, as if being seen with me had some secret value to him."

Malone wondered about that also, all the way back to Manhattan. And by the time the plane put down in the East River, he believed he had found the answer, had even known it for a long time. But it didn't seem to matter very much, now that Masters was dead.

There was the usual summer fog, rolling but not too dense. Malone drove carefully, in no particular hurry, handling the rented car with the casual disdain of a superior driver. He knew San Francisco well, having worked in the area for nearly two years early in his career. Yet he retained no sense of the place, no vivid memories or clinging sentiments; it had become just another city, another faintly remembered catalogue of experiences, of cases worked on and closed, of men and women left behind when he was sent elsewhere.

Malone turned onto the Bay Bridge. He'd come West on a hunch, hoping that the man he wanted might still be around. Joseph Wu, Chinese immigrant, forty-three years old, unmarried.

Wu had sent a letter to Senator Reese and signed it, using only his surname. Nevertheless, locating him had been comparatively simple. He had entered the country from Taiwan, nearly six years ago, never bothering to apply for citizenship papers. Soon after his arrival, he went to work for an importer named Leo Shelley, had been with him since. Most interesting, Wu was in New York on the night W. W. Masters was killed and from his letter it was clear that he hated Charles Reese, wanted him dead, had vowed to turn that wish into a reality. Malone saw in Wu a chance to put it all together into a neat and complete package, thereby resolving his need to make order out of chaos.

Malone had considered letting a local agent interview Shelley, try to find Wu; any information gathered could have been sent on to Washington or New York. But the idea troubled him; this was his case and he needed to be involved in every twist it followed. The killing had been *that* important to him.

In Oakland, he swung south toward the naval airbase and down to Central Avenue. A turn brought him onto a quiet street within sight of the Bay, a street lined with low factory buildings and warehouses. A sign read: Leo Shelley, Imports. Malone stopped the car and went inside.

A pretty Chinese girl sat behind the reception desk. She took his name and asked him to wait, went to an unmarked door, hips fluid under a miniskirt, and disappeared. Minutes later she returned, burnished cheeks glowing, and patting her fine black hair into place.

Malone showed no reaction. He watched the girl go back behind the desk and produce a mannered professional smile before she spoke.

"Mr. Shelley will see you now."

Malone thanked her and went through the unmarked door. Leo Shelley was a man put together out of concentric circles of flesh. The great, hairless head was set low on thick, curved shoulders, the bulging, flabby chest straining under a white silk shirt, a huge belly. His eyes were dark and round and his mouth puckered with a watchful sweetness that made him look like an animated Buddha behind his polished Chinese desk.

He rocked in his chair as if trying to stand when Malone appeared, but didn't make it, falling back with a wry exclamation. "Excuse me, sir, excuse me. I am a man of sensual indulgences, as my figure bears witness. I should not have kept you waiting." The curved shoulders lifted and rolled, sagged back into place. "Still, you saw little Gloria Chan. What a delight she is! Perfect in every way." He frowned. "A trifle too heavy in the flanks, you might say, and you would be correct. A racial characteristic. Chinese girls don't have good legs, you know. Ah, well, to expect everything is to be absurdly selfish. Would you care for tea, Mr. Malone? Gloria brews with rare delicacy and cherishes the opportunity for strangers to taste her good efforts. The tea is made in Taiwan from a bitter grass, Mr. Malone. Very excellent, very Chinese."

Malone said he would be glad to have some of Gloria Chan's tea and Shelley touched a button on his desk. The girl appeared carrying a tea service. She served each of them and withdrew, smiling behind her hand.

"Gloria and the tea set are both from Taiwan," Shelley explained. "I am a man who believes in mixing business and pleasure, finding equal enjoyment in both. I do most of my business with the Generalissimo's people, you know."

Malone had learned something about Shelley before flying to San Francisco. He imported such items as the tea set, and lace, small electrical appliances, toys, novelties. It was, Malone had discovered, a thriving enterprise.

A reflective smile curled Shelley's tiny mouth. "The Nationalists have performed miracles on Taiwan, you know. And as the quality of their workmanship increases, our sales charts rise. It is my hope, as it is the G'issimo's, that one day soon he will return to the mainland, overthrow the Communists, and place that marvelous country back in the high esteem which she deserves."

Malone had no interest in any of this, except insofar as it affected his work. The file on Shelley revealed that his official anti-Communism was intense, skillfully implemented. He headed the One China Group, one of several Nationalist China lobbies, whose annual five-million-dollar budget was spent to obtain favorable legislation.

Shelley eyed the cup in Malone's hand. "But you aren't enjoying your tea. It is too bitter, perhaps? I could have Gloria bring some coffee, or something stronger?"

Malone put the cup down. "No, thanks."

"It was most distressing, not being able to get to Washington for Mr. Masters' funeral. He was a great man. Working with him was a pleasure, sheer pleasure."

A faint memory came drifting back to Malone; it refused to come into focus.

"Business," Shelley said. " 'The business of America is business.' Calvin Coolidge said it, you know. People tend to misunderstand his meaning, but he was right, you know. My business, for example, Malone, so many people depend on my efforts. What happens to them if I make mistakes, or if the business goes bad? Why they're out of work and they go hungry." He giggled. "All those cute little Chinese girls working for me. Got to take care of them all." He glanced at Malone. "I suppose Masters explained everything about me to you . . ."

Malone waited. Waiting was so much a part of the job; people enjoyed telling what they knew, anxious to display their wit, their cleverness. All you had to do was wait and listen . . .

"But perhaps not," Shelley said. "One never knew for sure with Masters. He was complex and confusing, essentially a private man, secretive, but there was a greatness in him, don't you agree?"

"He was a giant."

"Indeed, a giant. 'It is excellent to have a giant's strength; but it is tyrannous to use it as a giant.' Shakespeare said it. Excellent sentiment, I believe." Shelley sipped his tea and watched Malone over the rim of the cup. He put the cup down and a look of triumph spread across his flabby face. "I thought so, Malone. You don't remember me."

Malone grew wary. That elusive memory . . . He tried to recall.

Shelley began to laugh. "I understand! You're a man who prides himself on remembering faces, names, putting them together. It's the job. But don't be too hard on yourself this time. I've changed. Oh, yes, changed radically. I was much more slender in those days and there was more hair on my head . . ."

Malone tried to see Shelley as he once was, to place him in another context, to recall their meeting. He drew a blank and experienced a thin discomfort. He held himself very still.

"Ten," Shelley said, enjoying the game, "maybe twelve years ago. But not here. In Washington. At the old Willard Hotel. They've torn it down, you know. Everything old, everything good, is being destroyed. 'The old order changeth . . .' Tennyson."

70

A filament of memory sparked and glowed in Malone's brain, flared brightly, giving off a defined picture. Malone had been working in Agency headquarters, then in a renovated townhouse on Massachusetts Avenue. He had been in charge of Congressional data, a job he found limiting and without challenge, but had done well nevertheless. Late one afternoon his phone had rung and when he answered he recognized the Director's voice ordering him to come to a certain room at the Willard Hotel. When he arrived, sunlight had been streaming through the blinds in rungs of brightness, making it difficult to see. Masters had introduced him to another man, to Leo Shelley. A quick, casual introduction, a flabby handshake.

"Ah," Shelley said. "By your expression, I see that you do remember. Very good."

"It had to with customs evaluations . . ."

"Exactly. You do have a fine memory. Business was not very good in those days. I was operating on the edge of bankruptcy most of the time. A friend of mine who held a post in the government arranged for me to meet with Mr. Masters. It was a fortuitous circumstance. Marine freight can be terribly expensive and I was buying goods in Taiwan in bulk amounts, being charged by the cubic rate. Cheap items mainly in those days and unless I could keep the price down I would lose out to the domestic competition. I explained all this to Masters and he said he thought he might be of some help. He sent for you—"

"Yes," Malone said softly.

"He said that cutting my shipping costs would require a change in tariff classifications, that this could be done only by changing the description of the goods . . . What a vital change came about as a result of that meeting! I became successful, Malone, and wealthy, thanks to Masters. I have always remained grateful . . ."

Malone remembered it all now. Masters had sent him out to San Francisco to discuss the matter with the man in charge of customs at the port of entry. A few easy changes in the records . . . and in a good cause, as Masters had explained . . .

"Masters and I grew close over the years," Shelley went on. "What a delightful man he was—cultivated, intelligent. He loved good music, you know, Wagner and Bach mostly, and he collected fine art." Shelley cleared his throat. "I introduced him to the mysteries of Chinese painting on silk. Soon after my fortunes changed, I was fortunate enough to come into a very rare, very exquisite work by Liang K'ai. Authentic Sung dynasty. A marvelous, delicate effort. It was my pleasure to make a gift of it to Masters. From time to time, there were other paintings and some rare porcelain, a counterpart of the tea set in front of us now."

Malone blinked once.

"A business such as mine," Shelley said, "depends on good information, contacts, assistance of different kinds. Perhaps one day, Malone, you may be able to help me. If that day should come, I would like to feel that we have an understanding. Masters, after all, is gone."

Malone made a strenuous effort to order his brain. "This visit has to do with the murder of Mr. Masters."

"If I can be of service, please call on me. But it seems to me that you are far afield."

"I'm looking for Joseph Wu," Malone said.

There was a flicker in the round eyes, a slight tightening of Shelley's small mouth. Then it was all gone and the fat face was again benign.

"Ah, Joseph, a good man. A hard worker. Unable, however, to adjust to life in these marvelous United States of ours. The language and our customs were barriers he could not overcome."

"Where is he?"

Shelley spread his hands helplessly. "Workers come and go, Malone. I don't keep track of them. He left my employ some weeks ago."

"Wu worked here as recently as a week ago."

"Yes, that's so. But he's left. I wouldn't know where."

Malone stood up. "This is official. Either cooperate now or we'll go down to the bureau. You'll be charged with complicity . . ."

Shelley grew pale and wet his lips. "You don't understand."

"Try me."

"Wu misused my trust, you know."

"Make the point."

Shelley's chest heaved, the flabby breasts moving. "He used my establishment for illegal activities and I could not tolerate that. He brought in contraband items."

"Drugs?"

"I had nothing to do with it. As soon as I found out what he was up to, I discharged him."

"When was this?"

"About two weeks ago. I gave him a chance to stop and he promised to do so. But he took advantage of my goodwill and continued these operations. I let him go."

"What else?"

"Well. Wu's political activities were a bit too . . . extreme for me."

"Explain, please."

"He voiced rather violent sentiments towards anyone who failed to agree with his own point of view."

"Made threats?"

"I put no stock in that. You see—"

"Did he mention Senator Reese? Did he ever threaten to harm the Senator?"

Shelley raised his brows and his eyes seemed to enlarge. "As a matter of fact, yes."

"Wu sent a letter to Reese. He said it was Reese who should have been killed. That Masters' death was an error. He said that Reese would be next."

"Surely you don't believe that Wu meant any of that! He might have written such a letter but he isn't a man who would—"

"The letter was postmarked at the GPO in Manhattan only hours after the shooting. Wu was in New York that night. He could have pulled the trigger."

"Well, yes, but so could anyone else who was there. Eight million people live there, tourists, visitors . . ."

"Wu was the only one who sent a threatening letter and signed it."

Shelley sagged in his chair.

"In concealing him, you're breaking the law."

"He told me he had had enough of America, that he wanted to

go back to Taiwan. The Chinese, they're so ethnic. It must be the cooking."

"Where is Wu?" Malone said.

"I don't see how . . ."

"He didn't go to Taiwan, that's known. He caught TWA flight number 424a out of Kennedy for San Francisco the day after the shooting. The Agency has checked out every ship that left this area since. Wu was on none of them. Where is he, Shelley?"

Shelley managed a wan smile. "Why would I hide him? Why—"

"Because he was a smuggler and you're associated with him, tainted by him. I'm sure Wu didn't want to go back to Taiwan. He wanted to stay here, continue his smuggling operations. Getting rid of him must be your idea, a way of dumping an embarrassment."

"Look here, Malone, I've been very tolerant but you—"

Malone placed his fingers on the desk, leaned forward. The slight movement seemed menacing to Shelley and he flinched.

"We are talking," Malone said, speaking the words slowly, "about the murder of W. W. Masters."

"You can't think that I had anything to do with that!"

Malone looked directly into Shelley's eyes, the unblinking stare that Masters himself had used with such good effect.

"You are connected with Joseph Wu. We are looking for Joseph Wu. He talked about killing a United States Senator. He put it down on paper. On rice paper that your company imports from Taiwan. He may have acted it out, missed Reese and killed Masters. The Agency will find out."

Shelley milked his fingers. He was frightened by what was happening to him, frightened by Malone just as he had been frightened by W. W. Masters. They were two of a kind, controlled men, apparently never acting close to the source of their emotions.

"How do I know . . . ?" Shelley began. He heaved himself to a standing position, breathing noisily. "If I give Wu to you, I must be sure that I will in no way be involved. No suggestion of blame must fall on me. After all, I am innocent of any wrongdoing. The smuggling was all Wu's . . ."

Malone straightened up, said nothing.

"There mustn't be any involvement with the police, you know.

That's why I decided to get rid of Wu. There's a ship out of Seattle in three days. Some of my people are going to see that Wu gets there, gets aboard. All the arrangements are made. The captain and I have a kind of partnership, so I can be certain he will hand Wu over to the proper authorities in Taiwan. That way, he will never return. Oh, dear me, Malone. I surely don't want any trouble."

"Where is he?"

Shelley sighed and reached into his desk drawer, withdrew some keys. He came from behind the desk, went out of the office, Malone a stride to the rear. Beyond the reception room was the factory area where lines of workers, all Orientals, mostly women, were busy assembling and packaging various items. In the far wall, a narrow, green door. Shelley unlocked it and they went down a wooden stairway. In the basement, an iron door. Shelley unlocked it and pushed it open.

They entered a small chamber. Four Chinese men sat around a card table, playing poker. One of them, seeing Shelley, grinned nervously and began to chatter in Chinese. Shelley answered brusquely. Terrified, the man's eyes darted to Malone.

"Joseph Wu," Shelley said.

Malone said nothing. But he knew at once that the Director had not been killed by this frightened little man.

VIII

BARNEY'S WAS on the corner of Eighth Avenue, half-a-block from the station house. It was a bar that served large mugs of cold beer at good prices and maintained an air of dark intimacy that encouraged serious drinkers, adulterers, and others requiring a cover of privacy for their activities.

Capolino arrived first. He settled down at a small, round table in the open back room where he could see past the long bar to the front door, and could be seen. Capolino believed in conducting his business in public, whenever possible; that way people were not likely to suppose that his dealings were either secretive or illegal. Capolino held that a good cop was as concerned about what people thought about him as about what he did.

Five minutes later, Hellman joined him. They drank beer and talked about the Mets' chances, about the heat and the pollution and the fact that Capolino intended to marry for the third time in September.

"When it's cooler," the detective explained. "I sweat too damned much. My second wife hated it, when I sweated. You should get married, Hellman."

"I did once."

"You run around too much."

"We're both promiscuous, Capolino, only you make it legal and I don't."

Capolino began to clean his glasses. "Being married can be a very good thing."

"For peace of mind and contentment, give me an ex-wife every time. That mistake still costs me."

"You're too bitter . . ."

"Six hundred dollars a month worth of bitterness."

"Marriage *is* a contract."

"In the eyes of man and God, you mean?"

Capolino adjusted the glasses into place. "You know I don't go to church."

Hellman grinned. "Why don't you pay your back dues in the Holy Name Society?"

"I liked your father a lot, Hellman. He wasn't a comedian."

Hellman raised his hands. "Sorry, Captain Capolino. No offense intended."

"You can buy me another beer to make up for it."

Hellman signaled the waiter for two more beers. They drank without saying anything. Finally Hellman broke the silence. "I'm into a new investigation, Joe."

"What is it this time—the alcoholic content in hair tonic or—"

"The Masters shooting."

The change that took place in Capolino was subtle, a stiffening expression around his mouth. "You're not a cop," he said, voice edged with toughness.

"That's a fact," Hellman said, trying to keep it light.

"Stay with truth in packaging. That's your field, not murder."

"The papers are full of it, Joe, the TV. It's all people talk about."

"Stay out."

"I can't do that, Joe. This is something I can ride. You can see that . . ."

Capolino leaned back, eyes almost invisible behind the thick lenses. "That's why you wanted to get together, about Masters . . ."

"Joe, you can help. Answer a few questions. Being able to quote a captain of detectives gives the story authority. I'll mention your name and—"

"Who is the story for?"

"Masses & Progress."

Capolino grunted. "Don't use my name. That lousy magazine doesn't like cops, acts like we're all animals. My name shows up in there and the PBA will climb up my back."

77

"Okay, your name stays out."

"I got nothing the papers haven't printed already." He thought about Jethro Stark on the wheel, being swung from one precinct to another in order to keep some smart lawyer from springing him, holding him for as long as was possible without leveling charges, hoping something solid would turn up. But Capolino wasn't going to tell Hellman about Stark; not yet.

"Let me tell you what I've got so far," Hellman said. "Then you fill in the holes. Or say where I'm off base."

"That won't be hard."

Hellman ignored the sarcasm. "I studied the murder scene. The hotel steps, the angle to the building where the shot came from . . ."

"Where the papers *said* it came from."

"Come on, Joe. You think I'd run a bluff on you? Gerber, Little and Kinderman, Theatrical Accountants."

"Where'd you get that? No paper had that name."

Hellman went on. "I duplicated the gunman's movements, Joe, into the building, up that fire exit, up the stairs. I retraced every step he took right into that side office."

"That room is off limits to everybody not officially involved."

"There are ways, Joe. My old man was seven years in the burglary division, he taught me everything he knew. Hell, with the tools he turned over to me I can open just about any lock in town."

"One day, when you get your ass in a sling, don't come running to me. I won't lift a finger, no matter how much your father meant to me."

Hellman laughed. "I'll remember, if it happens."

"You'll see, some smart rookie is going to bust you and find those tools and you'll buy three to five. You'll see."

"Is this going to be a law and order lecture, Joe?"

"Smartass. All right, what else you got?"

"Let's talk ballistics for a minute . . ."

"Has Tony Mante been running off at the mouth? I'll see he walks a beat in Staten Island for the rest of his time."

"Mante's not the only ballistics guy in the city. The point is, I've gone over the ground—trajectory, muzzle velocity, angle of fire, all of it. There are three windows in that office. One is too deep in the side street, impossible to make the shot from there. The police say the center window was used . . .”

“What do you say?”

“The center window makes sense only if the guy was after Reese.”

“We believe he was.’”

“Uhuh. It was Masters.”

Capolino jabbed a finger at Hellman. “Only amateurs try to make facts fit theories. There were scars on the sill of the window facing the Avenue, scars that could’ve been caused by the muzzle of a rifle, or the butt plate. The odds are it was a military weapon. He probably rested it on the sill, brought it down too heavily. Moved it around maybe.”

“Causing wood scars?”

“Right.”

“Well, don’t you see? He stood at the window waiting. From there he had a straight shot at Masters!”

“I don’t buy it. He wanted Reese.”

“No, no. I marked the position, Joe. Traced the path Masters and Reese followed out of the hotel. Masters was in the line of fire all the time, Masters was nearest to the gunman, Masters was who he wanted. Joe, it does make sense.”

Capolino breathed deeply, exhaled. “This is empty talk. We don’t even have the murder weapon. Get back to basics. Why did this guy want Masters dead?”

“Masters *was* a growing threat to the political left. Over the last few years he’s been putting the Agency more into the political scene. On the quiet. Agents infiltrating . . .”

“Hold on!” Capolino broke in. “That’s all cocktail party chatter. Your liberal pals may believe that crap but I know it’s not so. That wasn’t Masters’ bag. There are no IIA agents on campuses and they don’t go around taking pictures of everybody at a protest demonstration and they aren’t tapping the telephones of radical lawyers. No matter what you hear, it’s not that way.”

Hellman grew somber. “People believe otherwise, Joe, so it might as well be true.”

“What kind of logic is that? Sure, some nut can believe anything he wants. But the IIA operation simply isn't that widespread, or that up to date. Jesus, Dan, stack the Agency against a modern urban police department like ours and it comes off second best."

Hellman grinned maliciously. "I thought Masters was right up there as a folk hero to all cops."

"You thought wrong. In the beginning, he was okay. He created the Agency, made it into an honest and efficient investigative organization. Within limits, they did their job and did it damn well. Then Masters seemed to change. The Agency got sort of flabby. Efficiency dropped off."

"What happened?"

"A couple of things. Masters began to hire and fire according to how close people fit his personal ideas. That made for a particular kind of agent, able only to do certain kinds of jobs. Also, Masters got more concerned with keeping up the appearance of a good record than in performance." Capolino smiled. "But that's just my opinion. I can dig up a dozen guys in the Department who'll say opposite, that Masters was a top policeman in every way. Take your choice . . ."

"People talk a lot about Masters," Hellman said. "There's a story that the IIA uncovered a blackmail operation in Washington. One of the victims was supposed to be a high-level official in the State Department, a married man with a family. There were the usual photographs. But Masters kept it quiet, kept the man's name out of the papers. That man is a Governor today and I'm told he never made a major decision without first getting Masters' opinion."

"Yeah? Well, I never heard *that* one . . ."

"Let's get back to the politics, Joe."

"You're buying the beers."

"Suppose some freaky radical did go after Masters, and got him?"

"Okay, let's suppose."

"Joe," Hellman said after a moment. "Who was in the building that night?"

Capolino grinned. "So you haven't been able to find out *everything*?"

"Not everything, Joe," Hellman said. "I spoke to the night watchman and he said the nightbook had been impounded by the police."

"Well, isn't that amazing!"

"Come on, Joe."

Capolino rubbed his thinning hair. The pressures were building —public, private, political. There was no way of avoiding them, there never was. But this time Capolino felt an expanding threat, the need to defend himself. Right now he had only Jethro Stark and that didn't amount to very much. In this kind of a case, his ordinary sources of information were no help.

Meanwhile, the demand for a solution became shriller, more insistent, and intra-departmental conflicts made it imperative that he come up with something soon. If Hellman were able to supply any help at all . . .

"Remember," he said wearily, "you didn't get it here."

"My word."

"The building was virtually empty that night. The watchman, of course, and some people on the fourth floor in the Joyful Noise Recording Studios. But that's all."

"Who was there?"

"A rock group cutting some sides. Nothing to it."

"What's the name of the group?"

"Silas' Trippers. The leader's name is Jimmy Silas. He's black and as usual these days unfriendly."

"What else?"

"Nothing else. Dammit, that's the problem. We don't really have anything else."

"Maybe I can get it."

"You know, Dan, I don't actually trust you. There's nothing worse than a cop who's gone wrong, unless it's a cop's son."

"Very funny."

"If you come up with anything, I expect to be told about it, *right away*."

"You got it, captain."

"Remember, this is no garbage killing. This is very big stuff."

"Don't worry about me, Joe."

Capolino shook his head sadly. "Pay for the lousy beers, willya . . ."

That evening Hellman went over the information he had managed to collect. He wrote it all out, studied it carefully, and concluded it amounted to very little he hadn't known earlier. Only the presence of the Silas' Trippers in the building at the time of the shooting was new and had they been worth serious suspicion, Capolino would certainly have mentioned it. Also, a group of unknown rock musicians would have little appeal to the readers of *M & P*.

What Hellman wanted was someone whose name and words would provoke interest and excitement, controversy, someone instantly recognizable, someone whose political standing was clearly established. He reviewed his notes again and finally fastened on Henry Cardinal McCoy.

The Cardinal might be able to provide the required spark. His Eminence was considered a conservative in most matters religious and secular, a close friend and supporter of W. W. Masters, a man who might readily agree that Masters was murdered by his enemies on the radical left. Hellman picked up the phone and asked Information for the number of the New York Archdiocese.

Hellman pressed his hands against his trouser legs until the palms were dry. Very deliberately, he inspected the narrow antechamber. Everything about the room added to the impression of ancient wealth and on-going power. The walls were paneled in old wood, burnished by time and regular hand rubbings; the floor was made of Vermont marble with an inlaid sunburst at one end, a rendering of glowing angels in flight at the other. Behind the angels, alongside the short wall, next to the wide doors that led to the Cardinal's office, was a small desk at which a priest worked over some typewritten pages. As if sensing Hellman's curiosity, he lifted his head. He was a slender man, dark, with moist eyes and a patient expression.

"His Eminence should be with you soon," he murmured. "I'm sorry you had to wait so long."

Being surrounded by these totems of the Church made Hellman uncomfortable. He tried not to let it show. "Was it you I spoke to when I called?"

The priest nodded cheerfully. "I am Father Perez, one of Cardinal McCoy's secretaries. His Eminence is most anxious to see justice done in this awful matter."

"Perhaps he can help me."

"Mr. Masters was a dear friend, to the Cardinal and to the Church."

"Did you know him, Father?"

"We met only once. Briefly on that night. I escorted His Eminence to the hotel and waited outside the ballroom until he was ready to depart. I did some paperwork while I was waiting. It was perhaps twenty minutes prior to the end of the dinner when Mr. Masters appeared. He wanted to make a phone call but all the booths were occupied. He asked would I make the call for him, so that he could get back to the dais. I was pleased to oblige him."

"Go on, Father!"

"That's all there is, Mr. Hellman. All I did was to dial the number Mr. Masters provided and deliver the message."

Hellman wanted to pursue the matter, to insist that the priest make the phone call meaningful.

But before he could speak, before he could isolate his thoughts, bring order to the jumble of ideas and suspicions, the wide doors swung open and the Cardinal appeared. His eyes were bright and searching and he was smiling.

"Mr. Hellman, isn't it? Sorry to have made you wait. Won't you please come in?"

Hellman trailed the soft rustle of the Cardinal's robes into his office. He was reminded of the side chapels of St. Peter's in Rome. Here was the same musty timelessness, the air still, heavy, the wood old and dark, the statuary pristinely white.

The Cardinal, a lean man with a pinched nose and slightly

protruding teeth, appeared to fit his surroundings. A gesture of one pale, veined hand directed Hellman to a chair with a carved back. When he was seated, the Cardinal withdrew behind his desk.

He lifted his upper lip in a smile. "How good of you to visit, Mr. Hellman. You must be a very busy man." The words were issued with practiced ease and Hellman understood that he was to be allowed only a few minutes. "Father Perez tells me that you're going to write about Mr. Masters."

"I'm investigating the circumstances of his death. . . ." Hellman wasn't sure how to begin. "So many people seem to want to make Mr. Masters' death into an accident, a mistake."

"You believe otherwise?"

"Yes sir. I think the killer was after Masters, that there was no mistake."

The Cardinal made a steeple with his fingers and rested his chin on its apex. It was a pious attitude, but for Hellman not one that inspired reverence. It caused Hellman to recall a story he had been told as a child. The Baal Shem Tov, the founder of Hasidism, had once stopped at the threshold of a house of prayer, refusing to enter. He told his followers that it was crowded with teachings and prayers from wall to wall and from floor to ceiling. "The words from the lips of those whose teaching and praying does not come from the hearts lifted to heaven, cannot rise, but fill the house . . . How could there be room for me?"

"Why," the Cardinal said, "should anyone want to kill Mr. Masters?"

"He made enemies . . . especially on the Left, among intellectuals, radicals."

"Is that not your position, Mr. Hellman? Out on the Left?"

"Perhaps. But I'm not closed to the truth."

"Ah, *the* Truth, Mr. Hellman. So many of us are sure of it and yet how seldom we can match it with anyone else's truth. Tell me about yours."

"I believe the killer was after Masters for political motives."

"Masters was a patriot," the Cardinal said.

"A patriot," Hellman repeated. "A man who held old-fashioned but not discredited notions of what this country should be."

"And he was killed for those notions?"

"Yes."

"Mr. Hellman, I find that I hold a certain sympathy for your theory, if it can be proved."

"I hope to do that."

The Cardinal looked up at the high, carved ceiling. "Mr. Masters was meant for important things. Guilt must be established and justice done. I wrote this to the President in the strongest language. I will have a copy of my letter forwarded to you, Mr. Hellman. Quote freely from it, if you like, and from this conversation as well."

"Thank you, Your Eminence."

Cardinal McCoy frowned thoughtfully. "It seems to me, Mr. Hellman, that we exist in a climate that encourages people to excesses of all kinds. A sickness seems to have spread across our land. Mr. Masters' death is a symptom."

"There is talk the assassin was after Senator Reese."

"I have heard that. It is, I believe, an effort to divert us from what actually happened, to allow the guilty parties to escape unpunished. In your search, perhaps I can be of service."

"Can we discuss the night of the murder? I'm sure you've told the story a dozen times."

The Cardinal spread his hands. "And in this good cause I gladly tell it a thirteenth. It was, as you know, my birthday and Mr. Masters attended the celebration dinner with other friends, all of whom did me honor. The dinner was excellent, the speeches happily short and amusing, and it was over too soon."

"Was anything said by Masters to you, some suggestion of danger, some hint of why anyone might want to kill him? He was Director of the IIA for many years and no attempt was ever made before."

"You're wondering why he was killed at this specific time?"

"Exactly."

"I'm afraid I can't help you. It was a strange night in certain ways. Masters was preoccupied, as if his mind lingered elsewhere. I asked him if he felt all right. He smiled in that contained manner of his and assured me he was in excellent health.

Otherwise, he was his usual self, charming, gracious, amusing."

Hellman was disappointed.

"What about Senator Reese?"

"What about Senator Reese?" Cardinal McCoy said with barely concealed waspishness.

"He was at the dinner."

"Yes, and frankly his appearance surprised me. A telegram had arrived at the Archdiocese earlier that same day announcing his regrets."

Hellman straightened up, excitement taking hold. "You mean he wasn't going to come!"

"I assumed so. There were the usual declarations of regret, mention of other obligations, of an attempt to attend if . . . Why should this matter to you, Mr. Hellman?"

"The telegram, have the police seen it?"

"Of course. And the IIA."

"And what was said about it?"

"Nothing at all. No one else has shown any particular interest. It was treated as routine. But you seem to give it a special value. Why?"

"I'm not sure. If Reese wasn't going to be there, isn't it likely that the killer might have known? His planning was so thorough in every other detail."

"Which means what, Mr. Hellman?"

"Well, if Reese wasn't going to be present, then obviously he couldn't have been the target. It had to be Masters. That telegram, Your Eminence, could I see it?"

"I'll do better than that. I'll have one of my secretaries locate it and make a copy. Those Xerox machines, fabulous devices, don't you think? You'll have it in a day or so, along with a copy of my letter to the President." The Cardinal rose smiling, ushered Hellman to the door.

Hellman went directly back to his apartment. He realized his interpretation of the Reese telegram might be based more on hope for proof of his theory than on reality, but it *could* have been that the killer knew even a last-minute change such as this, and if so and he went ahead anyway, Masters had to have been his intended victim. . . . He was just about to turn the key in the lock when his phone began to ring. He hurried inside, picked it up.

"Hellman here."

"Dan," came the familiar gruffness of Joe Capolino. "I was trying to get you earlier, to save you some work. . ." There was a taunt in the detective's voice.

Hellman grew wary. "What do you mean?"

Capolino began to laugh. "We got him, Dan, the guy that shot Masters. He's signed a confession . . ."

IX

MALONE SETTLED into his seat for the flight back to Washington. He adjusted the seat belt, put his head back and closed his eyes. *"Sleep whenever you can. You can never know when you may have to go without for extended periods . . ."* Travel time, Masters used to insist, was for rest or for thinking ahead. Had it been Masters who said that, or his own father? Tension settled along Malone's body. How odd to remember John Malone at this moment. At any moment. How long since he had seen him? How long since he had even thought about him?

As a boy, Malone had loved his father, admired him, wanted to be like him. John Malone was a cheerful, energetic man who laughed a lot, who was very strong, a man who seemed to know everything, a man who could do almost anything. Or so it had seemed to his son. Peter had tried to emulate his father in every way until a day in January, three days before Peter's fifteenth birthday, when John Malone had failed to come home from work. Peter never saw him again. John Malone vanished without a word to Peter's mother or anyone else, gone into the large and frightening world that Peter knew nothing about. There was a rumor that John Malone had departed in the company of a robust nineteen-year-old girl, but that had never been established as a fact.

For almost a year, Peter waited for his father to return, certain he would reappear as abruptly as he'd left. But he never did and one day Peter stopped waiting and began to hate John Malone, to hate everything he was, his sensual weaknesses, his cowardice, his betrayal of trust. And Peter vowed that he would never allow himself to become that kind of a man.

During his seventh year as an IIA agent—he had been working out of Charlotte, North Carolina—the receptionist had come into Malone's office to say that John Malone was in the waiting room, wanted to see him.

"Send him away," Malone had replied.

"But he says he's your father."

Malone had stared at the girl. "It's a mistake. I have no father."

Since then, he had never thought about John Malone, until this moment. He promised himself never to think about him again. He closed off his brain and tried to sleep. It was a futile effort. Josept Wu faded into view behind his lidded eyes. Joseph Wu, pathetic and defenseless.

Malone had come down hard on Wu. Wu had babbled and sobbed, insisted in Chinese that he was innocent, that he had killed no one, insisted that he had loved Masters, loved the United States, wanted to become a citizen.

Malone never doubted Wu's innocence. Still, after questioning him in Leo Shelley's basement, he took Wu to the IIA bureau across the Bay. There he kept Wu in isolation for nearly two hours. Then the little man was subjected to intensive interrogation by teams of agents.

Wu claimed he'd gone to New York to board a freighter bound for Hong Kong, where some friends would help him increase the scope of his smuggling operation. On the night of the Cardinal's birthday dinner, he had gone to the Hotel Americana with a companion, hoping to catch a glimpse of W. W. Masters, who, Wu said, he admired for his anti-Communist sentiments. He had seen Masters fall. Enraged, and determined somehow to avenge his hero, Wu had written a venomous letter to Senator Reese. In the letter, he threatened to shoot Reese, blaming him for Masters' death. After posting it, Wu recognized the enormity of the act and became afraid. He tried to board the Hong Kong-bound freighter, only to discover its departure had been put off for three days.

Wu panicked, flew back to San Francisco and put himself in Leo Shelley's hands. Shelley, recognizing the threat Wu presented to him, placed him under guard until he could arrange to have him transported to Taiwan.

While Wu was being questioned, his alibi was being checked out in New York. Herman Flood assigned a young agent named Benedict to the case. He tracked down George Lee, a waiter, who had been with Wu at the Hotel Americana. Lee corroborated Wu's story and Benedict was able to locate other witnesses who substantiated the major details. Satisfied as to his innocence, Benedict phoned Malone.

After almost fourteen hours of continuous questioning, Wu was told that he had been cleared. Wu began to cry, incoherent with joy. He tried to kiss Malone's hand in gratitude.

Malone had stepped back and surveyed Wu absently. "There is a Federal law which prohibits anyone from threatening the life or well-being of any Federal official," he said, as if by rote. "You'll be charged accordingly. In addition, information about your smuggling activities will be turned over to the Customs people."

Wu pleaded for mercy in Chinese laced with English. But Malone had stopped listening; he walked out of the room and confronted Leo Shelley. The fat man was pale and worried. Without emphasis, Malone told him everything.

"Wu can expect substantial prison terms on both charges," he finished.

Shelley mopped his brow. "What about me?"

Malone had asked himself the same question, tried to imagine how Masters would have dealt with the situation. He made an effort to recall Masters' exact words. Slowly they came floating back.

"The application of power is an exercise to be practiced and polished. A man who has power and doesn't use it is as weak as a man with no power at all . . ."

Malone stared at Shelley. "The evidence in this affair will be placed in a confidential file," he said, the words carefully spaced.

"No evaluation will be made on your role. Remind yourself of the facts—Fact: you were involved with Wu. Fact: Wu was a smuggler. Fact: a man in your employ made threats against the life of a United States Senator."

"I'm entirely innocent!"

Malone almost smiled. "No one is entirely innocent."

"That file?"

"The information in it will remain confidential. But there is margin for human error. Leaks have occurred in the past . . ."

Shelley protested. "Malone, listen to me! We can make a deal. Arrangements can be made . . ."

If Malone heard, he gave no sign, already walking rapidly away, his mind reaching ahead for what still had to be done.

When he arrived at National Airport, Malone called his desk at the IIA. A detached female voice answered and Malone identified himself, asked for messages. There was only one—call Captain Capolino, New York City Police Department. Malone hung up and called New York. He spoke briefly to Capolino, then went to the Eastern desk to board the next shuttle flight to La Guardia.

Two hours and seventeen minutes later, he stepped out of a cab and hurried inside a stationhouse in the Brownsville section of Brooklyn. The desk sergeant directed him to a rear stairway, at the base of which two officers examined Malone's credentials before allowing him to pass through an unmarked door. Malone felt renewed, alert, all senses tuned in, all weariness gone, all guilt dissolved, Joseph Wu and Leo Shelley neatly disposed of in some shadowed hemisphere of his brain.

The room was large and brilliantly lighted and it took a moment before Malone's eyes made the adjustment. A burly figure appeared out of the glare. Capolino. He needed a shave and he looked tired, but behind the thick lenses his eyes gleamed with triumph.

"Malone," he said, offering his hand. "Well, this time we got the sunuvabitch who did it!"

In the center of the room, floor-to-ceiling bars had been erected, forming a single cell. There, a hunched, pale man with large, luminous eyes and a wide contemptuous grin.

"Not so much to look at," Capolino said. "But we've got a confession . . ."

"How'd you get it?" Malone said.

"He gave it freely," Capolino said. "In front of witnesses, after being informed of his rights. He refused a lawyer."

"That's right!" the man in the cell said. "I don't need no crappy lawyer to defend me. I handle my own case better!"

Malone looked at the prisoner and he returned the look without flinching.

"His name is Roy Brewster," Capolino offered.

"A good American name!" the prisoner added cheerfully.

Malone turned away. Three other men were ranged against the far wall. One of them stepped forward; it was Herman Flood.

"Looks like this winds it up, Malone," Flood said. "The call came through to the bureau and I was informed, naturally. You don't mind my being here this way?" There was a suggestion of mockery in the words, and challenge.

Malone made no response. He brought his eyes around to the next man in line. It was Charles Reese. Malone concealed his surprise.

"Hello, Senator," he said.

"Mr. Flood called me, Malone, and I wanted to see the young man who so desperately wants to see me dead."

"Next time it *will* be you!" Roy Brewster said in a strong voice.

"Shut up," Capolino said wearily.

Malone examined Brewster. "What do you mean?" he said. "Why do you want Senator Reese to die?"

"He claims he's making the new American Revolution," a strange voice said. It was the third man, the man Malone didn't know. Malone turned to see him advancing, hand outstretched, aggressive and powerfully built, his arms extraordinarily long. "I'm Dan Hellman," he said.

Malone spoke to Capolino, not masking his displeasure. "What is this?"

92

"Dan Hellman," Capolino said, looking away. "A friend of mine. He has a special interest in the case . . ."

"You want another Dallas?" Malone said quietly.

"Dammit, I know my job!" Capolino said, voice gone heavy and morose.

"I'm researching the case," Hellman said. "Maybe we can help each other."

Malone measured him. "You're a newspaperman . . ." It was not a question.

"He's okay, I told you," Capolino said impatiently. "His old man was a cop, a friend. Come on, Malone, we've been waiting a long time for you. You going to talk to this guy or not?"

Malone walked over to the bars. The prisoner was young, attractive at close range. An ingratiating smile spread across his slender face.

"You must be somebody special, Malone," he said. "They been talking about you." His eyes went past Malone to the others. "Local fuzz, the press, the IIA. Hey, I always figured the Agency was just a rumor to scare cats like me."

"Why'd you want to kill Senator Reese?" Malone said.

Roy Brewster straightened his shoulders, grew serious. "You've heard of the Weathermen?"

"You're a member of the Weathermen?" Malone said.

"All power to the people!" Brewster raised his right fist.

Malone measured the other man professionally. Roy Brewster was ideally fashioned to end the charade, to stamp finish to the case. Unlike Joseph Wu, he evoked no sympathy in Malone, would fit the role in every way. The perfect murderer, the perfect victim.

There was no one else. Jethro Stark had been released after word came from the agent-in-charge of the Oklahoma City bureau—:

> Stark substantial citizen no criminal record.
> Decorated veteran Korea. Strong U.S. loyalties.
> No subversive connections.

Stark and Wu. False trails both of them. Common enough in a case like this; all the weirdos, the obsessive personalities, the cranks simmering with a sense of having been wronged, crying to be heard and seen, to take the spotlight.

Now this man of no apparent consequence—happy face, strong, large hands, white teeth. He offered himself up, wrapped himself in guilt. With some supportive evidence—and it would be easy enough to find—the case could be closed. A troubled citizenry would be reassured, could return to their usual pursuits, satisfied that justice had been done.

Malone walked away, kept his back to the cell. Capolino and Flood went after him.

"What have you got?" Malone said.

Capolino shrugged. "He lives by himself. There was a lot of Communist propaganda in his room. Lists of politicians and businessmen. He kept a journal and made comments on these people, made it clear he wanted to kill all of them."

"Reese?" Malone said.

"He'd made a list of people to kill. Reese was on it."

Malone hesitated.

"He's a good bet," Flood offered.

"I'm sure we can dig up more," Capolino said. "He's the kind who shoots his mouth off. There'll be witnesses. And we have got the confession."

Malone looked at Senator Reese.

Reese sighed. "The middle ground seems like a bad place to be. The Right sees us as agents of Moscow or worse and the Left puts us down as traitors, the cause of all the country's problems."

"You think this man tried to shoot you, Senator?" Malone said.

"It's too pat," Hellman said, coming forward. "I don't believe it."

"Why not?"

"The Weathermen are violent but they aren't into *political* assassination."

"Not yet," Capolino put in.

"Oswald was some kind of a leftist," Flood said.

"And James Earl Ray was a small-time hoodlum," Hellman said. "That doesn't prove anything."

"This isn't getting us anywhere," Malone said, dismissing them.

Hellman felt suddenly out of place, as if he weren't wanted, didn't belong with these people. He spoke swiftly. "I'm convinced that whoever did it was after Masters. If Brewster really is a Weatherman, a radical revolutionary, why wouldn't he have wanted to kill Masters? But no, he claims he was after Reese, that he missed. I don't think it makes much sense." He swung around to Brewster. "How good are you with a rifle, Roy?"

Brewster laughed. "I get lined up on you and I won't miss."

Malone moved closer to the bars. "Brewster, I think you're lying."

"What do you mean! I'm telling it like it is!"

"You're not the type, Brewster."

"What'sa matter with you! I thought you IIA guys were smart. You better believe it!"

"Whenever there's an important killing," Capolino said, swinging to Malone's position, "guys show up trying to make a name for themselves. But it's not so easy."

"You won't be able to handle the pressure, Brewster," Malone said.

"That's crazy. Both of you are nuts. I did it. Okay, so I goofed, right. My hand slipped and I missed Reese. I am filled with remorse, okay. Reese deserved to die before he could become President and hurt the people more. Liberals like him are the real traitors, the real sell-outs."

"It doesn't work that way," Malone said. "It has to be proved."

"I confessed, didn't I?"

"The law says there has to be a trial. You must be prosecuted, unless you plead insanity."

"No! I knew what I was doing. I'd do it again. Right now! Give me a gun and I'll kill Reese now!"

"Where's the gun you used?" Capolino said.

"When the time comes," Brewster said, "I'll produce it."

Malone turned away. "He didn't do it," he said.

"Wait a minute," Flood said. The blond face was grim. "We've got ourselves a pigeon here, a pigeon who confessed. He's provided us with his motive. Okay, there's no weapon. Maybe he broke it down, scattered the parts around town in various sewers or dumped them out in the bay . . ."

Brewster laughed. "Sure, I could've done it any of those ways."

Malone faced Flood. "No," he said.

Flood tightened. "The case also falls into my jurisdiction. Let's not give up on this guy so quickly."

"This man didn't do it," Malone answered. "We're wasting time."

"I agree," Hellman put in. "There's no logic to this—"

"Logic," Flood said, voice wintry, "has nothing to do with murder."

Malone addressed Capolino.

"Find out what you can about Brewster."

"All right. And meanwhile I'll keep him on ice. Where will you be, Malone?"

"A hotel. I'll let you know."

"Nonsense," Senator Reese said, smiling graciously. "I keep an apartment in the city, Malone. I insist that you use it. I'll be staying there tonight and it'll give us the chance to talk."

An evening with Charles Reese would be a welcome relief. Malone accepted the invitation.

Watching them leave, Hellman felt left behind once again. It had too often been that way for him. But when his investigation was finished, *everyone* would want Dan Hellman . . .

The Fifth Avenue apartment looked down on Central Park from a high floor. The full sweep of Manhattan was visible to the south and to the west, just beyond the jagged skyline, the Hudson River.

There was a reassuring, lived-in spaciousness to the rooms. Reese led Malone into a library that was all brown leather, old books, and paneled walls.

"This apartment is my favorite," he said. "I've always enjoyed New York and whenever I'm free, I stay here. When I was a bachelor—." He grinned. "Some brandy, Malone?"

The brandy was old and very strong and Malone enjoyed the slow, spreading heat throughout his body. "Senator," he said deliberately, "you realize that another attempt could be made on your life at any time?"

"Martin says the same thing. The risk goes with the job, I suppose. That means you're convinced Roy Brewster wasn't telling the truth?"

"I think he's trying to focus attention on himself. Instinct tells me he's not what he wants us to believe he is. He talks too much, for one thing, too easily, he's too anxious to have us believe that he's guilty."

"You think he's a fraud?"

Malone nodded. "Everything he says sounds too pat. Capolino will dig out the real story. His contacts in the radical scene . . . Then we'll know."

"Maybe you're right. Still, there is a kind of national hysteria. You heard Brewster; my moderate position somehow makes me the enemy. Dammit, Malone, there are too many public officials trying to make political capital out of an inflammatory condition and thereby making it worse. Some of my fellow senators are not exactly guiltless in this area . . ."

Malone liked that about Reese, the ability to see himself and his colleagues in a clear, objective light.

"What if you're wrong, Malone? What if that shot was intended for Masters?"

"There's no reason why anyone would want Mr. Masters dead, Senator. He was a fine man . . ."

"Surely he made enemies. Personal enemies. Criminals, perhaps."

"There have been threats. But most of that is talk. Criminals can't manage to build up much of a hate against enforcement officials. They expect to be caught, expect to spend a certain amount of time in prison."

"Occupational hazard?"

"Yes. Few of them ever saw Masters. Fewer ever met him. Still, somebody might have gone after him. The possibility exists, but it can't be given much credence."

"What makes you so sure?"

"Because very few people even knew what Masters looked like. He was a cautious man, a private person, and he stayed out of the spotlight. During the last ten years I doubt that one photograph of him was taken."

"Yet on that night . . ."

"Yes," Malone said. "He submitted himself to the press, the television people. But that changes nothing. Any potential assassin would have to know that he'd be there and Mr. Masters didn't announce his plans in advance. No, Senator, it was you the killer had to be after."

"You mentioned threats from criminals."

"There's a routine. Men who make threats when they're sentenced are kept under surveillance. Their prison files are flagged and just prior to their release the Agency is notified. They're watched. No man who ever made a threat ever tried to do anything about it."

"Still, Masters is dead.'

"Brewster didn't do it."

"What makes you so sure?"

Malone hesitated. "He's the third suspect we've turned up."

"There was Stark," Reese said.

"He's been released. One of those superpatriots given to talk and nothing more. Second was a Chinese national named Joseph Wu. He came out of that pile of mail you received."

"And?"

"He didn't kill anyone."

"And now Roy Brewster."

"He'll be another blind alley."

"How can you be so sure?"

"As I said, in this work, a man develops instincts, a feeling for guilt."

"That's interesting."

Malone's eyes were steady. "Consider this, Senator, all this may do you a great deal of political good. There's a sympathy vote in this country and you'll get it now. Wasn't it politics that brought you to the station house tonight?"

Faint amusement shone out of Reese's eyes. "Am I to infer that you think I arranged the shooting as a device to help my campaign?"

"Did you?"

Reese sank back in his chair. An ironic laugh came out of him.

"By God, Malone, that may be the most outrageous thing I've ever heard. If it weren't so far-fetched, I'd be alarmed. I assume it's your rather heavy way of testing me."

Malone waited.

Reese shook his head in disbelief. "I should be angry, I think. But I'm not." He laughed briefly, without mirth. "For a moment, a split second, I thought it was Masters talking. That same even manner, the words separated. Uncanny . . ." He stood up. "Now, if you don't mind, I'm tired, and you must be too. There's a guest room you can use. It's fully supplied, but if there's anything else you need . . ."

"A telephone?"

"In the room. Please make yourself at home. I'll be leaving early for Washington in the morning so we probably won't see each other. But I'm certain we'll meet again . . ."

When he was alone in the guest room, Malone undressed, folding his trousers neatly over the back of a chair, hanging his shirt and jacket in the closet. He went into the bathroom and showered, the water as hot as he could stand. He soaped himself thoroughly and rinsed off, repeated the process twice more. Satisfied, he let the cold water run over his body. It hit with shocking impact but he held steady. After a while, he lifted his head, the water pounding against his face, keeping his eyes open for as long as possible.

Afterward he dried himself briskly and went back into the bedroom. He called the New York bureau of the IIA and asked for the night agent-in-charge.

"Benedict speaking," a voice said over the wire.

Benedict was the agent Flood had assigned to check out Wu's alibi. "This is Malone."

"There was one call for you, Inspector. From Oklahoma City. No name, just a phone number."

Malone didn't like that. The bureau chief would have left his name; and Malone was acquainted with no one else assigned to that station. A vision of Jethro Stark floated to mind, that pale, tough face; he would be back in Oklahoma by now.

"Give me the number," Malone said. Benedict repeated it and Malone wrote it down. "Keep this to yourself, Benedict."

"There's a record kept of all incoming calls, Inspector."

"Have you entered it yet, Benedict?"

"No sir."

"Don't. If there's any flap, I'll handle it."

"Yes sir."

Malone hung up. That had been a mistake. Benedict worked directly for Flood and he had been drilled to believe that any business of the Agency was the business of his immediate superior. It would have been better not to have singled out the call. Malone breathed slowly in and out. It was late and he was tired, not functioning at maximum capacity. He picked up the phone and dialed Oklahoma City. A male voice answered tentatively.

"Yes?"

"This is Malone."

"Inspector, I'm sorry to disturb you this late . . ."

"Who is this?"

"This is Fleming, sir. Edward Fleming, Oklahoma City bureau, Mr. Malone."

The name meant nothing to Malone. He supposed Fleming was a recent graduate of the IIA academy, someone he'd never met. In the early days, he'd known all the agents to speak to, was familiar with the details of their private lives, their habits and pleasures. But close contact among agents disappeared as the Agency grew until bureaus were established in cities large and small across the country and thousands of agents were assigned to them. Fleming was one of that faceless army.

"What is this call about?" Malone said. It was not the responsibility of an agent in the field to make direct contact with anyone from headquarters. Any business Oklahoma City had with Malone should have been transacted by the bureau chief. The wisdom of using chain command was deep in Agency tradition, established early by Masters, its use unquestioned. "Is this an Agency matter?"

"Yes sir."

"Has this call been authorized?"

In the brief silent interlude, Malone understood that Fleming had been made afraid, was questioning his breach of custom.

"It's about Jethro Stark, Inspector."

Malone spaced out the words for maximum impact. "Mr. Conrad's report cleared Stark."

"Yes sir."

"Do you contradict that report?"

"Not exactly, sir. Well . . . it's just that there's more to it. I mean, the report as submitted was incomplete."

Malone knew how difficult this had to be for Fleming, to bypass his superior, to criticize an official bureau report. Malone wanted very much to know what Fleming had found out about Jethro Stark, but he would not make it easy for him.

"There are things about Stark," Fleming went on, his voice cautious. "His predisposition for violence."

"The bureau report said he had no police record."

"That's true, technically. Stark's been arrested on four separate occasions and each time charges were dropped. Once he beat a man almost to death. No record was made."

"Explain how that could be."

"Yes sir. You see, out here, the Reverend Tate exercises a great deal of influence. People listen to him, do whatever he wants done."

Tate, Malone remembered. Willie Joe. Creator and maximum leader of the Continental American Patriots, the group Stark had been proselytizing for. Tate was one of those fundamentalist preachers who had gotten involved in politics, but his reputation was strictly local. His activities were known to the Agency, of course, but Masters had placed him out on the ineffective and nondangerous edge of the right-wing movement.

Masters had said: *The CAP and Tate don't concern us. They're the kind who march in Loyalty Day parades and support Conservative candidates in local elections. They're for prayer in the schools and against obscenity. No danger there . . .*"

"The Agency knows about CAP, Fleming," Malone said tonelessly, "about Reverend Tate. And about Stark's connection with them. That occasions no alarm."

"Yes sir," Fleming said automatically. "But there may be things that you don't know."

Fleming was no longer defensive; he had decided not to back off. Malone remained silent, interested but unable to encourage the younger agent.

"Sir," Fleming said, after a long beat, "I have cultivated an informer. A soldier in the United States Army. He's been involved with Tate and CAP, but he wants out. He's been very helpful and I promised him protection . . ."

"Protection against whom?"

"My informer insists that Tate is dangerous. That he's a real threat to national security."

"What's the form of this threat?"

"Yes sir. It seems that Reverend Tate has recruited his own private army, Mr. Malone. He is training people . . ."

"To do what?" Malone interrupted.

"Sir," Fleming said, voice crisper, less wary. "I have information about stolen weapons from a U.S. military post turning up in CAP's arsenal."

"Where does Jethro Stark come in?"

"My contact says Stark is in charge of security for CAP, that he is Tate's number one muscleman."

"This information should have been turned over to your superior."

"It was. At least, some of it was. When I began looking into Stark's background and discovered he was connected with Tate, I informed Mr. Conrad. He told me to forget it, that CAP people were friendly and they weren't to be bothered. But if they're dealing in stolen Army guns . . ." He broke off, his breathing harsh. "Sir, it is my conviction that Mr. Conrad's report on Jethro Stark was at the very least incomplete . . ."

"Has he been supplied with all the facts . . ."

"The bureau chief knows that Stark was with CAP. He knows about Stark's record of violence. Around here, Stark has openly threatened every public figure he disagrees with, and that includes the President. Mr. Conrad has all that information. He chose not to forward it to you."

"You're talking about your superior, Fleming."

"Yes sir," Fleming said, no apology in his voice. "I believe Mr.

Conrad's report was a distortion of the facts as I know them, a deliberate misstatement—"

Malone summoned up a vision of Jethro Stark as he had first seen him in that precinct cell, the bony, hostile face, the stony cast to his bulging eyes, the look of a fanatic. And suddenly Malone wanted Fleming to be right, wanted to be able to place Stark's finger on the trigger of the murder weapon. Fleming was sketching in a suitable background; only a few more specific details were needed . . .

"Mr. Malone," Fleming was saying. "I know it's unorthodox, but I'm trying to do my job, the best way I can. I can't explain it yet, but I believe there's a connection between Tate, Stark, and . . . and somehow the Army is involved. I have reason to believe—"

A weariness settled into Malone's flesh. He felt bloated, sluggish, with a crawling discomfort at the sides of his wrists. His fingers tingled.

"Could you come out here, Mr. Malone?" Fleming said. "If you would talk to my informant. Your authority would go far to—"

Malone committed himself and having committed closed off his mind. "In the morning," he said.

"Thank you, sir."

"And Fleming, you'd better be on to something." Malone hung up and switched off the light, stretched out on the bed. But there was too much tension in his body and hours passed before he fell asleep.

X

THE ARTHUR Woodson Round Table was taped in a former bus garage converted for television programming and painted pink and green, inside and out. Men of all ages wearing pink-and-green shirts and wide ties strode along the antiseptic corridors, absently fingering their sideburns.

At the receptionist's desk, an elderly man with the profile of a movie star and the voice of a radio announcer greeted Hellman and spoke his name resonantly into the intercom. "Someone will be out in a moment," he said.

Hellman sat down in a soft, leather sling chair. Moments later, a competent-looking young woman appeared. She wore tie-dyed bell bottoms that fitted tightly to her thighs, and her breasts were displayed in outline under a Mexican peasant blouse. Hellman stood up.

"Mr. Hellman," she began, all pelvic thrust and cocked shoulder. "How good of you to come on such short notice. Arthur was so pleased when I was able to tell him you'd accepted our invitation."

Hellman took her hand and studied the clear outline of her right breast. "I've been a fan of Arthur's for a long time."

"How good of you to say! I'm Lynn O'Neill, production assistant, jill-of-all-trades, y'know!" She gave a short, breathy laugh. "Anything I can do, please call on me."

Hellman tried to look down the front of her blouse.

She stepped away. "I'll take you to make-up now and explain how Round Table operates."

They went down a narrow flight of steps, along a cinderblock passageway, turning into a large room with lighted mirrors on the walls. An elderly woman with frizzled gray hair acknowledged Lynn O'Neill's introduction glumly and ordered Hellman into a chair. She tucked a Kleenex under his collar and applied make-up base to his face.

Lynn O'Neill stood to one side, spoke swiftly. "Max Linden was supposed to be on Round Table today. The noted behaviorist. What a really marvelous man he is, so many original ideas! But poor Dr. Linden, he was struck down by a taxi this afternoon and he's in Beth Israel with his leg in a cast . . ."

"How lucky for me," Hellman muttered.

"What?"

"Please go on," he said blandly.

"Oh, yes, well, all right. I suggested you to Arthur at that point. I've been in contact with Wayne Murdoch and he hinted, barely hinted, at what you were into. How exciting! I mean, with the world like it is, we need more men like yourself who at least try to put things right."

"I agree completely," he said, and smiled.

"The piece you're doing for Wayne, it really sounds neat."

"Neat," Hellman repeated.

"It fits perfectly with our subject for today's program."

"I doubt that," he said.

"What?"

Hellman closed his eyes. She was out of her time, a minor character in a twenties novel.

"The subject of discussion?" he said.

"Oh, yes. The advertised topic is 'Violence for Good or Evil.'" She took one step forward. "As a result of recent events, we've subtitled it . . ." She waited.

"Yes?"

"'The Death of W. W. Masters, Antecedents and Results.' It will make for a fantastic show, don't you think?"

"If I told you what I think you'd blush."

"Oh, Mr. Hellman. My mother is past president of the Virginia Dressage Society and I grew up around horses. When a girl is raised on a horse farm, she stops blushing by the time she's ten."

Hellman decided Lynn O'Neill was unreachable. "What position does Arthur Woodson take? Does he believe violence is for good or for evil?"

"Oh, Arthur avoids any public commitment on principle. Otherwise his objective position would be compromised. He will, when the situation calls for it, act as sort of a devil's advocate, but only for the sake of a more stimulating discussion. Arthur is quite brilliant, you know."

"Who else is on the show?"

"A fantastic company! There's Louis Berger, the Sigmund Hesse Professor of Political Science at the City College. And Sam Batsford, the nationally syndicated Washington columnist. And Joanna Cook, and you . . ."

"Who is Cook?"

"You're putting me on! Joanna used to be a model before she turned to writing. A simply fantastic woman! Very beautiful, very brilliant. She's a free-lance journalist."

The make-up woman stepped back and surveyed Hellman gloomily. "There. That's it. You're not exactly Paul Newman."

Hellman stared at his reflection in the mirror. She was right; nothing helped. His rough, pocked cheeks and hooded eyes made him appear bored, debauched, menacing.

"You've made me look years younger," he said.

She scowled. "And you're not very funny either."

"Well," Lynn O'Neill said brightly, "shall we go upstairs?"

The studio set was simple. Five chairs in a semicircle facing a round table. Behind the cameras, veiled beyond the nimbus of bright lights, the studio audience.

Arthur Woodson, in the center seat, suave, ruggedly good looking, stared into a camera and introduced his guests one by one, cataloguing the credentials of each. A camera rolled up in front of Hellman and when Woodson spoke his name a red light went on. Hellman made a powerful effort to project an image of detached confidence. But sweat broke across his shoulders. Very slowly, he placed his hands in his lap in order to conceal his quivering fingers, fighting the apprehension, the unaccustomed stage fright.

This was Hellman's first network television appearance and he intended to take advantage of it. He had done local shows in New York and elsewhere, but they had failed to provide him with a suitable forum. The Round Table was different; here was a chance for some instant fame. He forced his mind to work, to assess the situation, to plan his strategy. In the beginning he would say little, allow the other guests to make their positions clear. Only then would he commit himself, hope to make the strongest possible impact on the millions of viewers.

"Violence for good or evil," Arthur Woodson was saying into the camera. "It is indeed a fit subject for our experts to discuss. Are we a people violence prone by nature? Have our laws and philosophies, our religions, fallen so far short of their purposes that license has replaced restraint? These are some of the questions our guests deal with in their day-to-day affairs and it is something that we shall explore here this evening. Let us begin with a statement. Given: There are more homicides by gunshot in the United States than in any other nation in the world. Lady, and gentlemen, how say you to that?"

Hellman drew a blank, forgetting the inhibitions he had put on himself earlier. It became vital suddenly that his voice be heard, that he become the focal point of attention.

"It's the John Wayne syndrome," he said in a sly, serrated voice.

Louis Berger, an impish man with bright eyes and quick, fluttery hands, leaned forward in his seat. He laughed and spoke. "But John Wayne, Mr. Hellman, has grown old in the saddle and fat, slow on the draw, no match for an urban guerrilla."

Hellman felt he had been wounded, damaged by the diminutive college professor.

On the far wing of the semicircle, Sam Batsford. The columnist was a rugged man with a weathered face. "In my part of the country, folks' respect for Mr. Wayne has in no way diminished. He was and is a symbol of righteousness and justice."

"Bravo!" Louis Berger responded. "There is what may be the common view of John Wayne, a positive force for good."

"You understand me, Professor."

Joanna Cook interrupted. She sat with her spine tucked in, legs tightly wound, elbows against her sides. Her fair features were precisely arranged, and her dark eyes glowed defiantly. "How typical this exchange is of American men, reducing the complex aspects of this nation's disposition for violence to the level of comic-book and Hollywood stereotypes."

Hellman struggled to collect his thoughts, regain his confidence. His attempt at humor, to call attention to himself, had backfired. He suddenly felt inadequate to the situation and wanted to retreat to a protected position. Then he remembered why he had come and was compelled to assert himself once more.

"Miss Cook is too serious," he said, not looking at her. "John Wayne represents a way of life that never existed, except in the imagination of the script writers."

"Mr. Hellman is correct," Joanna Cook replied in clipped accents. "I am indeed serious. Seriousness is appropriate for those of us who care and would like to change the kind of world we have today."

"Bravo!" Louis Berger said.

Joanna Cook continued. "As for John Wayne, he influenced a generation and a half to settle a difference of opinion with a punch in the nose, to prove manhood with a gun."

Louis Berger said with sprightly cheerfulness, "To this I say, yes and no. With Miss Cook I agree in part, with Mr. Hellman not at all."

Hellman's impulse was to lay hands on the little professor, shake him. Instead, thinking that there might be a camera pointed at him, Hellman arranged a cool smile on his wide mouth.

"John Wayne, Mr. Hellman, did indeed exist. He was the American image grown to lofty proportions, twelve feet tall and in Technicolor, with a gun on each hip and prepared to fight on the side of law and order."

"Law without trial," Joanna Cook said. "Order that conformed to those who controlled the power."

"Now, Joanna," Sam Batsford drawled. "Aren't you being a mite harsh on us Americans?"

"There is something worth examining in this," Louis Berger said. "After all, Wayne was not so much a cause as he was a reflection. Was our national philosophy of Manifest Destiny anything but the rule of one people over another by the exertion of violent force? I think not."

"We committed genocide against the Indians and stole their lands," Joanna Cook said.

"Well, now," Sam Batsford said, rolling the lapels of his white gabardine suit. "I suppose you're going to say that an American started the Spanish-American War by blowing up the battleship *Maine* . . ."

"It wouldn't surprise me."

"And I guess the Mexicans didn't attack the Alamo . . ."

"History can be a lie, Mr. Batsford," Joanna Cook said.

"Again I agree," Louis Berger said. "But back to John Wayne . . ."

Arthur Woodson touched his right ear and the control room ordered a camera to be pointed at him. "It is evident," he said, "that the homicidal tendency of Americans toward each other and foreigners clouds the entire span of our history. Many people grow convinced that violence in all its dehumanizing forms is accepted in this country."

"Gloom and doom," Sam Batsford intoned. "The vast majority of us are decent and law-abiding. The Congress has passed laws to halt the growth of crimes of violence."

"The Congress," Joanna Cook said dourly.

Arthur Woodson directed himself to Sam Batsford. "Is it pessimistic to recognize and point out the realities of life and death in our land?"

Louis Berger laughed, his face wrinkling and making him resemble a lively gnome. "America and violence. To speak of one and not the other is impossible. We see violence etched in our history. It has shaped our attitudes and directed our national course. Miss Cook suggested some of our more violent exercises. There are others—Guatemala, Santa Domingo, Nicaragua, the list is not a short one. How many people have heard about William Walker, the greatest of the filibusterers? He attempted to create a nation of his own in Central America by conquest. The venture was doomed, not by the people he sought to dominate but by the government of his own country at the urgent request of an embittered rival for power and profit—the good Commodore Vanderbilt."

Sam Batsford snorted in disgust. "Walker is a minor figure, of no consequence."

"Only a journalist of little sensitivity and less knowledge of his own country's history would say that," Joanna Cook snapped, uncrossing her legs and crossing them again. "In Latin America people remember Walker and others like him who tried to exploit those countries."

"Aren't you being a little harsh?" Hellman felt obliged to say.

"Accurate," Louis Berger corrected. "Imperialistic violence. Police violence. Criminal violence. All these we tolerate. The only violence we seem to abhor is that which is directed against property. I make that out to be unchristian. But of course," he added, grinning wickedly, "I am only a Jewish atheist peacenik with a predisposition for Bach, Strindberg, and the films of Jean Luc Godard."

Hellman thought he saw an opportunity. "There it is, the heart of the matter. Since the Greeks, civilization has disapproved of violence against property."

"*Western* civilization, Mr. Hellman. Europeans enjoy the fable of their own gentleness, but like ourselves are disposed to violent reactions when their property is threatened."

"And only violence can put a stop to it," Joanna Cook said.

"Peace is war," Hellman said. "Is that what you mean? And hate is love. Or it depends on whose ox is being gored . . ."

"I'm only suggesting—"

Hellman cut her off. He had decided that she was too icily pretty, too obviously cerebral, too aggressive, and ripe to be made the target for his attack. He was sure her manner didn't sit well with the television audience and that opposing her would create sympathy for himself.

"Miss Cook, you've managed to distort the vocabulary of peace and love to your own ends, no different from the extremists who run wild, claiming their destructiveness will produce a better world."

"Don't put words in my mouth—."

Arthur Woodson signaled and a camera swung his way. "Joanna, I know you've been exploring contemporary uses of violence as a means to short-term ends, politically speaking, that is. Won't you tell us—."

"My faith in America's ability to reform itself has rapidly diminished," she said quickly.

Hellman inspected Joanna Cook. It was apparent that she had spent a great deal of time in achieving that carefully groomed look. Yet she presented a modest, almost old-fashioned picture, her clothes simple, her jewelry discreet. He found her physically desirable, but clearly a bitch, and he wanted nothing to do with her.

"How sad it is," Sam Batsford was saying, "that a young woman so lovely to look at is at the same time bitter and closed off from the truth."

"My opinions come from my travels, the people I've talked to, the awful conditions I've seen in this country, Mr. Batsford. Do your column and your readers a service and get out of Washington, talk to the people. The *real* people, Mr. Batsford. The streets are crowded with them, poor, frightened, frequently hungry, Mr. Batsford, and often angry. Do that and you may discover that United States senators are not the only source of information."

"Now I resent that," Sam Batsford said, fingering his wide, yellow tie. "Elected officials can be—."

"Mr. Batsford, I no longer believe in the good intentions of the men who rule us, nor in the words they speak. We have been disappointed too many times to trust politicians."

"Do you trust anyone, Miss Cook?" Hellman said.

Her lips came together and she glanced down at her hands. Very slowly, she opened her clenched fingers. "I once trusted my teachers," she said, almost absently. "They lied to me. I trusted my parents and—I'm sorry to be personal—they failed me. I trusted men that I met; they used me. I trusted the institutions that governed my existence; they didn't recognize me as an individual human being."

Hellman was unable to look at her. In a few seconds she had managed to transform herself from a bitch-goddess into a sympathetic character, and at his expense. He had been severely damaged.

"I believe in our Constitution, however damaged," he replied aggressively.

There was applause and Hellman was embarrassed; it was, he conceded, a cheap shot.

Sam Batsford leaned forward. "Let me express the feelings of an old cynic. To hear a young man talk that way, Hellman, well, you're to be congratulated."

"Unfortunately," Louis Berger said, palms upraised, "the splendid document you mention possesses no more value than it is given by the men who run the country. When a Vice-President, for example, demands that the Congress always allow his President to do as he wishes, he exhibits no understanding of or concern for the constitutional separation of the branches of government. Nor of the responsibilities of the different branches. Such a man surely is more interested in furthering his own stay in office than in protecting the rights of the people. The Constitution, the Bill of Rights, I would remind us all, were created in order to protect the people *from* their rulers. That is a fact often forgotten."

Hellman said, "Yes, and a government has the right, the obligation, to protect itself from anybody who would change it outside the established legal forms."

"And the people," Joanna Cook said quietly, "also have an obligation. To themselves and to their futures, to work and fight to change a government that can't or won't respond to their needs. Only in change is there any real hope. The old politics are just no longer relevant."

Woodson displayed no emotion on his face. "Miss Cook, you sound like a revolutionary. Are you?"

"I've had it, Mr. Woodson, with men and institutions that send young boys off to be killed in war, who do nothing to provide jobs for the jobless, who permit—make that *encourage*—the economic and social exploitation of minorities. I am afraid in a country in which political assassination plays a major role."

"Which brings us to our specific concern of the evening," Woodson said smoothly. "The death of W. W. Masters. Who would like to begin?"

Louis Berger shifted forward in his seat, bright eyes directed toward Joanna Cook. "You believe the killing of Masters was motivated by what forces, Miss Cook?"

She shook her head, long brown hair rippling to her shoulders. "I'm convinced that Masters' death was a mistake, that the bullet was meant for Senator Reese."

"That is nonsense!" Sam Batsford exploded. "The evidence is there—Masters was killed because of what he stood for!"

"I agree," Hellman said.

"John Kennedy," Joanna Cook said. "Bobby Kennedy, Martin Luther King, oh, what's the use! In this country the pattern of killing off progressive and liberal leadership is very clear. No one can deny it. Masters doesn't fit the pattern. Senator Reese does."

"Your political prejudice is showing," Sam Batsford said. "Millions of good Americans know why Mr. Masters was murdered and they want his death avenged."

"Let me suggest something to you, Mr. Batsford," Joanna Cook said briskly. "The very nature of the Internal Investigative Agency precludes an assassination attempt on its Director. As I understand it, Masters kept the Agency operating in the shadows. Unlike the FBI, Masters allowed no public relations efforts to get his name and photograph into the newspapers every week. My God, there's an FBI badge in every box of corn flakes turned out by Battle Creek."

"Yes, Miss Cook," Batsford said. "And that ability to remain obscure, to mask off IIA operations from public scrutiny, made Masters more effective against the enemies of the United States. They were afraid of him, wanted him out of the way . . ."

"It was that very secrecy that made him more of a threat to our freedoms, to the national welfare."

"It seems to me," Hellman said carefully, "that since we all acknowledge Masters' craving for secrecy, for avoiding public attention, it becomes obvious . . ."

Joanna Cook broke in. "It becomes obvious that the gunman was trying to kill a very public and unsecretive man, Senator Reese."

Hellman began to see the dangers that existed in either argument. To side with Joanna Cook would place him further on the Left than was politic just now; yet to support Batsford would taint him with the columnist's well-known conservativism. Hellman desired neither label.

"My analysis of the situation," he said, "has led me to certain conclusions. But fairness demands that we proceed carefully before making any charges."

Arthur Woodson presented a cool smile of encouragement. "I understand that your investigation will reveal some stunning surprises. Can you give us a preview . . . ?"

Hellman resented Woodson's words, felt impelled to fulfill that boast, yet had little to deliver in the way of facts. He produced a youthful smile.

"And I intend for people to read those revelations in *Masses & Progress*. But I will say this much. In my opinion the extremist elements in the country are more active than ever before, more militant."

"When people are forced to the wall," Sam Batsford said, "they will defend their homes and their families. Miss Cook would have us believe that some fringe conservative was after Senator Reese and killed Mr. Masters by mistake. The facts contradict that idea. I happen to know that at this very moment a committed radical revolutionary is being held by the New York City police, and he has confessed his guilt. When the facts become known . . ."

Hellman summoned up a vision of Roy Brewster. "The man you're talking about," he said, wanting his own discovery, "is not guilty. His confession is an attempt to make himself appear important, to focus attention on a cause he believes in. But it won't stand up, I can assure you."

"My contacts say otherwise," Batsford said dryly.

Hellman spoke in a calm voice. "It's easy to make unfounded

allegations. I don't want to do that. We must be careful to deny no one his rights under law. At the same time, I'm compelled to support Senator Leland Abernathy's Order in the Nation bill, now in committee. If we don't restore justice in the cities, we're all going to be in serious trouble. I recall Rousseau's words—'Man is born free but everywhere is in chains.' "

The audience applauded.

"Beautiful," Joanna Cook said. "What does it mean?"

"We all know what freedom means," Sam Batsford put in.

"It does not mean the shooting of students," Louis Berger offered.

"Nor the killing of Vietnamese peasants," Joanna Cook added.

"Nor," Louis Berger went on, "the jailing of those whose politics disagree with prevailing sentiment."

Hellman said, "We must distinguish between legitimate dissent and illegal activity."

"Aren't we avoiding the guts of the argument?" Joanna Cook asked. "The most liberal and forward-thinking of our leaders are being murdered. It seems to me that we've gone beyond coincidence to conspiracy."

"Ah," Sam Batsford said sarcastically. "The Establishment conspires to kill off those who threaten the status quo. Also to heave dissenters into concentration camps, correct? And President Nixon was going to cancel the election in 1972. Whatever happened to that one?"

Hellman spoke quickly. "It wasn't so long ago that people saw plots and conspiracies of the Left in every dark corner, Sam. Remember, Eisenhower was accused of being a Communist agent and fluoridation was a Red plot . . ."

"Just where *do* you stand, Mr. Hellman?" Joanna Cook said tightly.

"Where the truth lies," he answered without emphasis. "I believe Masters did present a grave threat to certain radicals. He commanded a highly efficient organization that, once mobilized, would be very effective against the extremists. And it was being mobilized. Masters had ordered action taken against the bomb-throwers, the rioters . . ."

"Translated," Joanna Cook interrupted, "that means the young and the poor and the blacks."

"It means those who make revolution and violence. Masters was a definite threat to them."

Louis Berger spoke. "You surprise me, Mr. Hellman. I know a little about your work in consumer affairs and I've read one or two of your articles—the one about the unconscious collusion of the public with those who corrupt the ecology. It was well thought out, well-researched and written. Yet now—" He shrugged. "You surprise and disappoint me, Hellman. I expected more insight from you, more compassion."

Hellman flushed, held himself still. "I'm very much involved in this case," he said. "I have been able to gather information and opinion from a variety of sources. Study of the available evidence convinces me that Masters was the target. To reach that conclusion is not to betray any political philosophies held by me previously."

"All this talk around the subject," Joanna Cook said curtly. "Give us one plain, uncorrupted-by-opinion fact, Mr. Hellman."

"Very well," Hellman replied. "One singular piece of information which you might have discovered yourself, Miss Cook, had you taken the trouble. But you didn't extend yourself and neither has any other member of the press . . ."

"We're waiting, Mr. Hellman. The television audience is waiting."

Hellman breathed in once and out again. He had to use it. He had nothing else. "It was never the intention of Senator Charles Reese to attend the celebration of Cardinal McCoy's birthday."

Louis Berger scowled. "How could you possibly know that?"

"He couldn't," Joanna Cook said. "But then truth is not Mr. Hellman's primary concern."

Hellman wondered what it would be like to have that beautiful face and body, hostile and full of rage, squirming naked under him.

"Senator Reese," Hellman began, "sent a telegram to His Eminence earlier that same day regretting that he and Mrs. Reese were unable to attend the dinner. He wasn't going to be there, Miss Cook! It is not unreasonable to assume that the assassin, a careful man, to judge by his actions, would surely have known that, if he was after Reese."

"But Charles Reese did attend the dinner."

"Exactly the point. He had a last minute change of plans, arrived unexpectedly."

"That's supposition!"

"Common sense," Hellman said, realizing it was going over better than he'd hoped. "The killer was after Masters from the start. He waited for him in the window of the office belonging to Gerber, Little & Kinderman, waited with a loaded rifle, certain that Masters would appear. And when he did, the man with the rifle shot him."

"Can you produce the telegram?" Joanna Cook said.

"I can and I will," Hellman said. He was making news. Tomorrow reporters would be checking with Cardinal McCoy, with Senator Reese, and with Hellman himself. Things were beginning . . .

Three minutes later, Arthur Woodson announced that time had run out. He thanked them all for providing a most interesting hour and said he wished they would all return to the Round Table in the near future. This said, he began reading the closing commercial . . .

The show over, Hellman looked for Sam Batsford. The columnist was a good man to know, his connections in Washington were excellent; but he had already left. Disappointed, Hellman walked off the stage. He noticed Joanna Cook standing in the wings, watching him. Away from the harsh, hot lights, she appeared very young, and alone, the hostility and anger washed out of her face. He went over to her.

"You made a few points," he began. Her eyes examined his face and he smiled. "Make-up. I guess I look a little faggoty."

She looked away. "No one would dare suggest that, Mr. Hellman. You wear masculinity like a suit of armor."

That was more like it, he told himself. The kind of reaction he was accustomed to from young women. He examined her features —composed, perfect.

"I could use a drink," he said. "How about you?"

"There's something about you, Hellman," she said pleasantly. "A very sexual scent. You reek of it. But it's got little to do with me. You only need someone to empty yourself into." She swung away and disappeared behind some scenery; Hellman felt as though he'd just taken a severe beating. He swore softly, then broke off. Lynn O'Neill was striding across the stage. He went after her.

Hellman drifted between sleep and wakefulness. Next to him, Lynn O'Neill changed her position. He opened his eyes and measured her narrowly. She met all the standard requirements; shape and texture, proportions, all very good. Even without make-up, she was exceptionally pretty. She had strained to please him, her body strong and athletic.

But something was missing. Too often recently, something always was missing for Hellman. Orgasm was no longer sufficient and the satisfaction he craved seemed out of reach; frequently there was a pervading guilt, as if he had committed an outrageous, an unpardonable act.

He sat up and lit a cigaret, tried to remember the last woman who had refused to go to bed with him. Only Betty came to mind, and he'd married her. And even when it was legal and proper, she'd given him fits, acting as if each time was the first. But Betty belonged to the distant past and she came to mind only when he was forced to write a check for child support. How odd that he seldom thought about his son or felt like a father.

The telephone rang. Lynn O'Neill rolled over and moaned. "Is it time to get up?"

Suddenly he wished she weren't there. "It's late," he said. "Get dressed, I'll put you in a cab."

"I can stay all night."

"The cleaning lady comes in early," he lied. "She's pretty straight . . ."

The girl sat up and yawned. "Are you going to answer the phone?" She went into the bathroom.

Hellman waited for the door to slam shut before he picked up the phone. "Yes?"

"Hellman," a male voice said.

"Who is this?"

"Martin Williams, executive assistant to Senator Charles Reese."

Hellman tried to anticipate the reason for the call. "I've been meaning to call you, Mr. Williams. I met the Senator recently and I'd like to arrange an interview. I can come down to Washington or—"

"Senator Reese asked me to call. You were wrong on Round Table tonight."

"Wrong?"

"About the Senator's telegram to Cardinal McCoy. To begin with, it was no secret, as you suggested. Surely His Eminence told you that the police know about it. It was always the Senator's intention to attend the dinner, Hellman. His admiration for Cardinal McCoy is a matter of public record and he would do nothing to slight his old friend . . ."

"You mean he didn't want to abuse the Catholic vote in Connecticut?"

"I mean," Martin Williams said, "that you deliberately misinterpreted the meaning of that wire. It was purely congratulatory."

"I've got a copy of it," Hellman said. "Reese said he was going to Bridgeport—."

"The wire read the Senator had *obligations* in Bridgeport and he hoped to be able to postpone them. I wrote that wire, Hellman, I sent it. Bridgeport was a purely political occasion and the Senator had no intention of putting politics before friendship. I'm putting out a statement to the press—."

Hellman thought rapidly. He wanted desperately to turn the call to his advantage. "Williams, I'm sure Senator Reese wants to get at the truth as much as I do. At least the wire was subject to misinterpretation. Let's arrange a meeting—."

"Not a chance. The Senator doesn't approve of your efforts to exploit Masters' death."

"Dammit! You call me up at midnight and question my ethics! To hell with that! You tell Reese that I—."

The phone went dead. Hellman sat back. Obviously Reese's interests would be strengthened by the public conviction of an assassination attempt, and he would do anything to keep the idea alive. He was a politician seeking high office, and a sympathy vote would help him get it.

A rising excitement gripped Hellman. Williams' call was a good sign, made him feel he was right. He was beginning to attract attention from important people. All he had to do was keep pushing until things began to break. This could be a straight, fast trip to the top of the mountain . . .

He was wide awake when Lynn O'Neill came out of the bathroom, shiny, clean, and smelling of bath soap. Suddenly there was no reason to send her home. He watched her thighs rub together as she walked toward him. He raised his eyes and saw that she was smiling.

"My, my," she said. "What a nice surprise . . ."

XI

MALONE PHONED the IIA bureau from a booth at Norman Airport.
An operator answered in the usual way: "May I help you?"

Masters had decided in his first year as Director that all the
bureau telephones should remain unlisted, that the burden of
locating the Agency would rest on the caller. The procedure
eliminated almost entirely the nuisance calls most police agencies
were plagued with and maintained the official remoteness he
desired.

"May I help you?"

"Edward Fleming," Malone said.

"Mr. Fleming is out," the detached voice reported. "He should
be back within the hour. If you'll leave your name and number,
I'll have him call—."

Malone hung up and rode a cab into Oklahoma City. At Cali-
fornia Street, he got out and walked down Dewey Avenue. He
went into the Union Bus Terminal, phoned the Washington Hotel
and reserved a room. He tried the bureau again; Fleming was
still out. He went to the hotel, shaved and showered. This time,
when he called, Fleming came on the line.

Malone identified himself. "I'm at the Washington Hotel. Let's
talk."

"Be out front in fifteen minutes," Fleming said. "I'll be in a
Ford sedan."

Fleming was a tightly knit man with an unlined face and eager
brown eyes who reminded Malone of someone. *Who?* No answer
came. Neither of them spoke until the car passed beyond the city
limits, heading into open country. The dull, buff land was flat,

without color or points of interest, and it made Malone uneasy.

"All right," he said.

Fleming kept his eyes on the road ahead. "This isn't what I wanted, going over Mr. Conrad's head. But I had to do what I believed was right."

"Root out evil . . ."

Malone saw the face of W. W. Masters as it had been reflected in the windshield years before. So elegant and cool, the eyes remote and all-seeing, the mustache beginning to turn gray.

"This thing is really bothering me," Fleming said.

When Malone had been with the Agency for less than eighteen months, he'd been assigned to narcotics work. He'd kept a dealer under surveillance for days, followed him to Philadelphia where he'd made a purchase, then to New York where, on a Hudson River pier, he'd met with another man. Money exchanged hands. Malone had recognized the second man as a veteran IIA agent. Shocked, not wanting to believe that an Agent could be so involved, he did nothing for three days before deciding to act. He bypassed the bureau chief, bypassed all the levels in the chain of command, went directly to the Director himself.

"The Agency demands more than honesty of a man, it requires purity. You did right, Malone, rightrightright . . ."

"It goes beyond Jethro Stark," Fleming said, as if completing a complex explanation.

Malone brought his attention back to the present. "Say again."

"This country, it doesn't seem like very much." They were winding through low, brown hills, bald except for occasional patches of weed and sparse brush. "Less than thirty miles from downtown and—" Fleming broke off, afraid to speak frankly, afraid of what Malone might think, of what he might do. "All that out there, it belongs to Reverend Tate, that is, to his Western Fundamentalist Baptist Church."

"Have you found out anything new about Stark?"

"Yes sir. Not only is he in charge of defense for CAP, but he's been cleared by their security board for what they call high risk assignments."

"What does that mean?"

"I'm not sure. But there's a great deal of talk around here among CAP people about eliminating their enemies. Mr. Malone, these people take heavy military training. They have modern weapons. They learn how to use explosives. And they're operating under a strict military discipline. On Veteran's Day, they put on a parade in a town nearby and every man was fully equipped for life in the field. It looked like an infantry battalion. Three companies of Army Reservists marched along with them, including mobile units. I spoke to Mr. Conrad about it but he told me to mind my own business . . ."

"Your business is the business of protecting the nation and its citizens . . ."

"Have you made a connection between Stark and the death of Mr. Masters?"

"No direct link, Inspector. But I believe Stark is dangerous, capable of anything. If ordered to do so, he would shoot *anybody*."

"Get back to that military hardware."

The road swung north and they were climbing toward a spiny ridge. "Up there is where Tate trains this army of his. He's brought some of the worst boys in the area together. Hardheads, all of them. Roadhouse brawlers. The kind who fight and hunt from the time they can walk. Playing soldier is what they do best."

"Why haven't there been any updates on CAP?"

"That's just it. All reports go directly to Mr. Conrad. He submits the updates."

Malone stared at the younger man. "You're suggesting that the agent-in-charge is withholding information?" Malone gave him a chance to answer, then went on. "A bureau chief evaluates material from the field, synthesizes it, and then reports. That's his function."

Fleming nodded. "Mr. Malone, I'm no flake, but CAP comes across to me as a clear and present danger to the country. The first time I mentioned it to Mr. Conrad he described them as a few country boys marching up and down practicing close-order drill, said it wasn't worth discussing."

Malone faced front again. A rabbit skipped out into the road, stopped. Malone stiffened, anticipated the impact. Fleming blew his horn and the rabbit hopped to safety. Malone felt the tension drain away.

"Sir," Fleming said with the conviction of a man willing to take a risk. "I want to say that Mr. Conrad has failed to alert the Agency properly to the situation out here."

"That is your opinion, Mr. Fleming. Have you accumulated facts to support such an allegation?"

"My informer, Corporal Herbert Donahue, was stationed at the Maxwell Armory, outside of Wayne, Texas. That's where the weapons and ammunition were stolen from."

Malone had almost forgotten about the missing guns. That troubled him; he took pride in his ability to store away fragments of information, to recall them as needed.

"About those weapons?"

"Donahue said they were M-16's mainly. Also mortars and a few bazookas, large amounts of ammunition."

"Assuming Donahue is right, where's the link to Tate?"

"That's just it, the way it began. Donahue's brother-in-law is a member of CAP. He tried to get Donahue to join. He boasted that Tate was getting all the guns he wanted. He talked of this most recent shipment, of Army trucks bringing the crates to a point in the badlands about a hundred miles south of here where Tate arranged for a transfer to his own vehicles."

Against the uneven skyline, Malone imagined he could see men with rifles, crouching as they ran, signaling to each other, disappearing beyond the crest.

"Around here," Fleming said, "folks don't pay too much attention to CAP. They know it exists but nobody is about to dispute Tate and what he does and says."

"What does he say?"

"Tate makes no secret of his ideas. The man uses the pulpit to propagandize his politics. He claims to be God's Chief of Staff, and people eat it up."

Malone accepted that. Tate would not be the first religious leader to take an active role in politics.

"He's a fanatic," Fleming remarked after a short time. "In religion and politics. And very smooth, very good at what he does.

And CAP is getting stronger, in equipment and in numbers. Those people are so convinced they're right that even political assassination might seem like a patriotic act to them."

"You're suggesting Tate ordered Masters killed?" Malone said quietly.

Fleming seemed shocked. "Oh, no, sir! Not Mr. Masters. But maybe Senator Reese."

"You think Stark was after Reese and missed?"

"Senator Reese seems like a pretty good bet to be elected President in November and he's too liberal for Tate. The time to get him would be before he's in office, before the Secret Service moves in."

Malone's mind raced back. Capolino had suggested the same thing, had wanted to charge Stark. Capolino had wanted it to be Stark, perhaps rightly. Stark and Tate and that assembly of patriotic fanatics. They shouted freedom and would deny it to other people. They opposed violence and prepared themselves to destroy and to kill . . .

"Let's talk to Corporal Donahue," Malone said.

"That's part of it," Fleming replied. "I promised Donahue protection if he talked. I told him he wouldn't be damaged in any way."

"That can be arranged."

"Not now, Inspector. Donahue was run down by a hit-and-run driver. He died this morning without regaining consciousness."

Malone waited in his hotel room for Fleming to call. He showered, ate a room-service steak, tried not to remember how much time he had spent waiting in other hotel rooms, or in parked cars, or on street corners. All the meetings with informers, all the rumors and guesses and misleading information.

But now he was as optimistic as he ever permitted himself to become. Fleming was arranging for him to meet Donahue's brother-in-law. With his help, Malone might be able to assemble all the various pieces of this puzzle, create a logical blueprint of murder and subversion that would hold up in a courtroom. As a target for assassination, Senator Reese made sense; Masters did not. Masters' carefully worked out obscurity was an important element in Malone's logic. On another level, Malone was unable to believe that anyone would want to kill Masters; he was someone to be admired, perhaps envied, his perfection something to be aspired to but never destroyed. Malone shivered. He yearned for an ending to the case, an ending that would provide some meaning, some value, to Masters' death.

At midnight, Malone decided to get some sleep. Fleming was young, but well trained. He seemed competent, would be able to take care of himself in any situation. Satisfied, Malone closed his eyes and willed himself to sleep.

Sunlight streaked into the room and Malone sat up, instantly awake. He swung out of the bed and looked at his watch; almost nine o'clock. He'd slept through the night. He called Edward Fleming at home; no answer. Malone ordered toast and coffee sent up to the room, then shaved. There was a sensual pleasure in the glide of the blade over his skin, in the resulting smoothness, the faint shadow that tinted his lean cheeks. He showered, dressed quickly, and was almost finished when his breakfast arrived. He carried the coffee over to the bed and sat down, dialed the IIA bureau, asked for Fleming.

"Mr. Fleming is expected shortly," the same detached voice reported. "May I have your name and—."

Malone hung up and sipped some coffee, reviewed what had happened, tried to assess the possibilities. When he left the hotel, he felt alert and strong, glad it was no longer necessary to wait for someone else to act.

The office of the local bureau of the Agency was on the third floor of an old building in a district that was partly residential. In keeping with the Director's insistence on a low profile, there was no identifying legend on the door. To that end, agents were expected to keep their names and photographs out of the newspapers, to submit to no interviews, never to appear on radio or television. By remaining anonymous, each agent thereby increased his usefulness.

Malone identified himself to the receptionist and she announced his presence to the bureau chief. Moments later, Robert Conrad appeared, pumping Malone's hand enthusiastically. "Malone! Why wasn't I told you were coming? It's been too long since the last time—three years."

In fact, four years had elapsed since the two men had worked together, but Malone made no effort to correct the mistake.

"It was Cincinnati," Conrad said, leading Malone into his office. "That gambling set-up in Covington, Kentucky, right? A beautiful job. You were beautiful, Malone. You always were special. Very special."

Conrad positioned a chair for Malone, a disciplined smile on his wide, flat mouth. He was a stocky man with short brown hair and slitted eyes and gave off an impression of immense physical strength. Yet Malone viewed him as weak and undependable; it was an intuitive judgment, as yet not influenced by Fleming's charges.

"This is nice," Conrad said.

Malone watched him settle behind his desk, his movements abrupt, as if anxious to get them over with. The unannounced appearance of an inspector out of headquarters would do nothing to improve a bureau chief's feeling of security. Especially now, with the Agency in an uncertain state.

As if to emphasize that point, Conrad's face squeezed together. "I don't have to tell you how shocked I am about what happened."

"Everyone is."

"He'll be missed. There's no way to replace a man like Mr. Masters."

"Shipley is in charge now."

"Yes. But not permanently. With Masters out in front, Shipley was okay as number two. But he doesn't have the quality. You know that, Malone."

Malone's face showed nothing.

"You," Conrad said, as if making a discovery. "They should

appoint you Director. You've got it all, everybody always knew that, Malone. It was common knowledge, Masters was grooming you."

"There isn't anything you can't become, Peter, if you want it enough. If you set your mind, your spirit, and are willing to pay the price."

Malone let his chin drop slightly. "The Agency wants the man who killed Mr. Masters."

Conrad set his jaw. "I get calls every day from newspapers as far away as Flagstaff and Wichita Falls and Fort Smith. Everywhere in the area. People are stirred up, Malone. They're demanding action. Results. I tell you, Americans are fed to the teeth with what's going on, the violence, the killing, the disrespect for law." He stopped and his manner became confidential. "You're the right man for this business, Malone. There isn't a better agent around. You and Masters, as close as you were, you deserve the case."

Malone didn't acknowledge the compliment.

"What can I do to help?" Conrad said.

Malone looked into the bureau chief's eyes. "The report you turned in on Jethro Stark, it didn't do the job."

Conrad hesitated, leaned forward. "It dealt with the pertinent data, everything I had."

"No," Malone said.

Conrad leaned back in his chair. "I think I'll let you do the talking, Malone."

"Your report whitewashed Stark. It didn't mention his membership in the Continental American Patriots, the key role he plays. It didn't indicate his background of violence and threats of violence against public figures."

"I don't know where you got that but—."

"Stark is Willie Joe Tate's muscle."

"Well," Conrad said. "My man may have failed to do the job."

"None of that came through in response to my query."

"You've been talking to Fleming," Conrad said after a moment. "He's a disappointment to me, Malone. Not a very good agent. Not really dependable. Is that why you're here? Because of Fleming?" He laughed, an abrasive hacking. "You made a mistake, Malone. You can't rely on people like Fleming. It isn't the way it used to be, Malone, when we started out. Masters practically hand-picked every man. Now all kinds of people come through the training school. Fleming is not thorough. He makes excuses for his own failures. I won't be responsible when inexperienced and incompetent people are assigned to my command. Oh, you better believe it, Malone, things are different. Law enforcement has changed. It's the Supreme Court, of course, that's been largely responsible. All the changes."

"You withheld information," Malone said quietly.

"Withheld! I wouldn't say withheld. My supervisory judgment was exercised in a manner I considered proper." A placating grin. "Oh, what's the point, Malone? We both know better. What I did, there's nothing new about it, right? People in our positions, we take care of our friends. Tate and his people are friends. Come on, we both know how Masters felt about Reverend Tate . . ."

Malone blinked rapidly and a succession of dim images shifted in and out of focus until a complete and lingering picture was formed. A restaurant, dark and cool, situated on the outskirts of Georgetown, empty of patrons at this hour of the afternoon. In a rear booth, Malone and Masters and Senator Hugh F. Pears, Republican of Idaho.

Malone had been honored to be present, flattered at the attention the Director was giving him. After only four years in the Agency, it was generally agreed that he was one of the most promising of agents, one of the Director's protégés.

Senator Pears had wasted no time in getting to the reason for this meeting. His sad face grew sadder and his voice was plaintive.

"I'm in serious trouble," he said to Masters. "This election, I'm going to lose it."

"I'm sorry to hear that, Hugh," Masters had said. "I've always considered you a friend."

"That's why I asked you here," Pears said quickly. "You see, I don't have a decent campaign issue. The trouble is, I'm not sophisticated enough for politics, just a country boy."

"There's a place for country boys in the American political

scheme, Hugh. All that has to be done is to convey to the electorate your sincerity, your patriotism."

"I've got to find an issue, a guaranteed vote-getter. I hoped you could help."

Masters had turned toward Malone, that elegant face cool, faintly mocking. "Perhaps you can help the Senator, Peter."

"Is there much unemployment in your state, Senator?"

Masters squeezed Malone's forearm. "There you are, Hugh! Peter is concerned with the welfare of your constituency."

Senator Pears sighed. "I did have an idea about pensions, beginning at age fifty-five. Maybe two hundred dollars a month."

Masters lifted his wineglass, inhaled delicately. "I don't think so, Hugh. Giveaway programs serve only to further weaken the national character."

"You're right."

"It would be nice to be able to keep you in Washington, in the Senate."

"I want to stay."

"There is a situation which troubles me," Masters said. "An insidious infection in the government that must inevitably destroy the country if permitted to go unchecked."

Pears shifted closer. "What is that, Mr. Masters?"

"I refer to the vicious, alien conspiracy that eats at the fiber of the country, tearing down the traditional supports that have made America great, Hugh. I am talking about the political and moral subversion which gnaws at the foundations of society."

"Communism!" Senator Pears said. "You mean Communism."

"At this point in time, Hugh, I am mainly concerned with the traitors and foreign agents in the State Department's diplomatic corps, people who set and execute national policy, too often to the advantage of the Soviets."

Senator Pears shook his head. "I agree," he muttered. "It's very bad."

"I'm sure you believe that such foreign elements must be exposed, made to pay for their crimes."

"I do indeed. But how?"

"It occurred to me that you might do the job, Hugh."

"Me? How could I do that?"

"By attacking these enemies of America, Hugh."

"But I don't know anything about them."

"Of course you don't," Masters said thoughtfully. "But you can be taught. You'll become a national figure, Hugh. A genuine hero."

"How . . . ?"

"You have senatorial immunity, Hugh. Use it. Accuse, demand, threaten. Become angry, Hugh, inveigh against the subversion that has infested our national life. Expose it, unloose your passion, your indignation, until the people rise up behind you."

"I don't know where to begin."

Masters smiled. He patted the Senator's hand. "Files filled with data about various individuals are available. Peter here will see that you are supplied with information. Names and numbers, Hugh. Everything you need to serve the nation and at the same time to get yourself re-elected. You'll become quite important in the Senate."

Malone had been surprised that Masters would make unevaluated files available to anyone outside the Agency. But it never occurred to him to question the Director, or to fail to obey him.

And later, when they were alone, Masters had laughed that remote, velvety laugh of his and said, "There you have it, Peter. We will make Pears into the most important man in the Senate, a *force,* and a very good friend who will one day be pleased to repay this debt . . ."

Malone blinked his way back to the present, to Robert Conrad, an expanding uneasiness taking hold. "Mr. Masters never dealt with people like Willie Joe Tate," he said.

Conrad grinned slowly. "More than anyone else, you know better than that."

The telephone rang before Malone could reply. Conrad answered, face closing protectively. He hung up and looked at his visitor.

"That was Highway Patrol," he said. "They just found Edward Fleming. On Route 7a. A hit-and-run driver got him. He's dead."

XII

HELLMAN FELT spent; the results of the Round Table had finally all been negative. The exchanges with Louis Berger and Joanna Cook had damaged him. He had been outwitted and outfought by them both.

Even more troubling was the reaction to the Reese telegram, as it had come to be known. In the two days since Round Table was broadcast, the newspapers had been following up on the debate. Reporters had questioned Senator Reese and he insisted that he had always intended to be at the birthday dinner. The result was to make Hellman look foolish and inept. Even more depressing, his presence on the program had made only a minor impact on the viewing audience. Less than three percent of the comments received by the network had even mentioned Hellman.

His depression lasted for nearly thirty-six hours. He saw no one and refused to answer the telephone. He tried to persuade himself that a conspiracy existed to silence men like himself, men of his caliber and opinion.

On the second morning, the mail brought an advance copy of *Masses & Progress,* featuring his article. Seeking reassurance, he read it hastily. Then more slowly. He recognized the gaps in judgment that had been masked off by flamboyant prose and the faulty conclusion based on supposition. Nevertheless, he refused to surrender his theory of the shooting.

But it was impossible to ignore the fact that so much of what he had done was wasted effort; the rewards and acclaim he had hoped for were being denied him.

He left the apartment and walked rapidly, hoping to work off the tension, the sense of defeat, trying to think ahead, to find some fresh approach that could be used to advantage.

At Hotaling's, he bought a number of foreign journals, some American magazines and newspapers. Somewhere in all those printed pages he hoped to locate an idea that he might be able to use. Back in his apartment, he settled down to read; minutes later the phone rang. It was Sam Batsford.

There was a derisive edge to the columnist's drawl. "You must be a busy man, Hellman, so I won't waste time. My copy of M & P came this morning and I scanned your piece."

"And you intend to tell me what's wrong with it!"

Batsford chuckled. "Slow down, fella. Things ain't that way at all. I wanted to say that I appreciated the article for what it was, for what it tried to do. I said as much to Senator Leland Abernathy this morning when I had breakfast with him. I was sure you wouldn't object."

Apprehension and anticipation fought for supremacy in Hellman. Abernathy could do a man a great deal of good. Or harm. He smiled into the telephone.

"Was the Senator pleased?"

"Senator Abernathy is not like other men, Hellman. He takes no real pleasure in the aspects of life that affect most of us. He views people and events in terms of relative value, present and future. He finds them constructive or destructive, from his particular viewpoint. He is either for you or against you and acts accordingly."

"What did he say about my story?" Hellman persisted.

"That's not the first question," Batsford said. "First comes this one—where do you stand in relation to Abernathy?"

"You make it sound as if I can help him."

"Favors are the currency of business and politics."

"What favor can I do for Senator Abernathy?"

"The Senator is a man who can perform great and marvelous wonders, when he so desires. I have suggested that he might like to aid you in your search for truth."

"I don't get it. What are you after, Batsford? We barely know each other and we're not exactly on the same side of the fence, yet you're pushing me. Why?"

"Unimportant details. At this moment in time, we seem to be striving toward a similar end and that transcends any existing differences. The Senator agrees with me. Like-minded persons should be in serious communication. I suggested that you and the Senator should get together, talk, and he agreed . . ."

Excitement broke over Hellman. With a man of Abernathy's influence at his back, there was no limit to what he might accomplish, how far he might go. He hesitated; he had always considered the Senator from Alabama to be a political grotesque, a man opposed to progress and justice, an enemy . . .

"This afternoon at four," Batsford was saying. "In the old Senate Office Building. Be on time; the Senator doesn't tolerate people who aren't prompt."

Hellman started to answer, but Batsford had already hung up.

At some almost forgotten period in the past, Leland Abernathy's office had been part of an ornate passageway. But as the need for additional office space grew, it was determined that the amount of traffic through the corridor did not warrant its continued use. Workmen were called in to convert it into offices, which were used by junior Senators from the smaller states. But later this particular suite came to the attention of Leland Abernathy and when he achieved the proper amount of seniority, he arranged to have it assigned to himself. He felt comfortable within its confines, at home with the alabaster profiles of Revolutionary heroes that graced the high, arched ceiling; pleased by the pink-marble walls laced with black and gray. He had arranged for an Oriental rug to be moved in to cover the tile floor. That had been twenty years ago and he'd never regretted the choice.

An immense black-marble fireplace with fluted pillars and embossed angels served as a backdrop for the Senator's desk. Draped on one side of the fireplace, an American flag; a Confederate banner decorated the other side.

Senator Abernathy remained seated when Hellman entered the office, watching him out of tiny eyes that stared like unblinking black buttons. The milky skin, the small features, the sagging jowls made Hellman think of an animated snowman.

"Be seated, Hellman," Abernathy said, clearly a command made soft by a syrupy drawl. He studied his visitor. "I saw the Woodson program. You appear younger in the flesh, less like a gangster. Hah! You've been told that before? You have the glowering persona of a criminal, that simmering energy, the kind of thing women so respond to. That Woodson, an ass! A witless weakling issuing platitudinous pronouncements as if he were Moses passing on the commandments."

Hellman felt the need to respond. "I've always considered Woodson to be an intellectual pincushion, accepting critical barbs as if they were manna from heaven."

"Hah! That's good, I like it! Intellectual pincushion. I'll use it, if I may." The tiny eyes squeezed shut. "You fancy yourself a contemporary man, Hellman, and at the same time you see me as a fusty old curmudgeon standing athwart the advance of social progress! That's so, is it not?"

Hellman took one deep breath. "What is it you want from me, Senator?"

The tiny eyes rolled open. "Better, Hellman. Much better. From such a beginning, business can be done. You want something from me, I want something from you. An equitable exchange can be negotiated."

At once Hellman's fear was gone; he was glad he had come. "I'm flattered that you think I can help you, Senator."

"Good Lord, Hellman, don't be flattered yet. Be curious, hopeful, trepidatious, perhaps. You must wonder why you, a muckraker of the second rank, a man torn between being the People's White Knight and making his fortune at their expense, you must wonder why you have been sought out by the influential and antediluvian Senator from the deep South."

Hellman forced himself to be silent.

Abernathy fell back in his seat, chin tucked down. "Have you nothing to say, sir? Very well, I shall continue. My stock in trade,

Hellman, is ideas. They are my inventory. On the Round Table, and in your article, you provided me with fresh thoughts, new ideas. That is why I summoned you. Here, I said to myself, is an exceptional young man, one capable of putting aside his attitudes in pursuit of the truth. Most of us force the facts into the mold of our preferences. You have gone beyond. You are a capital-L Liberal, sir. But you have not become a prisoner of your ideology. I thought as much when I saw the Round Table, and again this morning, when Sam Batsford delivered to me your article, my opinion was confirmed. You impress me, sir."

"Senator—."

"Allow a garrulous old man to continue. Many folks accept the premise that Mr. Masters died by accident, that the intended victim was Senator Reese. Why this unacceptable conclusion? Because they can find no immediate and pressing motive for anyone to kill Masters."

"That is a problem."

"But you intuit that the sniper was after Masters. *Very good.* I will supply you with a reason which, should it ever come to light, I will deny having said. Mr. Masters had been stung by the queen bee of ambition; he wanted to become the President of these United States of America and was functioning to bring that fact about."

Hellman was stunned, found the information difficult to accept. Yet it made sense. Why not Masters, a man who for so long had wielded a great deal of power? He must have been bored on the back benches of authority, believed himself better equipped to rule than those who gave him orders.

"And you would have supported him, Senator?"

"My boy, your perspicacity and persistence do us all service. Let us assume that word of Masters' intentions had leaked out. In certain circles that would be greeted with immense alarm."

Hellman wished Abernathy would come to the point, but dared not say so.

The great head rocked from side to side. "Hellman, your investigation, your attitude, are of interest to me. I view the death of Mr. Masters as but one eighth of the polluted iceberg that lies beneath the social and political surface of these United States of America. In those murky depths an evil genius is at work spreading poison among the people, hoping to destroy the power and authority of the nation.

"A bomb in a university, the murder of a policeman, a riot, looting, the erosion of order and the destruction of the university system. All the same. Threads in the same fabric. Morality is dead, respect is lost, honor and patriotism are words without meaning. Noble attitudes toward women, all dissipated, turned to dross. Consider Mr. Masters' mother—."

Hellman felt lost in a rhetorical forest.

"She was a mountain of strength and purpose," Abernathy went on. "An institution of a woman. Proud, determined, she created the man Masters became. She made certain that he received a proper education in the home and in the schools, made certain he learned the verities. And Masters respected her. He visited her regularly, even during her declining years, obeyed her dutifully."

Hellman's interest picked up. He tried to imagine where this would lead.

"When the time came for Mr. Masters to marry, his mother arranged it. Don't misunderstand—she made no attempt to impose her choice on the young man. She did see that he met the right kind of young women and when Masters decided finally he submitted the lady to his mother for her blessing and approval.

"Unfortunately, as you undoubtedly know, Mrs. Masters, the younger, had a mental breakdown. But Masters was loyal to her through the difficult years and never, never, was he touched by even a hint of scandal. He was an exceptional man." Abernathy, breathing hard, paused. "You wonder why I tell you this? I want you to comprehend fully the kind of man W. W. Masters was so that you may understand how his death has impoverished the country. Time is killing off the giants, Hellman, time and the assassin's bullet."

"Senator," Hellman said deliberately, "this is all very interesting. But what I need in order to pursue the case are some good leads."

"Leads. Yes. It is my intention to persuade segments of America whose political leanings differ from my own of the correctness of my position. In that effort, I require assistance. Men like you, Hellman, men who can reach an audience. You, solidly respected on the Left, have such an audience. They trust you, will listen to you. You can be an instrument through whom the truth can be communicated."

"I won't write anything I don't believe myself."

"Good Lord, man! Nor would I ask you to. It is *because* of your integrity that I have sought you out."

Hellman examined that pale face for some indication of irony. It was barren of expression.

"I'm still listening, Senator."

Abernathy smiled briefly. "Do you know Hillary Smithson?"

"The book publisher?"

"Smithson and I have been in contact frequently over the years. Our concerns overlap, you might say. Our causes are the same. Earlier today, I phoned Hillary and in the course of conversation mentioned that I was seeing you at this hour. I told Hillary how expertly you handled yourself on Round Table, of your article. I said I admired your attitudes, your verbal skills, your vitality. I suggested that you were bound to become an important literary figure. Hillary was impressed."

Hellman took a chance. "Impressed enough to commission me to write a book for his company?"

"How quickly you strike to the heart of the matter. Smithson expressed more than a mild interest and if you were to contact him upon your return to New York, I am sure it would prove to be of value. But a word of caution, sir. Hillary is not a fuzzy-minded, intellectual publisher. He is a hard-headed businessman. You will have to convince him that you are pursuing correct leads that would result in a book to his liking."

"And to yours, Senator?"

Abernathy smiled softly. "I am not unconcerned."

Frustration. Here was the most important opportunity of his life and he wasn't sure he could take advantage of it. He recognized that the *M & P* article was fat with innuendo, leaning heavily on Reese's telegram, shaping the ballistic evidence to make

Masters out to be the target. But the article could never be stretched into book length. Hellman brought his attention back to Abernathy.

"I suggest that some insidious subversion is at work to divide and destroy our way of life, Hellman. Do you agree?" Abernathy went on without waiting for a response. "I am convinced that out of those depths came the plot to kill Mr. Masters. But the enemies of America failed to reckon with the fervor of this Senator and his friends. My resources have been gathered. I am armed for the battle. Will you enlist under my banner?"

Hellman hesitated, but Abernathy paid no attention.

"Dark deeds, dark people," he said. "Since the Supreme Court set itself above the Constitution, went into the business of making rather than interpreting laws, the blacks have run wild. Guilt-ridden urbanists, the spectrum of Left-oriented intellectuals and academics, would have you believe otherwise. Hah! They have coddled the Malcolm X's, the Panthers and the Muslims, unwed mothers *and* the NAACP. All are instruments of a conspiratorial web spun to subvert the Christian ethic that made this country. The aim? To bring us down, Hellman! To destroy our greatness." The large, pale face grew tense and the black eyes glowed brightly. "Within the radical black movement is the black finger, the very finger, that pulled the trigger of the gun that killed W. W. Masters."

Hellman exhaled. He had not anticipated race becoming part of it; he had found nothing to indicate it belonged. Yet why not? he asked himself. An angry black militant would find it easy enough to build a case against Masters. Masters, a product of his time, of his class, reflecting for a black the white bias that was part of America. Hellman's mind went backward and a dim memory flickered and came alive. "The night of the shooting," he said. "A rock group was recording in the building the killer used. The group is called Silas' Trippers, the leader is Jimmy Silas. They're all black, of course."

Abernathy looked into Hellman's eyes. "Yet you failed to explore such an obvious lead. You disappoint me, sir."

"You knew about the Trippers?"

Abernathy rolled his huge shoulders. "The coincidence factor, Hellman. It seems too much to accept. Silas. There is Silas, a black rabble-rouser, a dispenser of evil and trouble, a revolutionary. Woody Silas. Woodrow, I imagine. There may be a connection between these two Silases, Hellman, and a wise man would explore it with dispatch and thoroughness." Abernathy heaved himself erect, presented his hand.

Hellman rose. Woodrow Silas. *He* was the reason for this encounter. All this talk was designed only to put Hellman onto Silas. Hillary Smithson—the promise of a book, of future rewards. It was apparent now—his background, his acceptance on the Left, made Hellman an ideal agent for Abernathy. Hellman knew he should protest, declare his principles, vow to be his own man doing his own thing. Instead he accepted the proffered hand and offered his thanks.

"I'll contact you as soon as I know anything," he said.

Abernathy withdrew his hand. "That isn't necessary. Should there be questions, or problems, talk to Sam Batsford. He will make himself available day or night and if something seems sufficiently pressing, Batsford will make certain I learn of it. And do contact Hillary Smithson. You two will undoubtedly have much in common . . ."

Hellman stepped out of Abernathy's office into the wide corridor, emotions in conflict. Abernathy was using him, dangling a tantalizing carrot to gain his cooperation, and Hellman hungered for that carrot. He felt soiled and weary. But underneath the weariness was a quickening expectation and he was ready to catalogue the rewards that were suddenly within reach.

Hillary Smithson was the promise and the prize. A publisher with a limited and highly selected list, he promoted and advertised each book intensively, dispatching authors on nationwide publicity tours that made them famous and placed their books high on the best-seller lists. Exhilarated by the possibilities, Hellman increased his pace and so failed to notice the chic, dark-haired woman who studied him curiously as he went by. She hurried after him.

"Mr. Hellman!"

At the sound of his name, he swung around, recognized Joanna Cook. That pale and lovely face, the precise features; he felt at once as if he'd done something wrong and flushed.

"What are you doing here?" he said.

"Politics is my beat and I'm on a story now. I didn't expect to see you in these hallowed corridors."

He shrugged. "Just getting some background material." The words sounded unnatural to him.

"From Leland Abernathy?" she said lightly. "That old pirate will take your eyeballs and fit you for a new pair of glasses at the same time."

"Abernathy knows the Washington scene," he protested, matching her manner, but upset by her presence. That defiant tilt of her chin, the bold expression in her eyes. He took a step away. "I've got a plane to catch—."

Her laugh was surprisingly open and full-throated as she moved after him. "You're taking the shuttle back to New York?"

"That's right."

She linked her arm through his. "Well, then, catch a later flight. I'd love some good company. You might offer to buy me a drink . . ."

He hesitated. Like Abernathy, she wanted something. But unlike him, she could do Hellman no particular good. Still, it might be smart to discover what she had on her mind. There was no reason for him to hurry back to New York. And she was a very beautiful girl . . .

"Let's go," he said.

They went to the Hotel Congressional, a block away from the Capitol. At the bar, Hellman ordered Rob Roys, dry and on ice. The drink was perfect and the glass felt comfortable in Hellman's hand. This was familiar turf and he assessed Joanna Cook with rising confidence.

In these surroundings, she looked different. Her mouth was at rest, full of sensual promise, her eyes softer, vulnerable. No, he corrected silently. The look of it, perhaps, but she was too protective, too prickly for real vulnerability. What he saw might be desire, need, femaleness. Not that Hellman wanted more than that. He arranged a smile on his mouth and wondered if he would be able to arrange for a hotel room this late in the day.

She returned the smile. "Why were you seeing Abernathy?" she said.

"Background on the Masters' story," he said easily. "Abernathy knew him as well as anybody."

"What did you find out?"

"That Abernathy thought he was a great guy." He shifted closer and caught the fresh warm scent of her. "I'm glad we met this way," he said.

"Do you think Masters was a great guy?"

Hellman decided it would be a mistake to move too quickly. Perhaps with another drink she might become more amenable. He drained his glass and ordered another round.

"Tell me about yourself," he said.

"Tell me what Abernathy had to say about Masters."

He made a face and she laughed, watching him all the time. He lit a cigaret and gave it to her, lit one for himself. It was a corny gesture, she remarked to herself, reminiscent of a nineteen-thirties movie. Yet he managed to make it seem natural and right. She focused on his words.

"The Senator talked about Masters' mother a lot. According to him, she was one of those flinty old matriarchs who were behind the men who made America what it is today. American Gothic. Tight-lipped and tempered iron, I suppose."

"Momma kept Masters living with her until she found a suitable girl for him to marry, then transferred him to the girl's bed."

"You make it sound like a Greek tragedy."

"Well, Momma did choose her son's wife." When Hellman offered no response, she went on. "The Masters traveled all over Europe together for two years until Momma found someone suitable. Her name was Samantha. A delicate girl given to making samplers and playing Beethoven's *Moonlight Sonata* on the piano. Proper family background and all that. Including money. Momma forced the situation, kept her dear son and Samantha in close contact. When Samantha's father was transferred from Geneva to New York on business, Momma sent Masters after them with orders to marry the girl."

"Oh, come on!"

"That's how it happened."

"Masters proposed and Samantha, a romantic ninny, succumbed."

"He was an attractive man."

"Too cold, too cerebral for me. I had the feeling he never went for a walk without planning exactly where he would place each foot."

He laughed and there was an appreciative softening at the corners of her mouth.

"What else have you got on Masters?" he said.

The defensive expression returned to her face. "His wife managed to survive marriage for almost eight years . . ."

Hellman frowned. "What are you talking about! She's still alive, in a mental institution—"

"If you call that living."

"Well, it wasn't Masters' fault she went off the deep end."

"Don't bet on that!"

"What are you trying to say?"

"That Masters had her committed for his own reasons, that she was glad to get away from him. That for her the institution was truly an asylum."

"Beautiful, baby!" He shook his head and swallowed some of the Rob Roy. "Masters wasn't one of my favorite people, but you really go overboard putting him down."

She eyed him steadily. "I don't read you, Hellman."

"Meaning what?"

"Meaning you've got the name but you don't play the game. You say all the right words. Publish in the right journals. You bill yourself as a man tuned in to what's going on, to what's wrong, a man against the Establishment. Yet in this affair you seem to be right in the middle of the political nut-farm."

"That's crap and you know it."

"I'm not so sure. Look at the way you're operating. Eating out of the same plate as Sam Batsford. Cozying up to Leland Abernathy."

"I'm not in Abernathy's bag."

She wanted to believe that. On the Woodson show, she had judged him to be an opportunist trying to score, had been offended by him. Now she wasn't so sure. There was a rugged charm about him and she enjoyed the way those hooded eyes assessed her from time to time; no furtive glances for him. She recognized him as a man for many women, a man spoiled and arrogant, someone very much aware of his maleness. It was easy to dislike him, but almost impossible to suppress a visceral response.

"Then why go to Abernathy?" she heard herself say, voice familiarly caustic. "You won't get the truth there."

"You're a reporter," he snapped back. "You know the twists and turns a story can take."

"Okay. But you keep avoiding the most obvious explanation. Reese was *supposed* to die. They don't want him to become President. They can't afford it."

"*They?*" he said sharply. "They me no theys," he added, almost in apology.

She grinned sheepishly and ducked her head. When she looked up, she was unsmiling. "I could name names and so could you. But with factual evidence—" She broke off, began again. "Look at the war industries; they're all afraid of being phased out of business. Look at the generals and admirals; without suitable enemies to alarm people there would be no wars for them to fight; and without wars what kind of careers would they have? Look at the self-serving politicians who keep themselves in office by crying wolf, by frightening their constituencies, by declaring themselves the only ones able to protect the Republic. Look at the adolescent patriots who measure Americanism in simplistic terms that fit only themselves."

"Okay," he said, raising his hands in mock surrender. "But that's not where it's at for me."

"I'd like to believe that," she said in a small voice.

He reached for her hand. "Why don't I get a hotel room, stay

144

in Washington overnight?" She turned away. "I don't have to go rushing back to New York, if I have a good reason to stay."

She swung back to him. He did it so well, voice rough with desire and sincerity, his eyes penetrating, his manner intimate. She supposed he'd had lots of practice, lots of success. Not that it bothered her.

"Shall I stay?" he said.

She removed her hand. It was so easy to deal with most men, not to consider them as men; but Dan Hellman made that impossible. His masculinity was pervasive, attention-getting and provocative. She wondered if he would want to see her again, would come after her.

"Well?" he said.

"Go back to New York," she said. Then more gently. "I've got a dinner date."

"Right," he said. "Meeting this way was a fluke anyway."

She looked away.

"Suppose I call you. I'll buy you dinner some night. Are you in the Manhattan book?"

"I'm listed."

He lifted her hand to his lips. "Soon," he said.

Bad, she commented to herself. Corny and obvious. Drenched in male chauvinism. No different from a hundred other men she'd known, focused on his own needs and willing to do anything to fill them. The prospect of his attention frightened and delighted her.

XIII

In the blue dusk of the summer day, the shingled church looked newer and less scarred than in the bright sunlight. It sat on a low hill, an American flag sagging from a pole in front, a cemetery to the rear, with parking areas on either side.

Inside the air was still, oppressive. More than three hundred people had forced their way into the narrow wooden pews, lined up in the aisles. There were old men in rimless glasses and farmers with pinched mouths and far-seeing eyes, laborers in overalls and blue workshirts, clerks from the Piggly-Wiggly, couples with babies, storekeepers with round faces and slack mouths. They sweated and fanned and paid attention.

Malone stood at the back of the church and studied the man who had caused these people to come together. He was tall and awkwardly erect, with the cardboard features of a male model. His eyes glowed and were never still and he spoke with the manufactured friendliness of a life-insurance salesman.

The Reverend Willie Joe Tate.

He stood now on the raised platform near the plain, wooden altar, legs planted wide apart, a Bible in one hand, a small American flag in the other.

"As always, I speak in the name of Christ Jesus," he began in a low, urgent voice. "On this night, however, I ask you not to pray. Not now. Not here."

An anticipatory rustle went through the church and people settled into their places and only the sibilant movement of fanned air could be heard.

Robert Conrad leaned over, spoke into Malone's ear. "You're

going to hear something. You won't be sorry you came. Reverend Tate, he gets right to it, no ranting and raving for hours. Short and to the point. You just listen . . ."

Malone kept his eyes fastened on the man on the platform, willed his mind away from the dead Edward Fleming. From Corporal Donahue. From W. W. Masters. Malone forced himself to concentrate on the job he had to do, to do it properly, as he had been taught to do it.

"I am here," Willie Joe Tate said, "to ask something of you, my friends. I have come to ask you to . . . *fight*. Fight, my friends, for I know you are a fighting people, every God-blessed last one of you. I am sure of *that*! I ask you then to fight harder for that which is most precious.

"What is it that calls peaceful Christians to battle? Ask yourself the question and surely the answer will come to you as it does to me. A threat, my friends. A living danger. To your homes, to your families, to your own self, to your religion, and to your country. These are the fighting causes!" He paused and looked at his listeners. They waited without moving. "Your country," he said finally. "Your country and my country. The U-nited States of A-merica! Long may she live! I am here to speak to you about this sweet and precious jewel in God's firmament . . ."

Malone stopped listening. He had wanted to speak to Tate, to confront him, and Conrad had tried to talk him out of it. But Malone insisted and in the end Conrad had made some calls; and they had driven nearly seventy miles to this little country church to hear Tate speak.

"You've got to see him with the people," Conrad had said. "That's when you'll get to understand this man, learn what he's all about, Malone, about his greatness."

Malone brought his attention back to Tate.

"Do you know *what* I am?" The tall man demanded of his listeners. "Do you recognize that fundamental truth? Let me tell you, my friends." His voice fell off dramatically, almost to a whisper. "I am a laborer in the vineyards of the Lord. Oh, yes. I am an evangelist in the marrow of my bones. I am a preacher of

God's unadulterated true word in this earthly kingdom and I walk in His way and believe in His holy book." Tate placed the Bible and the flag down on the altar.

"So now you know me, my friends. I am Bible-inspired and were it not for that good and beautiful book I would be a living terror to behold. Oh, yes, I do not deny it. It was the Bible that saved me, the Bible and the Reverend Frederick P. S. Ridenhauer who snatched me away from the Devil and set me straight on the righteous path toward salvation. Otherwise, I would be a fearsome tiger in this human jungle, wronging man and woman alike, seeking the pleasures of the flesh in all things instead of emulating the example set by our Lord Jesus Christ himself, amen . . ."

"Amen," the audience echoed.

Tate gazed out into the pews, the blue eyes fixed and piercing. One hand rose toward the sky and his long, tapered fingers closed into a rocky fist. "God's army must stand bravely against the legions of evil!"

"Amen . . ."

"Did you know?" Tate shouted. "Did you know that that false preacher Martin Luther King denied the truth of the Virgin birth? Yes, the very same Martin Luther King who misled his people in illegal assemblies and marches that defied the legally elected and appointed authorities of the states in which they resided. And did you know that today there isn't a black man who doesn't believe that the Virgin birth is little more than a white man's trick? Those poor black folks are doomed to hell with such filthy notions in their heads and it is up to us to save them.

"And did you know, that in schools across the nation, *everywhere,* innocent boys and girls of six and seven are looking at pictures of sexual *organs,* of men and women doing what God Himself intended for them to do only within the sanctity of matrimony and in *private* . . .?

"And did you know that the National Council of Churches has refused to support our fighting men in Vietnam while giving holy tithe money to draft-dodgers and cowards?

"Did you know these things? And if not, why not? Why are you steeped in ignorance while your enemies tear down the essential structure on which this great country was built? Your conscience demands the answer!"

Tate stepped back and took off his seersucker jacket, folding it carefully, draping it over the altar railing. He smiled, an ingratiating flash of white.

"Trust in the Lord with all your might, always acknowledge Him and He will light your way."

"Amen," the audience murmured.

"My friends, I direct your attention to the awesome disasters that have befallen this country of yours and mine. Our young people disobey their parents, they burn the campuses and riot in the streets. They destroy their brains and their bodies with insidious drugs, they defame sacred institutions, and spit on the flag, our beautiful Stars and Stripes. Do not allow yourselves to be convinced that such terrible occurrences are accidental, a series of coincidences. Oh, no, they are *planned, directed,* supported in every way, the same way that a military campaign is planned and supported. My friends, the battle is joined for the minds and hearts of our young people. Not in the memory of man, good people, have we witnessed such a battle.

"Ask yourselves who is behind it. For an enemy *does* exist, a secret enemy, an evil and cunning enemy. He has raised an army of our own young to fight us and he has subverted them, supplied then with false philosophies, with drugs, with money.

"Who is the enemy, you rightly ask? You *know* the answer. Who has been trying to take over our country and alter our God-given commandments? Who has prevented our children from praying in the schoolroom? Who protects criminals but not the victims of the criminals? Who has spent and spent and taxed and taxed until your dollar, so strenuously earned in hard labor, is worth next to nothing? Who stands in the vanguard of this devilish army?

"The liberals! Atheist liberals! Godless Communists! Traitors! *The enemy!*

"Your world is being polluted, my friends. The air you breathe, the water you drink, the land you live on. You, God's people, God's Christian people, the dear people who gave Western civilization to the world. It is your world that is being spoiled by this godless enemy.

"No *good* American is burning down the cities. Or the universities. No *patriotic* American is blowing up police stations or looting.

"You have been ignored by the politicians and you know who they are and where they come from.

"They want to take away your guns, my friends. By legal means, or otherwise. But you must not let them do it."

Tate leaned forward. "We are at war. A holy war. Every possible weapon is being used against us. Against *you!* Do not trust the press. Do not trust the men who speak to you from the pulpit. Do not trust the politicians, for the central government has already been captured by the enemy. We must assemble our forces, arm ourselves, be ready to fight back when the day comes.

"And come it will! The Republic is threatened. We alone can save it. We cannot allow our common beliefs to be fragmented. Hold on, people! Hold on tight to our values. Our *common* values, without which no society can successfully exist. Stand against the snobbism from the East. They hate ordinary people back there. They want to reform us, change us. Well, we don't need changing or reforming. We're all right! There is deceit in high places, treachery. Our leaders lie to us and it is time Christians put an end to it.

"The Gospel exhorts us to surrender to Christ Jesus, the word of God, spoken from the beginning of time. The eternal struggle between Christ Jesus and Satan for the souls of men continues today. Christian soldiers must gather round, girdled in virtue, tested in Christ, prepared to do battle."

Willie Joe Tate broke off, looked around. "Pray now, brothers and sisters. And while Brother John Crawford plays *What a Friend We Have in Jesus* on the Hammond organ, the ushers will move among you with envelopes. Give what you can, my friends, to save your country. The battle is expensive. Give to the Continental American Patriots who stand resolutely in the vanguard. Give your money, folks, as much or as little as you can. We're not proud, we'll take your dollars and we'll take your pennies. All in a good cause. To save your country. I want more from you, Christ Jesus wants more. We want your time, your bodies, your prayers, along with whatever is in your pocketbooks."

He produced a gleaming smile. "It sure was nice talking to you all and we'll be meeting again real soon, I'm certain. Bless all of you in the name of the Lord and His only begotten Son. Amen."

Willie Joe Tate recovered his seersucker jacket and stepped down off the platform, strode out of a side door, and disappeared. Malone motioned for Conrad to follow and went after him.

Night had settled down and the air was cooler. Malone circled the church and caught up with Willie Joe Tate as he was about to step into a powder-blue station wagon. Conrad hailed the preacher and he turned back. Conrad introduced the two men.

"Nice to meet you, brother," Tate said. "As you can plainly see, I'm in one heck of a hurry. Ain't got much time to pass the time of day."

"Malone is with the Agency," Conrad said carefully. "Out of Washington."

Tate measured him. "Well, I am pleased to meet you, sir. I'm on my way over to Twin Forks for another meeting. The work of the Lord our God and the nation keeps me on the run."

"This is Agency business," Malone said.

Tate glanced at Conrad, who looked away. The tall preacher displayed his white teeth. "Tomorrow, Malone. Sometime before noon. On the training grounds. Robert, you see that he gets to there. Now I must go. The Lord's work won't keep . . ."

West over the bends and dips of the two-lane road, past the buff-colored hills, turning north finally, Conrad directed his green Mustang with controlled abandon. Malone sat alongside, hands coiled in his lap. Edward Fleming had driven him over this same road less than twenty-four hours earlier, the same road on which the young agent had been killed.

Rage settled around Malone, a stifling anguish. Fleming had been young and pure, unstained by the savage truths of the world, by the deceits and the charades. Fleming and Corporal Donahue.

Two men dying in the same way; the coincidence was unacceptable.

"Murdered," Malone said aloud.

Conrad went around a steep bend in the road without slowing the Mustang. "Who was murdered?"

Malone's mind raced. Donahue and Fleming. If, as he believed, they had been murdered, it had been done by the same people. Should it become known, or even suspected, that Malone followed the same trail, he might also become a victim. Killing both men the same way might even have been a warning from the killers to him—an arrogant warning. His simmering rage cooled and his brain began to function crisply.

"Do you think Fleming could have been murdered?" he said reasonably.

"An accident," Conrad said. "There was no reason for anyone to kill him."

Malone decided not to respond.

Conrad took a long bend at eighty-five, wheels screeching, fish-tailed into the straightaway. "Donahue and Fleming," he said. "Both knocked off by hit-and-run drivers. It bothers you, Malone. Okay, I can see that." He smiled thinly. "Fleming thought Donahue was his secret, but he wasn't, you see. I keep close watch on what my agents are up to. Especially someone like Fleming. Let me tell you about Fleming. He didn't cut it. He was careless, took chances, turned in sloppy reports. This bureau is an education, Malone. Masters used it as a dumping station. All the second-rate people. I never objected. It was a challenge and I met it, made it work for me. I'm not sure Masters ever understood the situation. He was back in Washington sending out his memos, insisting on detailed reports . . ."

"Masters knew how to run things," Malone said.

"Well, sure he did."

Masters was dead, Malone reminded himself. And he alone might have prevented it from happening, had he been where he belonged, at Masters' side. Guilt and shame dulled his senses, made him weary and uncertain. He braced himself; *Find the killer, Malone, put the blame where it belongs . . ."* That had been Shipley's command. Malone took air into his lungs and exhaled deliberately, seeking that inner calm which was so necessary to re-establish the control Masters had always demanded.

"Jethro Stark," he said.

The Mustang seemed to leap ahead, running too fast for the road they were on. "That's why I want you to talk to Tate. Get it from the horse's mouth. That's what you're after, Malone. The truth, I mean?"

In the low rays of the morning sun, Malone's eyes were without color, empty, fixed ahead. "You take chances, Conrad, and that is dangerous for a man in your position. The way you drive. Slow down."

Conrad put both hands on the wheel and lifted his foot off the accelerator. "Didn't mean to scare you, Malone. Anyway, we're almost there."

The Mustang swung onto a narrow dirt trail that circled into the hills, climbing gradually. After about fifteen minutes, they broke into a bowl shielded on all sides by higher ground. Here a double row of green, pyramidal tents had been erected with military precision, forming a company street. At the head of the street, a Quonset hut. Conrad stopped the car and they got out.

A husky youth, pimples splayed across his chin, appeared from behind the hut, a rifle clutched in his big hands. He brought the weapon to port arms.

"Hello, Henry," Conrad greeted him. "How's your father these days?"

"Comin' on, Mr. Conrad. Doc Sweetan says as how he's goin' to make it agin."

"Say hello for me, Henry."

"I'll do that, Mr. Conrad. Reverend's inside waitin' on y'all."

Conrad led the way into the Quonset hut. Willie Joe Tate came from behind a small desk to greet them, looking younger than his years in starched khakis and combat boots. A Bowie knife was attached to his belt.

"Mr. Malone," he began, taking Malone's hand in both of his. "Was I abrupt with you last night? Please understand. Good works demand time and energy and I've too little of both. The seconds just keep ticking away. Two, three, sometimes four meetings a week. And five radio shows each week; thank the good Lord we tape those. The monthly TV special is live and that means a great deal of hard work. And there's our newsletter which is mailed out to the folks and summer school for young people. And all the other printed matter which has to be written and edited and produced. We do pamphlets, books, bumper stickers, and the like. Sometimes it just wears me down thinking about it all, but the Lord Christ Jesus blessed me with a strong back and the will to go on doing His work. Please sit down and have a Dr. Pepper."

"Nothing," Malone said.

"Forgive the lack of creature comforts, Malone, we deal with the harsh sides of reality in this place. Here we train Christian soldiers to do battle in behalf of Christ Jesus and the Christian way of life, amen." The brilliant smile materialized and the long-fingered hands lifted up as if to embrace some heavenly manifestation. "Please accept my fanaticism, Malone, for I confess to being a fanatic. Oh, yes, I am. A God-fearing, flag-waving, one-hundred-and-one-per-cent fanatical American." He sat back down behind the desk and looked from Malone to Conrad and back again. "All of us here are actively defending our great and beautiful country, you men in your way, me in mine. The techniques may differ; the grand purpose is the same. I have always prided myself on being a close friend and ally of the Internal Investigative Agency, a supporter of the fine work of W. W. Masters, may eternal peace be his in the embrace of Our Lord Christ Jesus. How may I serve you, Malone?"

"This visit is official," Malone said.

Willie Joe Tate smiled again. "Mr. Masters informed me once that a good agent was never off duty."

Malone stared at the carefully sculpted cardboard face. "You knew Masters?"

"Very well, indeed." He looked at Robert Conrad and to Malone it seemed like an intimate exchange, a secret shared. Malone became aware of the muscles across his middle growing taut.

"Whenever I visited the nation's capital," Tate was saying, "I dined with Mr. Masters. Those conversations are prized memories.

Naturally we did nothing to publicize those meetings, for neither Masters nor I sought unnecessary attention. With the forces of the anti-Christ so securely insinuated into our national existence not even W. W. Masters could be too careful."

Malone closed out the sound of Tate's beguiling voice. He imagined covert encounters between Tate and Masters, saw them huddled in shadowed hideaways, voices guarded and wary. The vision troubled him, though he wasn't able to explain why to himself. He forced his attention back to Tate.

"An IIA agent was killed yesterday," he said.

"Mr. Fleming," Tate replied soberly. "I met him, of course. A pleasant young man, I thought. Somewhat caught up in silly notions about the operations of CAP, however."

Conrad said, "Malone believes Fleming was murdered."

"Murdered! That inoffensive young man? How horrible! Have you arrested the killer?"

"Malone's the only one who thinks it was murder," Conrad said. "The police have Fleming down as a hit-and-run victim."

Tate turned to Malone, earnest and sober. "I don't understand, Malone. If the police say—"

Malone interrupted. "Fleming made contact with an Army corporal named Donahue. That was a few days ago. Donahue was also killed, also a hit-and-run victim."

"And you believe both men were deliberately run down?" Tate said. "The automobile seems like a clumsy weapon for murder."

"Not when it works," Malone answered. "Then it seldom rouses most people's suspicions. Just another highway death."

"We have no proof," Conrad said.

"The roads in these parts *are* very bad," Tate said.

Malone let his eyes roam over Tate's plastic features. It was a face most Americans would have found reassuring: resolute, ruggedly handsome, and trustworthy, almost the face of the Marlboro man.

"There could be some mistake," Malone said, keeping his voice casual. "Fleming was a pleasant young man, as you said. The death of any agent affects every other agent."

"That's true," Conrad put in. "That's very true."

"I shall speak of Agent Fleming's sacrifice at my next prayer meeting," Tate said. "I shall pray for his immortal spirit. I have always believed in the efficacy of prayer. But enough of this talk of death. Let's turn our attention to life, to the preparations we are making here and elsewhere to reclaim our country from those alien forces which seek to steal it from us. Would you like to see our little establishment, Malone?"

Malone blinked; Tate had anticipated him. He nodded.

Tate left the Quonset hut, Malone and Conrad following. A jeep was waiting and Tate climbed behind the wheel, motioned for the others to get in.

"Ordinarily," he said, "we don't seek attention to our activities. But our friendship with the Agency has always been close. Now, with Masters gone, we want other agents to know about us, about our deep patriotic sentiments."

The jeep rolled over the uneven road, climbing into the hills. Malone was disturbed by the casual confidence Tate displayed. Even the announcement that his visit was official had failed to shake the evangelist. Malone continued to wonder if Donahue and Fleming actually had been the victims of highway accidents.

"Look around, Malone!" Tate said happily. "To the untutored eye nothing out there—dusty hills and wastelands. But look again! There, Malone! To the west—those are guards with automatic weapons, keeping everyone who travels this road under surveillance. And higher up—those men, an infantry squad running a training exercise. Oh, yes, we are preparing ourselves for the day when the battle is truly begun and on that day we shall conquer with the help of Christ Jesus."

The jeep was bouncing along now, parallel to a small, clear stream. Tate made a sweeping gesture. "The weeds grow with the good plants, Malone, and often choke the life out of them, unless they are protected, kept separated." He glanced at Malone. "It is said that before the end of the world comes, Malone, many false prophets will spring up. The worst will be the anti-Christ and many will be deceived that he is greatest prophet of all. The corrupt philosophy of Marx and Lenin is the anti-Christ, Malone, and we must fight it with all our power. God is on our side and His will be done. We shall turn back the flow of international Communism and the insidious communalism that has captured so many of our young people. All the dupes must be dealt with, all the fronts and fellow travelers." He smiled graciously. "Further along, we've dammed this stream, created an artificial lake. It is quite pretty. There we rehearse our land-sea operations, train our frogmen, teach our recruits to swim. Look to your left, Malone."

Malone jerked around. A dozen women in combat fatigues were running an obstacle course.

"We learned that from the Zionists," Tate said complacently. "They utilize all their human resources; we are not too proud to learn from our enemies."

"You consider Jews the enemy?"

Tate smiled, this time not displaying his teeth. "A diabolically clever people, cleverer than we Gentiles, Malone. They have a powerful lust for survival. A relative handful of them got America to fight on the wrong side in World War II. Our guns should've been directed at the Soviets, you know. See ahead, Malone! Our people are taught all the manly arts of war—judo, karate, hand-to-hand combat. And now——." The jeep skidded around a dusty turn, entering a spacious, cleared area. "The firing range!" Tate said. "We've expanded our facilities, made them much more competent." He braked the jeep to a stop and climbed down.

Malone surveyed the scene. Two dozen men were on the firing line, shooting at targets that appeared suddenly out of safety pits, then vanished again.

"Each man has four seconds in which to locate his target," Tate explained, "and fire. It trains a man to estimate distance, windage, elevation, quickly and accurately. The enemy isn't going to stand around waiting to be shot, is he, Malone? Some of my boys can shoot the eyes out of a mountain goat at four hundred yards. We give thanks every day for the foresight of the Founding Fathers in giving American men the right to bear arms. It's a right we're going to fight to keep."

"Impressive, isn't it, Malone?" Conrad said.

Malone looked at Conrad, then back out to the range. Three targets were raised up at varying distances, were fired upon, and pulled back down. Malone spoke to Tate. "Were those photographs on the targets?"

Tate laughed cheerfully. "Faces of the enemy. The protectors of black revolutionists, of campus radicals, and the intellectuals who would tear down the nation."

Malone turned back downrange. Targets popped into view, brief glimpses of faces familiar and unfamiliar. His mind fixed on one picture—Charles Reese.

"Our people," Tate said, "fire on both stationary and moving targets and each man must shoot more than four hundred rounds before he qualifies."

"Four hundred rounds," Malone said in that spaced-out manner. "That is a great deal of ammunition."

Tate brought his hands together in a prayerful pose. "The Lord provides for his children even as he provided manna for the children of Israel in the desert during their journey to the Promised Land." Tate climbed back in the jeep. "Shall we go on?"

Malone moved to obey when he spotted a slender youth coming out of a small shack midway along the firing line. He was cradling a weapon in his arms. Malone recognized it at once as a U.S. Army M-16.

"That man," Malone said.

Tate followed his gaze, made a quick gesture; the man ducked back in the shack.

"He was carrying an M-16," Malone said. "The Army hasn't released them for general use."

Tate responded calmly, a faraway look in his plastic blue eyes. "You're mistaken, Malone. Our gunsmiths are quite skillful. They modify old models, make them look like new."

"Let's get out of here," Conrad said. "I've got a desk full of reports to go over."

Tate settled behind the wheel, started the engine. "You saw a World War II carbine, altered for the better, but old for all of that. We'd very much appreciate a supply of modern weapons

—bazookas, grenades, machine guns. But there is no legal way that can be arranged, is there? It is one of the handicaps we must overcome in our struggle. Shall we go?"

Malone suppressed his desire to pursue the subject; he climbed into the jeep for the ride back. ". . . *the Maxwell Armory,*" Fleming had told him, *"outside of Wayne, Texas, sir. That's where the weapons and ammunition were stolen from . . ."*

That night, Malone lay in bed and went over all that he had discovered. The investigation had produced its usual quota of false leads and that was to be expected. But Jethro Stark, Willie Joe Tate, the Continental American Patriots—they represented a deeply disturbing element.

Tate's relationship with Masters was especially unsettling, as was his close connection with Robert Conrad. It was the Agency's job to study and report on men like Tate, on groups such as CAP. Malone made CAP out to be as much of a danger to the country as the Weathermen, the KKK, the Minutemen, the Black Panthers; self-deluding visionaries, all of them, captives of their own violent rhetoric.

Malone considered Jethro Stark. When linked with Tate's militaristic patriotism, a strong circumstantial case could be established against him, considerable indirect evidence assembled; the file remained open.

And Fleming and Donahue. Their deaths would stand as accidents unless someone proved otherwise. And there was no one but Malone to do it.

Malone forced his mind to go blank. And in the darkness of the hotel room, concentric black and white circles exploded into view, went spinning and rolling out of sight. Targets. Slowing now, one loomed up larger and larger, coming to a trembling halt. An elegant visage faded into view, a face appealing and familiar—Senator Charles Reese. At once the target was shredded by gunfire, the face torn apart. Malone opened his eyes and stared into the night . . .

There, Jethro Stark, a sniper's rifle in his massive hands. Behind him, Willie Joe Tate, issuing silent orders. Tate, dedicated to his private vision, in command of a trained and fanatical body of men, might have decided on a rash of assassinations that would rid the country of men he viewed as dangerous.

At once Malone was convinced that Tate was not alone; surely he was supported by friends in high places. Too many questions were going unasked; and it seemed to Malone that most of the answers were locked away in some shadowed portion of his brain, waiting to be revealed.

Tate's guns. Someone wanted him to have them, wanted him to create an army, to make it increasingly impossible for the Federal authority to function. Once that happened, an alarmed citizenry might accept more drastic measures: a state of emergency could be declared and martial law instituted, all power in the hands of a single man. In some undefined way, Jethro Stark seemed to embody all the danger, the deadly tip of the arrow; yet to arrest him without conclusive evidence might backfire, bring down on Malone the wrath of all Tate's concealed supporters. Malone reached deep into the past, asked himself what Masters would have done, what the Director would expect of him. And able to ask the question, he knew the answer.

XIV

CAPTAIN CAPOLINO ushered Hellman into a cramped interrogation room at the rear of the station house. There were no windows in the room and the only furniture was some straight wooden chairs. In one chair, a black man, hands manacled behind his back. A uniformed officer leaned against the wall and watched him suspiciously.

"Okay, Collins," Capolino said, and the officer left, closing the door behind him. Hellman took his place against the wall.

The man in the chair kept his eyes fastened on the floor.

Capolino dragged a handkerchief out of his pocket. He mopped his neck. "I hate summer in New York worst of all," he muttered. "This specimen is Woody Silas. Woody, this is Dan Hellman. He wants to talk to you."

Silas didn't respond.

Hellman studied him. He was a burly man with powerful shoulders and a strong, deep chest. "Will you talk to me, Silas?"

Silas kept his head down. "I'm entitled to legal counsel."

Capolino sighed. "Be nice, Woody."

"I'm a writer," Hellman said.

Silas looked up. His face was broad, the cheekbones prominent, his mouth wide and thick, his nose short and strong. His eyes were withdrawn, the eyes of a man who expected the worst and usually found it. "You aim to buy my personal story for *Life* magazine, mister?"

"Be nice," Capolino said.

"I'm taking a close look into the Masters killing."

"Another honky dead don't bother me."

161

"Smartass," Capolino said. "That's gonna sound real good in a courtroom."

"Courts don't mean shit to a black man."

"Nobody's trying to railroad you, Woody," Hellman said.

"That raid was a phony. Pigs are after any black man that stands up straight. I'm entitled to make a phone call."

"Maybe we can help each other," Hellman said, suppressing his growing guilt.

"Don't need honky help. Honky help put me in here. All this jivin' is so much bullcrap. You want to help a black man, get off his back."

"Be nice, Woody."

"Joe," Hellman said. "Let me talk to him alone."

Capolino inspected the handcuffs that locked Silas into the chair, then left the room without speaking.

Hellman sat down in front of Silas, examined him closely. He looked intelligent and tough.

"Capolino says he can put you away," Hellman said.

"The hell he can! The pigs busted into my pad without warrant or cause. Any good lawyer'll get me off." He spoke with a soft precision, less hostile than before.

"The word is you had an arsenal in your apartment."

Silas laughed. "Oh, man, that is always the reason for breaking into a black man's home. Arsenal my ass! A shotgun and two machetes. That, and a rusty old hunting knife. Somebody wanted me hassled and the pigs are running scared. Ain't the first time they been put onto me."

"You're the head of Black Freedom Now. You don't deny that it's a Marxist revolutionary group."

"We follow Chairman Mao. Marx wrote the text, Mao interprets. We execute." He grinned swiftly. "You dig it, man?"

"You're in serious trouble."

"Huh?"

"Believe me, it isn't that shotgun that Capolino's interested in."

"Then why'd he come around?"

"Let's talk about your brother."

Silas' face closed up. "What's Jimmy got to do with this?"

"I saw him, talked with him."

Silas said nothing.

"So have the cops."

"Jimmy doesn't rap with pigs."

Hellman allowed a sly smile to play across his mouth. "True. But some of his Trippers are not such heavy cats. *They* talk. I've listened to them myself."

"They don't know anything about anything."

"Come on, Woody. The Trippers were cutting an album in the building from which Masters was shot. The same night. You were in the building too. At about the same time . . ."

Silas stared at Hellman. "You're running a game and I ain't playing." He looked away. "You trying to pin the Masters thing on Jimmy? No way, man."

"Don't try to tell me Jimmy admired Masters."

"Shit, man, nothing to admire there. Masters was a pig murderer . . ." He broke off.

"You hated him?"

Silas grinned. "Why, I do believe you are trying to connect me with the shooting. Sorry, baby, it just won't stretch."

"Capolino thinks it will. The D.A. feels he can get a conviction."

"Forget it."

Hellman held himself steady. Silas was smart; he understood that Hellman was guessing, trying to get him to admit his presence in the building. As yet, no one had placed him there. None of the Trippers had mentioned Woody Silas when they were questioned. None of them had even heard the shot. None of them knew Masters was dead until the police had told them.

"You were there," Hellman said quietly. "You entered the building with the Trippers, as if you were one of them. The watchman didn't even notice you . . ."

"All us niggers look alike . . ."

"The cops put your finger on the trigger, Woody," draping the lie in his most sincere manner. "They're interrogating a couple of the Trippers now. Both of them are hung on smack, Woody, and they haven't had a needle in twenty-four hours. They'll break. You know they'll break. They'll say anything . . ."

Silas looked at Hellman from under heavy brows. "You're fishing. You got nothing."

Hellman stood up. "Suit yourself. The cops'll charge you, place you in the building. And," Hellman added, taking a calculated risk, "you never made any secret of your feelings about Masters, did you, Woody? Not even now." The black man's eyes flickered and Hellman knew that he'd struck a key note. "It won't be hard to prove motive, Woody. Not in your case."

"You been doing your homework."

Hellman held himself steady, hoping, anxious, but showing nothing.

"Okay," Silas said finally. "Sure, I was in the building and sure I'm glad Masters got burned. I already said that. Plenty others said the same. But I didn't do it. I was much too busy at the time."

"You'll have to prove it."

"Like falling out of bed, man, which is what it was. About the time old W. W. was getting his brains splattered I was putting it to a pretty little gal who'll be proud to bear me out."

"What's her name?"

"Uhuh. I keep the name to myself until the bread's on the table. That chick'll make a first-rate witness for me. First rate. You see, man, she is white and white is right, right?" He laughed harshly.

Hellman sat back down. He believed that Silas hadn't done the shooting. Yet he couldn't rid himself of the idea that Silas was a vital element in the story. He reminded himself that it was Leland Abernathy who had put him onto the militant black man.

"Where did it happen?"

Silas laughed again, a soft, reminiscent sound this time. "In one of the empty offices on a nice, cool, leather couch. Very sleek, man. Just like the big executives do. Oh, man, it is no big thing. I went up there to rap with Jimmy, to listen to some good blowing and plucking, to find out what's happening. You know the music scene, always some groupies hanging around. I latched onto this yellow-haired chick who wanted to do her thing for interracial understanding, you dig it?"

"I might buy all this, Silas. Capolino won't. No cop would. You had the motive, and you were *there.* Somebody killed Masters, why not you?"

The dark-brown face drew down, the eyes masked, the voice heavy. "Oh, man, people won't look at where the real crime is. Where the injustice is heaviest. Shit, man, it's not black folks who've been lynching and raping all these years."

"Specify, Silas!" Hellman said abruptly. He resented finding himself in this position, resented acting as Abernathy's surrogate in this matter, resented the fact that he responded to Woody Silas, liked him. "Come off it, dammit! If you've got something to say, say it! I'll check it out. You've got nobody else."

Silas blinked slowly. "Man, you're uptight. You done something you're ashamed about?"

"You've had it, Silas," Hellman said, going to the door. "Capolino will take care of you."

"Okay, *okay.* Listen. A few years ago, in Alabama, a eensy-bitsy town called Lanston, a chick named Hilda Mann got herself shot in the back. Killed. Murdered."

"Hilda Mann," Hellman said slowly.

"A sweet gal who never did anything bad except get born black. Shot down in cold blood."

"You think Masters shot her?"

"He wasn't there."

"Then how . . . ?"

"Masters just reached out and put the hand of one of his Federal pigs on the trigger, pulled it long distance. Bang, bang, and poor Hilda is dead too soon."

"Why?" Hellman said. "Why would Masters care one way or another about some obscure black girl?"

"Maybe he didn't. Maybe there never was a Hilda Mann and it's all inside my head." He turned away.

"Tell me what you've got, Silas, and I'll dig out the rest. I'll make it public."

"Save it. Nothing's going to bring Hilda back. Nor any other black that's been killed. I'm putting it together in *my* way from now on."

Hellman opened his mouth to reply but no sound came out. It was clear from the expression on his face that Woody Silas had nothing more to say. "I'll do what I can," Hellman said, and walked out. Silas' mocking laughter trailed after him.

Hellman resented spending a lot for dinner. There was no need for it; he cooked reasonably well, was fairly sophisticated about French wines, and preferred dining in the comfort and privacy of his own apartment.

But not Joanna Cook. She insisted that they go to a restaurant and there was a guarded, discretionary quality about her that convinced him she would tolerate nothing that wasn't first rate.

But an expensive meal in a chic dining room made no dent in her defensive barriers. Twice she turned aside his attempts to take her hand and his verbal sex ploys went unnoticed. Or at least unremarked. When he said that a bottle of twenty-year-old brandy waited on the bar in his apartment, she provided an enigmatic smile.

From the start, the evening was a disappointment to Hellman. She responded tangentially to his questions, turning the conversation back on him so that he learned very little about her. At the same time, she was able to provoke him into revealing more about his private life than he had intended. Yes, he had been married. Nine years of it, and four years divorced. Yes, there was a child, a boy. No, he didn't see his son often; hell, lady, every man is not designed for fatherhood. Nor for husbandry. Or was it husbandship?

That had amused her and he played with the word. With other words. Soon he was telling her that he had taken his bachelor's degree at NYU, his law degree at Harvard, that he'd twice been elected to the New York City Council, only to discover himself being dumped by the political bosses when he announced his candidacy for the State Assembly. He listed his beliefs and prejudices for her as if filing a job application—he was in favor of complete abortion reform, was a champion of women's rights but not especially a supporter of hard-core Women's Lib, advocated full power for the black community, was an atheist.

"And you write," she said, "and appear on television talk shows . . ."

"When asked," he put in.

She smiled. "And lecture, especially at girls' schools."

"An agent books me."

"I imagine you do rather well with those impressionable young girls."

Hellman grew defensive. "I take what comes along. I don't have any rich relatives supporting me. Or one of those high-brow funds. I'm on my own in the jungle, scratching and clawing."

"We're in the same jungle, Hellman," she said gently. "You'll make it big one day. You want it *that* much."

"Don't make it sound like some kind of sin. I'm tired of looking up and always seeing somebody's ass staring down. I want to be on top, to look down."

She frowned. "I hoped you were into something else."

"What else is there?"

"Helping to change the society, helping the people."

"That's exactly where I'm at. But why get sticky about it? Hell, guys like Nader and me, we're the real enemies of the system, the ones who are really dangerous. I don't shoot my mouth off about killing cops and making a revolution, but I get things done. I'm out front, part of the People's Lobby . . ."

"Then why do you make noises like some ambitious business type?"

"It's no crime to want a share of the pie." She averted her gaze and he sensed an unspoken antagonism. "You're pretty damned hostile, you know that?"

"Because I speak my mind? That says a lot about your self-esteem! Where you see hostility there's only honesty."

"That Women's Lib notion of honesty doesn't jibe with mine. Bluntness isn't honesty. Bad manners isn't honesty. All night you've been putting me through a third degree, cutting into me, checking my insides like some kind of a social surgeon. What gives?"

Her lips tightened and the precise features seemed to harden in place. "I'm trying to get to know you. . . ."

"The hell you are! You're avoiding me . . ."

She folded her hands on the edge of the table. "You're angry because I didn't go to your apartment. Because I won't jump right into bed."

"Oh, come off it! You think I'm that hungry?"

"You're supposed to be an adult male."

Aware that he had lost ground, he tried to recoup. "Women aren't obligated to make love to me."

"Joanna Cook is my name. I'm not 'women.' "

"You're on an ego trip, but not at my expense, please. I offered you a drink, a nightcap. That doesn't mean I run a sexual service for any chick that comes around." He broke off, his voice sounding harsh in his own ears. He was afraid he'd gone too far, that he'd pushed her away.

She said nothing for a long time, her face expressionless, her eyes fixed on the table. Finally she spoke in a subdued voice.

"I'm sorry," she said, not looking up.

He reached for her hand and this time she didn't withdraw. "Don't misunderstand," he heard himself saying. "I mean, I'd be lying if I said I didn't turn on to you a lot. I think you're fantastic. Sure I'd like for us to make it right now. But I want more than that."

She disengaged her hand and lifted her eyes. "Could I have some more coffee?"

He concealed the triumph he felt and signaled the waiter.

Later, they strolled uptown on First Avenue, not talking very much until she mentioned W. W. Masters. "Have you been able to come up with anything new?"

He hesitated. She was a professional reporter, a competitor, and he asked himself if he could trust her. He shrugged away the doubts, anxious to impress her with his investigative skill, to draw her closer.

"There is something," he said. He told her about the raid on Silas' apartment, about his conversation with him; he described the death of Hilda Mann as Silas had told it to him, emphasizing Silas' dislike of white people in general and W. W. Masters in particular. But when he came to Leland Abernathy's role, he censored himself, afraid of telling too much, afraid of her disapproval. "But I don't believe Silas," Hellman ended up. "It makes no sense, the part about Masters ordering Hilda Mann shot."

"Why? Policemen kill blacks because they are black. Why not the IIA? Why not Masters?"

"Then you think Silas might have killed Masters?"

"I didn't say that." In the half-light, her eyes were streaked and strained. "Oh, I don't know. I've met men like Silas. Angry black men, desperate to make things right for their people. Willing to take chances, do anything. But I don't want it to be Silas."

"Why not?"

"Because I didn't like Masters and I'm sympathetic to the black cause. Okay, Hellman, it isn't rational or logical. But it's the way I feel."

"Silas looks primed for it to me. There were weapons in his apartment and he admits to having a motive—this Hilda Mann."

"I still don't believe it."

"Silas believed Masters was responsible for the death of his girl."

"You don't know that Hilda Mann was his girl."

Hellman didn't answer. There was so much he didn't know, as if an invisible wall prevented him from advancing his search, held him away from the information he needed.

"Hellman," Joanna said, almost pleading. "Haven't we done enough to black people in this country? Don't raise a cloud over the black movement. Be sure of your facts, double check . . ."

He waved her silent. "Spare me the advice! I know how to investigate a story. It's my business."

"That's it for you, a business. A way to lift yourself into the big leagues. I want to believe that you're a man of conviction . . . but you make it hard. You don't believe in a thing except your own greed."

"Thanks."

"Let Silas alone. Drop that angle, it won't go anywhere."

But he was sure she was wrong. Silas was his strongest lead, possibly the key that would solve the whole business. He couldn't explain his feelings to her because, he admitted to himself, they were largely hunches.

"I've got to check Silas out."

"And then what? You'll come up with enough random data to concoct some kind of a story. You'll hint and suggest and question until you put it together. Any good reporter can do it and you must be good. You'll publish and make a dozen TV appearances, turn it into a book and travel around the country talking to ladies' clubs and maybe a funky producer will make it into a movie."

"I'm not that bad," he protested mildly.

She peered into his face. "How bad are you, Hellman? That's what I want to find out. I gave up expecting to ever meet a man who was actually good. That's more than I deserve. Just somebody average corrupt . . ."

He produced his most appealing smile. "Then I'm your man. An average middle-aged lecher."

She didn't respond at once. "You're very American," she said at last, with neither animosity nor facetiousness. "The complete pragmatist, hooked on things. On success. You think everything goes, as long as you don't get caught with your hand in the cookie jar. Well, rest easy, Hellman, when it's all over, you're sure to be in the black . . ."

XV

SOUTHWEST OUT of Wayne, the road ran dusty and arrow-straight, a full day of Texas stretching in front of a traveler. The baked land was empty and ominous, reminiscent of American legend: Texas Rangers, Davy Crockett, the Alamo.

Malone sped along in a rented car staring into the shimmering heat, a preoccupied look in his eyes. Soon Maxwell Armory appeared on the horizon, a collection of military barracks and warehouses. The post seemed to have been set down complete, alien in the stark flatlands, all enclosed by a wire-mesh fence.

At the entrance gate, a husky MP saluted, asked politely the purpose of Malone's visit, matched his name against a list and directed him to the Headquarters Building. There Malone located the office of the commanding officer.

Colonel Ivan Wending was an affable man with a trim mustache and the slightly embarrassed expression of a thin man grown paunchy. He greeted Malone with brisk, military cheerfulness and remarked on the Texas heat and the privileges of rank that allowed him to have air-conditioned quarters. If he wondered why a man who appeared to be as sensible as Malone would come to Maxwell Armory, except under duress, he didn't say so.

For his part, Malone mentioned his nearly three years in the Marine Corps, his discharge as a major. The brotherhood of officers established, Colonel Wending felt relief and a renewal of confidence. He lit a cigar.

"Have to tell you," he declared, "this is a rare treat. Our establishment doesn't attract visitors as a rule. No reason for anyone to come. Most of my officers are a dull bunch. Bridge players, mainly. Clerks and bookkeepers, is what I call them."

Malone listened, his face expressionless.

"Duty here is routine," Colonel Wending said. "Receive weapons shipments, check them out, see that they get sent on to the proper posts. Sort of a way station, you might say, but to what purpose I've never figured out. Ours is not to reason why, and so forth. He laughed nervously. "You know the Army."

Malone agreed that he knew the Army. "That's why it might be smart to keep this visit quiet."

Colonel Wending pulled the cigar out of his mouth and leaned forward. "A hush-hush job? Well, all *right!* I can promise you there'll be no mouths around here."

"The Agency's received a tip."

Colonel Wending sucked on his cigar; it had gone out. He struck a match.

"This visit is to determine the value of our informant."

"Any help I can give . . ."

"Should all this be a mistake, it would be best not to embarrass anyone."

"I see." Wending massaged his flabby belly. "That's damned considerate. You can depend on my discretion, and cooperation. Just tell me what you want."

"During the last ten days, what deliveries and shipments have been made, and to whom?"

Colonel Wending manipulated the cigar like a baton. "Nothing, virtually. Not one heavy order for the last two weeks, in or out."

"The Agency likes reports," Malone said. "Details, dates, numbers . . ."

"I know, I know. Forms in triplicate. The Army too—swamps a man with forms. Why don't we get Sergeant Johnson in here? Career man. Johnson sees to things. My good right arm, you might say." He pressed a signal button in the base of his telephone and seconds later a burly master sergeant appeared.

"Sir?"

"Sergeant, this is Mr. Malone. Doing a special government job. We're to expedite things for him, without questions."

"Yes sir."

"Show Malone around, give him any scoop he wants. Clear?"

"Yes sir."

"Weapons shipments, Sergeant. Incoming, outgoing, whatever."

"Yes sir."

"There you are," Wending said to Malone.

Malone stood up, assessed Sergeant Johnson. He was almost as tall as Malone, a lumpy man with thick shoulders and a tight, closed face.

"If you'll come with me, Mr. Malone," he said.

"Anything you need, Malone," Wending called after them, "give me the word. . . ."

In the thick, still heat of the company street, Johnson pivoted around to face Malone. "Where would you like to begin, sir?"

Malone stared at the other man; there was an antagonism in his attitude that might only be the inevitable suspicion of a career soldier for a civilian. Or it might be more. "Weapons shipments," Malone said. "Incoming and outgoing."

"Sergeant Chisolm," Johnson said. "Chief supply noncom. He'll take care of you."

They discovered Sergeant Chisolm in a tiny, glass-enclosed office in Warehouse Number One. He was a wiry man, small and tense, who gave the impression of rapid animation even while at rest. His nose was a twist of gristle that had been broken many times and there was scar tissue above one eye. His yellow hair was combed straight back off a low forehead and neatly trimmed.

"Weapons shipments," he said, after Sergeant Johnson had departed. "You want to know about weapons shipments?"

Malone nodded.

"I'll pull the records. Last ten days. Okay? You can go through them for yourself. All routine stuff. So many received, so many dispatched. All counted and signed for. We're very thorough around here, the way the colonel likes it."

"Let's talk about M-16's," Malone said, watching Chisolm's face.

The broken features showed nothing. He went to the brown file cabinets along the wall and withdrew a folder, leafed through it, extracted a few sheets of paper. "Here's what you're after.

M-16's. Manifest says two hundred and fifty weapons were shipped to Fort McClintock on the eighth. Delivery accepted and receipted by the chief supply officer. Another two hundred were loaned to the National Guard unit in Parkersville for special target work. They go to camp in a few weeks and the CO is trying to shape them up. He'll never make it. Dumb bastards did a lousy job of cleaning up. Some of the barrels were lined with carbon and some were even pitted. My boys had almost three days of extra work. I recommended to the Colonel that we should cut that Parkersville bunch off our courtesy list."

Malone studied the manifest. "The Wayne High School?"

Chisolm's wide mouth lifted in a pleased grin. "Those kids are really something else! Best marching band in this part of the State. And they sent back every piece in first-class trim, cleaned and properly oiled. A bunch like that, you could teach 'em to be real soldiers. Four hundred and seventy-five crates in the warehouse, Mr. Malone. That's four thousand, seven hundred and fifty pieces altogether."

"Let's take a crate count."

Chisolm stared at Malone, nodded once. "Sure. A crate count. I'll put one of my boys on it right away."

"Let's make the count together."

"You got it. Sergeant Johnson says to cooperate with you and that's how it's going to be." He led Malone into the warehouse. It was a massive building constructed of rectangular sections of corrugated steel, bolted together. The flat roof sloped from the front to the rear. Along the back wall gun crates were piled up in stacks of five in a double row.

"You count, Mr. Malone," Chisolm said. "I'll check you out."

They moved down the line, each man counting to himself.

"Four-seventy-five," Chisolm said, when they finished. "Just like I said."

Malone didn't like it. The almost too-willing cooperation of the noncommissioned officers, the plain desire to have him make the count, the fact that his appearance had evoked no apparent apprehension. This operation was so well-organized, so well-protected that the men here felt they had nothing to fear. Or else Fleming and Donahue had been wrong.

"I'll escort you back to the Colonel's office," Chisolm was saying.

Malone stared into that fighter's face. Chisolm was a hard little man, his eyes stoney. But there was a triumphant note in his voice. His features swam out of focus and Malone saw Fleming standing there. He blinked and all was as it should be. He made an effort and visualized again the single M-16 in the fist of one of Willie Joe Tate's men.

"Let's take a complete weapons count," Malone said.

Chisolm rocked back on his heels, recovered. "I don't know about that. My authority is limited . . ."

"Colonel Wending's got enough authority . . ."

"Sergeant Johnson's my immediate superior. Why don't I call him?"

"Do that."

They went back to Chisolm's office and he made the call, spoke to Sergeant Johnson, then handed the phone to Malone. "He wants to talk to you."

Malone took the instrument. "What's the difficulty, Sergeant?"

"No difficulty, sir." Johnson's voice sounded the way he looked, burly and bloated, without emotion. "I can't give permission for a weapons count, Mr. Malone."

"Why not?"

"It means uncrating nearly five thousand pieces. That takes men and time. It's beyond my jurisdiction."

"The Agency wants that count."

"Yes sir. I'll have to talk to the Colonel about it. You wait right there, Mr. Malone. I'll get back to you." He hung up.

Malone arranged himself in front of the window of Chisolm's office and stared at the mordant flatlands. Nothing out there seemed to be alive; there was no movement, no variety, only endless brown to the horizon. After a while, he became aware of Chisolm looking at him and it was as if he could hear the silent laughter of the supply sergeant. Chisolm, Wending, Johnson, the overly polite MP at the front gate; they seemed a closed community that excluded Malone, diminished him in some undefined and painful way.

It was as if it had all happened before. A slow rage seeped under his skin and he struggled to contain his emotions, to close out the past.

The ring of the telephone jarred Malone back. Chisolm, an enigmatic lift to one corner of his mouth, answered. "Yes sir," he said after a moment. "It's for you."

Malone took the phone. "Yes . . ."

"Colonel Wending." The officer's voice sounded strained, almost frightened. "About your request . . ."

"Yes."

"It isn't going to be possible . . ."

Malone focused all his unrest and displeasure, the simmering rage, into his voice. He spoke without emphasis. "This is official IIA business, Colonel."

"Mr. Malone—I have orders . . ."

"What orders?"

"Direct orders. You are denied permission to continue your investigation on these grounds."

"Agency authority supersedes—"

"Mr. Malone, I'm sorry. I am ordered to prevent you from proceeding, by force, if necessary. Also, you are to remain where you are until your call comes through."

"What are you talking about, Colonel?"

"Mr. Shipley is calling you. From Washington."

"You spoke to Shipley?" Malone said evenly.

"No, no. You don't understand. General Terence Sain, you see. Armaments Procurement. General Sain was told of your presence on the post, Mr. Malone, and he was hopping. He climbed up one side of me and down the other, said this Shipley fellow would be in touch with you at once . . ."

Malone dropped the phone into its cradle.

Chisolm looked up at him, eyes bright. "Something the matter, Mr. Malone?"

Malone turned away, his agitation increasing. He had come under attack and ached to fight back, to put the world in order, to let go of his growing rage. Masters had warned him—.

"Hidden enemies constantly erode the national foundation, chip away at the spirit and strength of our people. Stay alert and vigorous, prepared to strike when the opportunity presents itself."

Malone shuffled collected bits and pieces of information around until a picture began to take shape. Fleming and Donahue, both dead, and Leo Shelley dealing for economic and political profit, Jethro Stalk and the plots of Willie Joe Tate, Tate's involvement with the Army, with people high in the government; they were all threads in the same conspiratorial fabric. But to what end?

And Masters' death? Did it play some subterranean role in this unholy design? Or was he merely being diverted from his original purpose? Malone understood that he had taken hold of a powerful, restless force, was unable to let it go; it was something he had known all along he would have to face.

The phone rang. It was Jason Shipley. He spent no time on amenities. "Malone, what are you doing in that godforsaken camp? What is the matter with you!"

Malone started to answer.

Shipley cut him off. "Whatever you're doing, I don't like it. This whole thing, people are very upset, they want a quick solution to the Masters affair. That's your job, not poking around some military installation that nobody ever heard of . . ."

"This is crucial—"

"What is wrong with you, Malone! There are generals on my back and Senators and you're fooling around. That's *our* Army you're bothering. I want you to stop it. At once. You get out of there!"

"Who got to you, Shipley?"

"Look here, Malone!" Shipley shouted in a high voice. "I am running this agency and you take orders like everybody else. Leave it alone. Don't give me arguments. Just do as you're told. Your assignment is Mr. Masters' death . . ."

"This is part of it."

"No! Keep away from the Army! Get on an airplane! Right away! Today. Get up to New York City. Sam Batsford has an office there. Contact him."

"Batsford!"

"Just do it! He's expecting you. He'll fill you in. And that's an order, Malone."

"Yes sir." Malone felt the heat close in around him. A constricting layer of moisture coated his skin and a thin, alien whine sounded inside his head. His eyes shifted, came to rest on Sergeant Chisolm. The fighter's face was open, innocent. And Malone was certain he was laughing at him.

"I guess you'll be leaving now," Chisolm said.

Malone reacted instinctively, launching himself across the desk, hands reaching for Chisolm's throat, bearing the soldier over backwards. He sputtered and plucked at Malone's tightening fingers.

As abruptly as it had come, the rage lifted and Malone pulled away. He stood up, helped Chisolm to his feet. When the sergeant's breathing returned to normal, Malone went to the door.

Chisolm, still shaken and full of respect, looked after him. "You were going to kill me."

Malone spoke without turning. "Sorry." Then he left, ashamed of what he had done, and afraid.

XVI

"Hellman, you *are* a bastard!"

Joanna Cook spoke quietly, not moving, eyes fixed on the ceiling of her own bedroom.

Hellman came up on his elbow, looked down at her with appreciation. She was, he told himself again, something special: detached, graceful, exceptionally beautiful. Her face, without make-up, was a healthy shade of pale, the lips delicate and slightly parted.

He grinned. "Was I a bastard an hour ago?"

"Don't let it go to your head. I'm not all that hard to get."

He found some cigarettes and lit one, placed it between her lips. Hellman kissed the tip of one breast and she shivered.

"Don't."

"You didn't stop me an hour ago."

"You're fixed on time, Hellman."

"I think you're fantastic."

"A good lay is what you mean."

"Don't knock it. I don't."

"We're a pair, Hellman, a couple of boudoir athletes. Are you going to ask me if you're the best I ever had?"

"What are you trying to do? Why spoil it?"

"Are we going to operate on a schedule? Odd days of the week. Or maybe weekends. Which do you prefer?"

"It's not like that."

She measured him. "You're not going to say it's love, Hellman?"

"I know this—you turned me on, and you weren't just going through the motions."

She made no answer and they shared the cigaret. When it

179

was burned down, she ground it out in the ashtray and they lay next to each other without speaking or touching.

"Hellman," she said after a long interval, "couldn't you let it go?"

He closed his eyes. "I don't know what you're talking about."

"You know. I don't have to spell it out." A vague smile lifted the corners of her mouth. "Maybe that's why it was so good with us, we understand a lot about each other without words."

He grunted, a deep, chesty sound.

"Let it go. Please."

"Dammit! You keep coming back, worrying it to death."

She sat up. "You say you're concerned with justice, Hellman, with truth. Okay, do right this time. Forget Woody Silas."

Without opening his eyes, he reached out, found her thigh. The flesh was firm, very warm. "Why are you so hooked on Silas?"

She shrugged. "After we spoke—I arranged to see him."

He came up to a sitting position. "What a dumb-ass thing to do! I trusted you. This story is mine . . ."

"Not for the story. Just to satisfy myself. I was sure you had to be wrong about this."

"And Silas convinced you?"

"Not really. He was tough and insulting. Revolutionaries, black and white, they're all male chauvinists. There's a lot of that in you, Hellman. I think you don't trust women."

"I just trusted you with the best I've got."

"That's not funny," she said, but smiled briefly in appreciation. "Silas wouldn't talk to me. But I came away convinced he wasn't the one who shot Masters."

"That's terrific! He told you nothing, but you're sure that he's innocent."

She looked away and he took the opportunity to study her. Sex improved Joanna Cook, softened the sharp lines of her face, blurred the aggressive edge of her voice, provided her with a wistful undertone. With her hair in disarray, without make-up, with all of her flesh exposed, she was prettier, more youthful, glowing faintly. Almost vulnerable.

The musty scent of her drifted into his nostrils and he remembered the first taste of her mouth. It had all happened so fast, a commitment fulfilled, as if action resolved problems and answered questions. He'd been pleasantly surprised in the beginning, but it had happened too rapidly to savor, and now Hellman wished the first time had yet to happen. It was an idea that startled and amused him.

"Silas is no challenge for you," Joanna said. "You can do better. Face it, there are plenty of people who stayed dry-eyed when Masters was killed. Any one of them could have pulled the trigger."

"I'm not accusing Silas."

"Not yet, but you will."

"All I'm going to do is look into his story."

She started to speak, stopped. Something strange and unidentifiable had taken place and she felt a sudden distrust of her own responses. She warned herself not to depend on Hellman; he was abrasive, offensive, and she didn't *like* him. Yet she had made love to him, wanted to make love again. No contradiction there . . . He was sensual, aggressive, and she was an extremely physical woman; she required a passionate man. But she was unable to shake off the lingering sense of wrongdoing, as if being with Hellman was a dramatic betrayal of her deepest personal convictions.

Why? The doubts had existed from the first moments on the Round Table. They were there that afternoon in Washington. The doubts were why she had held him off so long. Four times they'd been together, for lunch, for drinks, for dinner. And on each occasion she'd been careful not to let him get her alone. On each occasion except tonight. Tonight had been different. Her mind had been made up long before Hellman arrived at her apartment.

Hellman dropped his hand on her belly, a casual gesture of possessiveness. She resented it and enjoyed it. "What makes you sure it wasn't Silas?" he said. "Maybe it was somebody else in his outfit. They're an angry bunch, paranoiac."

"Men kill for a lot of reasons." She sat up and his hand fell away.

"What is that supposed to mean?"

She ignored the question. "Silas is tough and reckless in his anger. He deals in hyperbole; all activists do. That's how they get a reaction from a society that doesn't want to listen. But he's no fool."

"I've listened to that lecture before."

"Silas might think about killing Masters, but he wouldn't do it. He's too smart. He knows that dead, Masters would do neither him nor the black movement any good . . ." She broke off, as if in the middle of a thought.

Hellman said, "You're still hung up on the idea that the gunman was after Reese?"

She avoided looking at him.

"Pure crap, is what that is. Everything points the other way. All my professional instinct—."

Her laughter was warm and natural. "Masculine intuition, you mean?" She sobered rapidly. "Suppose you're right. That still doesn't convict Silas. Or any other black man." She lay back down, spoke bitterly. "You might do better cruising Third Avenue."

"Oh, come on! You don't believe that old bromide about Masters being a fag?"

"Some pretty hip people will give you good odds."

"I don't believe it. Rumor. Washington eats up that kind of thing. Anyway, Masters is married."

"Since when does that mean anything! That marriage was arranged to protect Masters."

"That does it!" Hellman exploded, remembering his conversation with Senator Abernathy. "Masters' mother was a woman of strong and maybe artificial social views. She wanted her son to marry a woman whose social and economic background matched his own. So what? We had a President named FDR with a tyrannical mother. You ever see more of a man than him? Besides, my sources are pretty good."

"If you mean Leland Abernathy, forget it. Suspect anything he tells you."

"I don't have to buy a man's politics to know when he's telling the truth."

"A beautiful sentiment. Irrelevant but beautiful. Masters wouldn't be the first homosexual who got married to give himself an acceptable front. . . ."

Hellman resented her attitude. He didn't choose to entertain any theory that contradicted his own, any idea that might interfere with his notion of how and why the killing took place. He didn't want to abandon Woody Silas as the prime suspect; he didn't want to begin over again. Besides, he felt she was reaching, had some special ax to grind . . . He raised his eyes.

Joanna was looking at him, an uncertain expression on her face. "I'm not claiming that the murderer was a homosexual. But it is a possibility." She studied a point in the middle distance with frowning concentration. "There was an article in the *Journal of Pragmatic Psychiatry* exploring a variety of rigid social structures. Hitler's Brown Shirts, for example. The author suggests that there is a high incidence of homosexuality, actual and repressed, in all such groups."

"Oh, great! That makes the U.S. Army a haven for queers. And the FBI and the IIA as well. Is that it?"

"You know what I mean."

"The hell I do. Okay, so a bunch of perverts joined the Brown Shirts. Why not? The whole Nazi idea was a perversion. And I know about men in prison and about sailors. But just as soon as they get back where women are available, they revert to type."

"Maybe," she said, voice thin. "I don't know any more. All I'm suggesting is that here is an aspect of Masters' life that ought to be examined. Oh, damn!" She clamped her mouth shut and closed her eyes, anxious not to go on, to hoard what was private behind a wall of silence.

When Hellman answered, his voice was caustic, each word issued with a sting. "Have you noticed, every woman past twenty-five likes to label a man gay if he isn't married? If he isn't leading an orthodox life. It gives them a ready excuse for their own social failures."

"That's not fair . . ."

"Masters isn't one of my heroes, but he was something special. The man was different from most of us, bigger than life. That doesn't make him queer." He shook his head. "The solution to all this is buried in the weird politics of this country, the screwed-up logic that allows some screwball to knock off one of life's winners and become a kind of minor-league hero. Sirhan Sirhan, James Earl Ray, even Charles Manson; you'd think they discovered penicillin the way some people lionize them." The rough face grew flushed and his eyes receded into the deep cavities. "Dammit, Joanna! Dammit to hell! Let it alone. I turn on to you and you to me. Why can't you just leave it at that?" He swung out of the bed.

She sat up. "What are you doing?"

"Fuck this noise! I've had it with beds that turn into battle-grounds. I'm splitting."

She watched him put on his trousers. "You fool! Stop *that*. Take off those ugly things and come back here. Don't you dare walk out on me. Don't you dare . . ."

That afternoon, Hellman boarded a plane for Mobile, Alabama. He ordered a rental car to meet him, for the drive down to the Gulf coast and Lanston.

During the flight, he tried to sleep but an evanescent image of Joanna Cook kept materializing. Something she had said continued to trouble him, but he was unable to call it back. Or perhaps it was something left unsaid. He was disturbed too because he was unable to stop thinking about her. After all, she was only another woman. Well, wasn't she? . . .

XVII

AT ABOUT the same time Hellman left for Alabama, Malone stepped aboard the plane that would take him back to New York. He felt an unusual ambivalence, began to doubt the value of his efforts. He considered the possibility of abandoning the entire case to those shadow forces over which he apparently had no control.

Not once since Shipley had offered him the assignment had he deviated from Agency procedures, operating always within the guidelines established by Masters. *"Evidence may be revealed haphazardly, but it reflects a logical and inevitable course of action. The agent must recreate that course and the criminal who traveled it."* Stark's arrest, for example; that had resulted in a routine query to the Oklahoma bureau, had brought Robert Conrad's incomplete report, had put Malone in touch with Edward Fleming and led directly to Willie Joe Tate, the stolen M-16's and Maxwell Armory. It had brought about the deaths of two men.

Malone had followed a straight, natural investigative line, acting, as trained, in the best interests of the Agency and the country. Yet he had been ordered off the trail; someone at Maxwell Armory didn't want him there, had complained to General Sain in the Pentagon. Obviously, he had carried the complaint higher, to someone of importance in the Executive Branch, perhaps a Senator, or a member of the President's Cabinet. Whoever it was had gotten to Jason Shipley promptly and effectively. Masters, Malone assured himself, would not have surrendered to such pressures. Masters would have sympathized with Malone's grievances; but he would *not* have tolerated his sagging commitment. Masters believed in meeting commitments, in performing up to expectations, operating according to the rules . . .

It was difficult for Malone to recall a time when he had not lived by rules set down by W. W. Masters, difficult to remember life before Masters.

Early on, Malone had understood that Masters was no ordinary man. He was not easy to be with, nor especially comfortable. He dominated, diminished other men by the simple fact of his presence. A flicker of his eyes or a half-turn of the elegant head was sufficient to indicate disapproval, to send the offender slinking away.

Nevertheless, people craved his approval and to receive it was to know a rich, warm glow of satisfaction. From his first meeting with Masters, Malone had been made aware of the Director's built-in superiority, had wanted to be near him. Here was someone to work for, to follow and obey, someone who promised that Malone would become a better man than he had ever dared hope to be.

Malone had never been able to resist Masters, had never wanted to. He had always seen the sense behind every move the Director made, the clear reasoning behind his arguments, the strength of his conviction, the power of his will. Masters had supported Malone and directed him, had shaped the course of his professional life, had kept him from diluting his commitment, had exposed him to a tremendous variety of experience.

It was Masters who taught Malone that an agent's work was a constantly changing thing, that no two assignments were ever alike, that there was an evolving, and often concealed, purpose behind every act of every agent. Duty required constant alertness, the utilization of all faculties, the ability to understand people and their motivations, the links between cause and effect.

One winter, Malone had been instructing recruits at the Academy in small arms fire and investigatory techniques when Masters sent for him.

"You're to go down to Richmond, Virginia," he said. "See the president of Oppenheimer Electronics, Incorporated. A personnel question has come up. John Ericson . . ."

Malone had worked with Ericson on three or four assignments. He was a cool man, competent and intelligent, the kind of man the Agency liked to keep. But Ericson had quit the Agency on short notice three years before and Malone had never heard his name spoken again by the Director until now.

In Richmond, Malone was ushered into the office of the president, a bespectacled man with thinning hair and a speculative expression on his oval face. He greeted Malone with cautious amiability.

"I didn't expect such a quick response to my inquiry," he said.

"The Agency enjoys helping whenever it can," Malone answered.

"I anticipated some sort of a form letter," the businessman said. "I'm not sure it warrants a personal visit, though I'm pleased." He located an employment application on his desk. "This fellow, John Ericson, he applied for a job as chief of our plant security. We're opening a new installation up in Maryland. According to his application, he was with the IIA for six years."

"That's accurate," Malone said, issuing words as if each was precious.

"He seems authentic. No black marks on his record."

A portion of Malone's brain turned backward to his last conversation with Masters, and he tried to evaluate his conflicting reactions.

"At one time," he said deliberately. "Mr. Masters held Ericson in considerable regard."

"Oh!" He pursed his soft mouth. "Was there some difficulty?"

"It's hard to pinpoint these things. Ericson left the Agency without explanation. The kind of abrupt departure that leaves a bad taste, although I've never heard Mr. Masters speak a critical word about the man. The Director believes it takes ten years for an agent to gain the proper experience, create a suitable emotional set, to mature. After all, citizens pay taxes, your taxes . . ."

"Yes," the businessman said. "Emotional maturity is vital."

"Dependability."

"The job we're trying to fill demands a person who is dependable."

"At the Agency, we like to believe that time eliminates those people who can't measure up. High-risk work requires courage and discipline. There is no room for weaklings."

"Weaklings," the businessman repeated. "Our new operation is sensitive, government contracts . . ."

"Mr. Masters wants to assist in any way he can."

"Convey my appreciation, please . . ."

Please . . .

Please fasten . . .

". . . Fasten your seat belts, please."

The announcement jarred Malone and his eyes went to the flashing sign above his seat. He obeyed the disembodied command. Below, New York City.

The plane was descending and the pressure in his ears mounted steadily. Pressure . . . because Masters was gone. Malone was concerned about the future of the Agency. Forces existed for whom the assassination was a good thing. Forces that wanted to block him from the proof he meant to gather and display. Cunning men maneuvered against him and he could not afford to be less cunning.

Malone was afraid that the system was breaking down without Masters to make it work. The future was unknown. A man needed an ally to protect him from surprise attack, someone trustworthy, someone strong. But it was not until the plane was on the ground and he was striding through the antiseptic confines of Kennedy Airport that he was able to come up with the right name.

Malone was pleased to be in the Fifth Avenue apartment again. The smell of old leather and burnished wood in the library made him feel almost as if he belonged there. He peered through the tall windows to the south and imagined he was able to see the United Nations. Today Reese had been there, lunching with the Secretary-General, was on his way back now. What would it be like to function at that exalted level where wealth was accepted as routine and power was exercised in the natural course? The concept was difficult to hold and after a while Malone gave it up.

Somewhere in the apartment, a door opened and he could

hear the vibrating thrum of masculine voices. Malone turned away from the window. Minutes later, Senator Reese came into the library, followed by Martin Williams.

"Malone," Reese said. "Good to see you again."

They shook hands. "If the timing is bad——."

"Not at all. Sorry you had to wait." Reese sat down and crossed his legs. "Your message said it was urgent."

"Have you found the murderer?" Martin Williams said.

"Martin," Reese remonstrated. Williams withdrew to a place against the wall.

"You might be interested in what has turned up so far," Malone said.

"Indeed."

Malone suddenly found it difficult to sort out his ideas. "There's so much happening . . ."

"Such as?"

"As an American . . ." he said, and stopped. The words sounded overblown in his ears. He tried again. "Sometimes a man does things he isn't proud of."

"We're all human beings, Malone."

"Masters insisted that an agent do nothing that wasn't in the best interests of the United States. He was a patriot."

"There are as many definitions of patriotism," Williams said, "as there are of love."

Reese glanced sidelong at the monkey-faced man. "Martin, it might be a good idea if Malone and I were left alone."

Williams left the room without a word.

Reese smiled in Malone's direction, spread his hands. "Martin is my aggressive alter ego. There are times, however, when his enthusiasm tends to diminish his good sense. Please go on, Malone."

Malone looked steadily at the other man. There was so much about Reese that reminded him of W. W. Masters. Perhaps he was making too much of the resemblance, had overestimated the Senator. Yet he had many of the same qualities of mind and character, and it occurred to Malone that in some way they might almost have been interchangeable.

As soon as he had stepped off the plane at Kennedy Airport, Malone had known that he wasn't going to contact Sam Batsford, as Shipley had ordered. First, Charles Reese.

Malone had phoned the Senator's Washington office and was told that Reese was in New York. A call to this apartment had raised a secretary who arranged this meeting.

Malone blinked once and Reese's face shifted into focus. There was no turning back now; he was forced to act. Masters was gone and no one had taken his place. Malone needed help, the kind of help Masters used to provide, the kind of help that only someone with great personal authority and moral stature could give. A superior man. Someone to trust and depend on. There was only Charles Reese. Malone decided to take the risk . . .

"From the start," he said, "this case has been complicated. Leads that went nowhere. Unexpected revelations. Fraudulent confessions."

"You mean Brewster?"

"Whenever someone famous is killed, some people are compelled to get into the act, even though it may cost them their own freedom."

Reese nodded but said nothing.

"A solid possibility now exists. A man who was held by the police for nearly seventy-two hours before he was released."

"You're talking about Jethro Stark?"

Malone straightened up. He'd forgotten that Reese knew about Stark, that he'd mentioned Stark himself during his visit to the Senator's Connecticut home.

"Why was Stark turned loose?"

"A check was run on him," Malone said, his face rigid, his voice toneless. He felt obliged to protect the Agency, to defend it against complaint. "The report that came in said he was clean."

"Now you think otherwise, is that it?"

"Yes. Subsequently additional information was made available. It led to Oklahoma . . ."

"What did you find there?"

Sweat broke along Malone's sides and the skin on the back of his wrists shifted and twitched. "There's a man named Willie Joe Tate, a preacher . . ."

"I've heard of him, of course. What's this got to do with Tate?"

"He's training a military unit under his own command. A private army. He has a pretty complete establishment and talks about making war against a radical takeover of the country. He sees enemies everywhere."

"Everywhere. Does that mean in the government?"

Malone summoned up a vision of the photographs on the target range. "Yes sir."

"For example? Who does the Reverend Tate consider as an enemy?"

Malone breathed out audibly. "You, sir."

Reese said nothing for a beat. "Do I understand you correctly? You think that Tate might have sent Stark after me?"

"Perhaps."

"What about proof?"

"Nothing that would stand up in court." He considered his options and decided to tell Reese everything. "The agent who connected Stark to Tate for me was killed. So was an Army corporal who supplied him with information. Both hit-and-run accidents, officially."

"You don't accept that?"

"One hit-and-run, perhaps. Two seems murder."

"Is there more?"

"Tate gets his weapons and ammunition from the Maxwell Armory, an Army supply depot in Texas."

"Surplus purchases, you mean?"

"No. At first it seemed the guns were being stolen."

"You no longer believe that?"

"New guns are shipped out of Maxwell Armory by military transport. Somewhere in that open, deserted country, they're transferred to trucks which carry them up to Tate's encampment."

"How can that be done? There are records—."

"Records can be altered, if the right men are involved—supply officers, noncoms, drivers."

"You're describing a serious conspiracy, Malone."

"At Maxwell, everything was friendly until the subject of a precise weapons count came up. Then, stalling, and someone got on the phone to Washington. A General Sain called from the Pentagon. He put an end to any cooperation by the commanding officer. There was no weapons count, and Mr. Shipley then ordered me up to New York to talk to Sam Batsford."

"The columnist? What's this got to do with him?"

"Maybe Batsford will answer that."

"If the kind of plot you are suggesting does in fact exist, it would include not only Willie Joe Tate and the people at Maxwell Armory, but would have to include a number of high-ranking officers in the Pentagon. Another thing, someone had to be able to get Shipley to pull you out of there. That could only mean someone of stature in the government. If that's true, then it's likely Shipley himself is involved, others in the IIA."

"If Masters were alive, this couldn't happen," Malone said, a pained look in his eyes.

Reese spoke as if to himself. "Traditionally political conspiracies haven't worked in America. Now I don't know. This is an unhappy period and men have given up the middle ground for the rhetoric and easy solutions of the fringes. Military coups have always occurred in other countries, arranged among politicians and generals and industrialists. Maybe our time has come." He measured Malone steadily. "You took a chance coming to me. I haven't announced it yet, but as you know I am running for the Presidency. I want the job."

The agent nodded grimly. Words skipped and skittered across his brain in wild patterns. He ached to release the constrictions that held him, unyielding and painful, to remember what he had managed to forget.

"I . . . trust you," he was able to get out.

Reese's aristocratic face underwent no change. "A public statement by me, an accusation—that would do no good."

Malone pushed himself erect, features pulled together, eyes frosted.

"Sit down," Reese said. "Listen to me. Try to understand. What the hell did you expect? Did you think I was going to get up on a soapbox and make a speech about treachery in government? If it's as big as it appears, then even a Senatorial investigation might result in a whitewash, get us nowhere. If what you say is true, then surely there will be political figures involved. Maybe a Senator or two or a dozen, for all we know. Dammit, Malone, even one man with the right connections, influence, could side-track any investigation, turn it into a public spectacle for his own benefit, make his opponents look like silly alarmists. We can't take that chance . . ."

Malone berated himself for underestimating Reese.

"Tomorrow," the Senator went on, "I'll invite a few of my colleagues in to see me. I'll tell them what you've told me, in confidence, of course. Among us, there are people who can help. Trained investigators, lawyers, politically knowledgeable people. I'll have a talk with Lindsay Murphy, the former Attorney General. I am sure of his sympathies and he knows where a lot of bodies are buried. We'll pull strings, Malone, we'll prod and we'll expose. Maybe we'll threaten a little bit. We might just be able to find out exactly what is going on, whatever it is, when it's supposed to happen. Maybe we'll be able to stop it." He started to smile. "I'm on the Committee on Military Appropriations. Suppose I arrange to have this General Sain subpoenaed? Under oath he might have something to tell us. If it's going to work, Malone, it'll have to be my way. What do you say, will you go along?"

Malone hesitated. There was no better man than Charles Reese to work the political side of this case. Meanwhile, Malone would continue doing what he had to do.

Later, when Malone left the Fifth Avenue apartment, it was with a rising sense of communion with Charles Reese, deeply moved by his practical idealism, his commitment to justice, and truth. The Senator could be a man to admire, to look up to, to believe in.

XVIII

WELCOME
TO LANSTON
Pop. 3,150
Speed 30

HELLMAN LIFTED his foot off the accelerator and the rented car slowed down. The road ahead widened, was lined with wooden houses painted white or a soft yellow, each with a broad porch and a lawn, some shade trees. He drove past a gray, stone church topped by a tall white steeple and a sign out front that read:

MIRACLE TENT REVIVAL, ONE MILE.

An arrow pointed left. Hellman went straight ahead.

The road opened into a square and Hellman parked in front of the Bon-Ton drugstore and got out. There was an eccentric stillness to the hot, slow air, as if presaging a thunder storm. A woman in hair curlers and Bermuda shorts came out of Andrew's Grocery and got into a station wagon, drove off. A young boy pedaled by on a bicycle. A wrinkled black man in a dark suit walked past, not looking up.

Across the street, a large, red-brick and granite building flying the American flag and the Confederate flag on poles out front. Near the sidewalk, a bronze statue of three Confederate soldiers, tattered and wounded, but still seemingly aggressive and looking for the enemy. Farther along, in a leafy circle of shade cast by an immense sycamore, two benches occupied by elderly men in Old Hickory overalls, faded work shirts, and straw hats. Their weathered faces were closed as they watched Hellman approach.

"Good afternoon," he said. "I'm looking for the sheriff's office."

The old men looked at each other and then back at Hellman. "Whut you want him for?" one said.

"Business," Hellman said.

The old men ingested that and one of them pointed toward the building behind them. "Go on up to the front steps, mister . . ."

"But don't go in," the other said.

"That's right. 'Round to the side's a entrance door. Jes' pass on through. McClung, he picked hisself about the coolest nest in the courthouse . . ."

The old men were right. The air in the narrow basement corridor was stale but cool and Hellman felt refreshed. He came to an open door. Inside, behind a wooden gate, a big-jawed man in sweat-stained gray chinos was slumped in front of a two-way radio, studying a copy of *Playboy*. Next to him, a second police officer, his chair tilted against the wall, his feet hooked in the rungs.

"I'm looking for Sheriff McClung," Hellman said from the doorway.

Neither man looked up. "Whut for?" the man at the radio grunted.

Hellman crossed to the wooden railing. "My name's Hellman. I've come down from New York to see the sheriff."

"New York," the second man said. "That's a long way."

"Sheriff expectin' you?" the first man said. He lifted his long head, appraised Hellman.

Hellman decided to stop wasting time. "Senator Abernathy seemed to think that Sheriff McClung might be able to help me."

Both officers straightened up at the mention of Abernathy's name. "Senator *Leland* Abernathy?" the shorter man said.

Hellman merely stared at him.

"Better tell the sheriff," the man at the radio said. His colleague went to a door at the other end of the room, opened it and looked inside. "There's a fella out here wantin' to talk to you, Ardis. Says the Senator sent him."

"Is that right! Well, what in the damned hell are you keepin' him out there for, John? Send the man in to me!"

John stood to one side and Hellman went past him. He found himself in a large, square room with an oppressively low ceiling. An ancient air conditioner wheezed and clattered.

Sheriff McClung stood behind an old oak desk, a wide man with faded yellow hair that fell limply over his ears. He wore a straw hat shaped like a cowboy's Stetson on the back of his head. His desk was littered with used paper coffee cups and against the wall there was a fully stocked gun rack.

Hellman offered his hand and said his name. McClung shook hands as if afraid of the touch of foreign flesh. He eyed Hellman with a sidelong look.

"You say you're a friend of the Senator?"

"I was in Senator Abernathy's office two days ago," Hellman said, putting a crisp authority into his voice. "In Washington. We had a conversation."

McClung made a noncommittal sound back in his throat. "John! Why in hell are you standin' around? Bring the man a chair so he can set down!"

"Comin' up, Ardis . . ."

John brought a hard wooden chair and Hellman sat down. John stood alongside, staring at him.

"Well, dammit, John," McClung said. "You mean to perch there all day? Git your butt on the hell out of here!"

When they were alone, McClung shifted around to face Hellman. He had a large head and features to match, with grayish eyes; a complex of blue veins formed a starburst in one cheek. His mouth lifted on one side when he spoke.

"How's the Senator feelin' nowadays?"

"In the best of health, when I left him."

"I surely do admire that man," McClung said. "You been friendly with him for a long time, y'say?"

"Not long," Hellman said, producing a smile. "Senator Abernathy invited me down to Washington so that we could talk about my work."

McClung leaned back. "Whut work is that, Mr. Hellman?"

"The work that brought me to Lanston, Sheriff. The murder of W. W. Masters."

A vertical furrow appeared in McClung's brow. "You're a peace officer?"

Hellman laughed shortly. "Will a cop's son do, sheriff? I'm investigating the circumstances of the killing. I do some writing . . ."

"A reporter," McClung said without enthusiasm.

"Not exactly. In any case, Senator Abernathy suggested I might get some help here."

"Don't see how. Nobody aroun' here had any part in the shootin', you can depend on it. Folks in these parts held Mr. Masters in high regard."

Hellman set himself, went on. "Senator Abernathy told me about man named Silas. A black man. Woodrow Silas. Woody—."

McClung's thick lips puckered, came back to rest. "Reckon I've heard the name. Whut about him?"

Hellman felt vaguely intimidated by Ardis McClung. Joe Capolino had always represented the ultimately tough cop to him; McClung introduced a new ingredient into the mix—meanness. But having come this far, Hellman decided not to back off. He leaned forward confidentially.

"Silas is the leader of Black Freedom Now," he said. "A revolutionary group."

Nothing showed on McClung's massive face. "Any nigger come aroun' here, he better say yessir to me and keep his eyes down."

"That's not Silas' style."

McClung grunted heavily, the pale eyes looking at Hellman as if across a large void. He yelled, "Bandifer!"

The officer who had been reading *Playboy* appeared in the doorway. "You call me, Ardis?"

"Bandifer, you know anything about one of them black militants name of Woodrow Silas?"

The long face grew longer, then brightened. "Shoot, yes, Ardis.

One of them outside agitators. You remember, he showed up a few years back and then took off like a big-ass bird."

McClung glanced at Hellman. "There you are. Silas ain't in these parts anymore."

"I know that, sheriff. He's in New York now. In jail."

"Well, good! Maybe teach the boy a lesson."

McClung's caution was commendable, Hellman told himself, but he was wasting time. Hellman decided to force the issue. "When Silas was in Lanston he tried to organize the local black people. Voter registration, school integration, and the like. Isn't that so, sheriff? There was a raid and a shot was fired . . ."

"Bandifer," McClung said coldly. "We ever do a raid on some niggers who were tryin' to foment a Communist revolution in these parts?"

"Well, shoot, Ardis, you know as well as me whut we did. We went on out there and sent 'em all packin'. Is that why you hauled me in here?"

"That's right," McClung said to Hellman. "It comes back to me now. They was puttin' together a nigger scheme to cause trouble. They was collectin' dangerous weapons, plannin' to rile up our good colored people. All that talk of votin' and integratin' . . . I mean, that ain't about to happen in these parts."

"That's for damn sure," Bandifer said cheerfully.

"A girl was killed," Hellman said.

"Was somebody shot in the raid, Bandifer?" McClung said. Bandifer nodded.

"Her name was Hilda Mann," Hellman said.

"Senator Abernathy, he told you that?" McClung said absently.

"It's true, isn't it?"

McClung looked inquiringly at Bandifer. The long head moved up and down. "It's like he says, Ardis. Hilda Mann was her name."

"Fomentin' a revolution is a dangerous activity. Somebody's bound to get hurt."

"Should've been Silas got it," Bandifer said, "'stead o' that good-lookin' nigger gal."

"That raid was one of the best ideas I ever had," McClung said. "Ain't been any suggestion of trouble since."

"Now, Ardis," Bandifer drawled patiently. "You know better'n that. Weren't all your idea. Come on down from the IIA bureau in Mobile. You remember?"

McClung grew thoughtful. "Reckon that's right. Must've been the doin' of that fella in charge."

"Herman Flood," Bandifer offered.

"That's the one. Old Herman was a good ole boy."

The name sounded familiar and Hellman's mind reached back to the detention cell in the Brooklyn precinct house, to Roy Brewster. Herman Flood had been there, a pleasant blond man whom Capolino had introduced as the agent-in-charge of the New York bureau of the IIA.

"Are you saying that the IIA instigated the raid?" Hellman said.

"I recollect it now," McClung said. "Ole Flood, he showed up with some of his people and told us what was on and how would we like to go along. Well, I tell you, we had a fine ole time scaring those niggers white."

"Isn't that sort of assignment unusual?" Hellman said.

McClung answered. "Anytime the IIA or FBI or any other Federal bureau wants us to help 'em out we are happy to oblige. 'Course, the IIA, you know the way those boys are—mostly going off an' doing things by their own selves an' not saying what they are up to."

"But not this time?" Hellman said, aware of a growing excitement.

McClung shrugged.

"Who shot Hilda Mann?" Hellman said.

McClung sucked air noisily. "A raid ain't no Sunday church meetin'. Those niggers wanted trouble, they got it."

"Else why was they there?" Bandifer added.

"That's right. Once the shootin' starts, somebody's bound to get hurt!"

"Who shot first?" Hellman said.

"Well, now, that's a good question," McClung said. "Maybe the niggers did. I'm inclined that way."

"Might've been one of the Agency fellas, Ardis," Bandifer said.

"Might've been. Maybe Flood hisself. But it damned well weren't none of my people. My men shoot only when I tell 'em to, not until."

Which left only Flood, Hellman told himself, to pull the trigger —or cause it to be pulled for W. W. Masters. But it made no sense. What connection could there possibly have been between Masters and Hilda Mann? Why would Masters want her dead?

"Anything else you want to know?" McClung said.

Hellman understood that he was being dismissed. He stood up.

"Not right now, sheriff. But if I think of anything, I'll be in touch."

"Reckon you'll be leavin' town now," McClung offered.

"I'm awfully tired. I need a good night's sleep."

"Lanston House is the best hotel in town," Bandifer said, grinning mischievously. "It's the *only* hotel in town!"

McClung looked at the deputy. "Whutever you say, Mr. Hellman. I'm sure pleased to help a friend of the Senator any way I can. And if you zoom out of here first thing in the mornin' 'fore I can say good-bye you carry my regards to the Senator, hear?"

"I'll do that, sheriff."

XIX

Two men unknown to each other, meeting in a deserted Manhattan street after dark on a summer night. The arrangements reminded him of an old gangster movie. Malone was beguiled; and mildly disturbed. He put his hand to his waist; the pistol holstered there was reassuring. During his twenty years with the Agency, he had been called upon to use the pistol infrequently, and he was grateful; Malone chose to be neither judge nor executioner.

Sam Batsford was where he had said he would be, behind the wheel of a gray Cadillac under the second street lamp in the block. Malone tapped on one of the tinted windows and Batsford examined him before unlocking the door. Malone climbed in.

"Malone?"

"That's right." In the dark, the columnist looked younger than his years. But there was a cynical set to his narrow face and folds of excess skin gave his eyes a reptilian cast.

"Lock the door, Malone. New York's a dangerous place to be at night." He turned away. "You look the way every agent should look."

Malone made no response. He seldom thought about the way he looked, had no clear vision of his own appearance. He took care of his body, fed it and cleaned it, kept it in working order so that when needed it would respond efficiently. It had never failed him.

"If they made a movie of your life," Batsford said, as if avoiding the reason they were there, "they'd get Henry Fonda to play the part." He placed his hands on the steering wheel. "You're making people unhappy, Malone."

2 0 1

"What people?"

"Important people."

"For example, Mr. Batsford?"

Batsford turned. "Senator Leland Abernathy, for example."

Malone let nothing show on his face, but there was an interior stiffness, his senses alerted to danger, searching ahead. This was the first time Senator Abernathy's name had been mentioned. Questions flashed across his mind, but he said nothing, giving nothing away.

"That business at Maxwell Armory," Batsford said wearily. "What were you trying to prove?"

The names were signposts in his brain: Conrad, Wending, Chisolm, Johnson, Sain, Shipley, Batsford. And now: Abernathy, Leland; majority leader of the U.S. Senate. What was it Charles Reese had said? *". . . Surely there are some political figures involved . . . a senator or two . . ."* Malone circled his wrist with his thumb and middle finger, rubbed hard.

"Where does Abernathy fit into this?"

"Use your brains, man!" Batsford said with unexpected heat. "Didn't Shipley tell you—some people are not to be rousted."

"This is an Agency investigation. Reports have come in from agents all over the country. Leads, clues, rumors. Everything is checked out. Some trails go nowhere, others stay alive. Nobody," he finished stiffly, "was rousted."

"Maxwell Armory," Batsford said. "That trail is nowhere, Malone. Wiped out. Nonexistent."

Malone stared at him. "An IIA agent was killed in Oklahoma. And an Army corporal. That brought me to Maxwell Armory, Batsford, and to you. And now to Senator Abernathy."

"Don't be a fool! There's nothing in it for you. Put that entire Western jaunt out of your mind. Forget it. That's good advice."

"Your advice, or Abernathy's?"

Batsford closed his eyes as if in pain. "Malone, I know about you. You're a first-class agent. You're smart. Think! I can tell you on good authority that Shipley is never going to make it all the way in the Agency. A man like you, on the other hand—you might. Consider that, Malone. Wouldn't you like to take Masters' place? Think about that!"

What a strange idea! Masters was the Director. Only Masters. Over the years Malone had competed with other agents, with Herman Flood, but that had been a manifestation of pride in his work, his desire to please Masters. At no time did he ever consider the possibility of taking Masters' place.

As if trying to verbalize Malone's thoughts, Batsford went on hurriedly. "Masters is gone. Someone has to do the job. Shipley is not the one. It takes a strong man, a good man, a man who is flexible and knows how to make the necessary arrangements. You were Masters' protégé, Malone, his friend. Who is there to look after your interests now? A Civil Service rating is no guarantee . . ."

Masters' words were echoed in Malone's mind. *"Prepare, Peter, for what lies ahead. Great tasks demand greatness of any man who would serve. School your emotions, your intelligence, learn to be a servant of the people, as well as their leader."*

"An agent goes where the case leads," Malone said slowly. "There is no other way."

"Times change," Batsford said. "Yesterday's idea won't work today. Yesterday's men won't do." When Malone made no reply, Batsford sighed. "You're not a reasonable man, Malone. I have some information that may throw light on the case. Shipley told me to give it to you directly."

"Yes?"

"You've been operating on the premise that the assassin was after Senator Reese. I agree. But it wasn't done for political reasons. I make it out to be a single man trying to avenge himself for suspected wrongs."

Malone's face was impassive.

Batsford looked away. "Do you know about Marie Craig? A lovely girl, very pretty, and a swinger. That is, she liked a good time. Well, which of us doesn't? I met Marie at a party. She drank pretty good and tossed herself around." He glanced at Malone. "This should interest you. Marie worked for Senator Charles Reese. The receptionist in his Washington office. One night Marie decided to take a walk. Out of a window. The window was on a high floor and did permanent damage to her. It killed her." He laughed at his own joke. "The window was in Martin Williams' apartment. Reese's executive assistant. How does that item grab you?"

Malone held himself very still.

"There was an investigation," Batsford said. "But nothing came of it. Closed doors, private testimony. Rumor has it that Marie was an acid head. LSD, Malone. Did you know that?"

"What's the connection with Mr. Masters?"

"A very good question," Batsford said brightly. "The word is that Marie Craig wasn't Williams' girl, that he was just a beard. And for whom, Malone? For that upstanding liberal Senator, Charles Reese. The way I hear it, Reese was making it with Marie and he was the one who was in that apartment with her when she took the plunge. How's that strike you, Malone?"

Malone braced himself against a swelling rage, allowed nothing to surface. "What else?"

"There's a man named Jim Cooley. He was Marie Craig's boy friend. He's a fireman and he lives in Queens, here in New York. Some of us believe that Cooley might have tried to kill Reese to even the score for Marie . . ."

"Is that Abernathy's opinion?"

"Let's leave the Senator out of this from now on. I'm simply indicating a certain direction for your investigation."

Malone felt as if some basic emotional shield was being systematically stripped away, leaving him exposed and vulnerable. A jealous boy friend; that was too simple, would leave too many loose ends.

"Why haven't you gone after this for your column?" he asked Batsford.

"Marie's father refused to talk to me. Said he didn't like newspapermen. Lots of people feel that way. I wonder why?" He grinned without humor. "I figured an agent of the IIA would do better."

"So you told Abernathy and he told Shipley and Shipley had to reach all the way to the Maxwell Armory for an agent you could talk to."

A grin appeared briefly on Batsford's face. "It's your case. There was nothing for you in Texas."

"Is that it, Batsford?"

"Are you going to talk to Cooley?"

Malone unlocked the door and got out of the Cadillac.

"Let me know how you make out!" Batsford called after him.

Malone never looked back.

XX

HELLMAN FELT restored. The old Negro waiter in the Lanston House dining room had suggested the pompano Louisiane with Chantilly potatoes and a wedge of pecan pie for dessert. Everything was perfect. He'd downed two cups of strong black coffee and tipped the waiter generously.

Satisfied, he stepped out for a stroll around the town. The streets were quieter in the late, low, summer sun and there were few people to be seen. He went past a movie theater heralding a new Elvis Presley picture. He studied the magazine rack in the drugstore and circled the courthouse square. When he came to his car, he got in and drove slowly along the main street.

After fifteen minutes, he turned off and soon the paved road ended. And so did the carefully barbered appearance of the lawns of the homes along the way. Here the houses were smaller, less sturdy, patched with boards that didn't match or sections of corrugated roofing material. To his left, through some trees, he spotted an inlet of the Mexican Gulf; the air was slow with moisture, cool against his cheeks.

He came on some black children playing at the side of the road and stopped the car. The children looked up, smiled expectantly.

"You kids know any people name of Mann?" Hellman asked.

"Sure, mister," a girl replied. "Next-to-the-last house over, up to the bay."

Hellman drove on and came to a shabby structure with an unsteady, unpainted porch. A small old man in overalls sat in a rocking chair and smoked a pipe, watched Hellman.

"Excuse me," Hellman said. "Is your name Mann?"

The old man took the pipe out of his mouth. "That's me, mistuh. The oney one left. Rudy Mann's my name, if you please, sir."

Hellman introduced himself, explaining that he was seeking information about Hilda Mann's death. The old man nodded thoughtfully. "That Hilda was a wild one, runnin' aroun' gittin' into trouble. Boun' to happen, her runnin' with all o' them trouble-makers. Yessir, it don' hardly pay to have chillun, they go off'n leave you to set and go hungry. Especially bad havin' a good lookin' daughter . . ."

"Hilda was your daughter?" Hellman had judged Rudy Mann to be the dead girl's grandfather.

"That's a fack. My oney daughter. They's the worst, good lookin' women. Jes don' pay . . ."

"I don't mean to revive painful memories, Mr. Mann, but I'm trying to find out exactly how Hilda died. There are conflicting stories."

"Shot in the back by some white bastard is how!" a harsh voice said in the darkness.

Hellman pulled around and saw four black men coming toward him. Even in the closing darkness, they looked as hard-eyed and angry as they sounded. He became aware of a cold sensation along his spine. He cursed himself for not anticipating trouble, for coming here alone, for coming at all.

"What the hell you after, honky?" one man said.

Hellman tried to collect his thoughts. He hadn't expected this kind of raw hostility from blacks this deep in the South. A part of himself had viewed them as remaining docile, accepting, keeping their place. He took a quick step away from the porch.

A husky black man glided between Hellman and the rented car, thick arms folded across his chest.

"Look," Hellman said. "I'm just trying to get some information. I'm a writer."

"What kind of information?" a slender man with a small, round head said.

The old man on the porch was on his feet, waving his pipe in the air. "Man came to see me, hear! Came to talk to me! You fellas scat out of here. Don't need no coachin' from you boys."

"Go to bed, Pa," the slender man said.

"Don't want to go to bed," the old man said.

"I'm trying to find out about Hilda Mann," Hellman said.

"She was murdered."

"Lynched."

"A clear case of lynching."

Hellman looked around. "I'm looking for the truth," he said. "Maybe you fellows can help."

Someone laughed. "I thought that by talking to Hilda's family I'd be able to find out what really happened."

"You talked to McClung this afternoon. You'll write his version."

"Not if it isn't true." Hellman's eyes went from face to face. "What's your version?"

The slender man stepped closer, his small head cocked curiously. "I'm Samuel, Hilda's brother."

Hellman glanced back at Hilda's father. The old man sucked on his pipe.

"The old man doesn't always remember things the way they are," Samuel said. "Since Hilda was buried, he's forgotten a lot. Maybe it's easier for him that way."

"We're wastin' time," one of the other men said.

"Hang loose," Samuel said over his shoulder. "Okay, mistuh, maybe you better say what's on your mind."

Hellman spoke in a low voice. "Woody Silas told me to come here."

That stirred the four young men. They moved in closer to Hellman.

"How come Woody be rappin' with a white cat?" Samuel said.

"I'm investigating the death of W. W. Masters."

"What's that got to do with Woody?"

"He's being held by the New York police."

"*Woody* burn Masters? That boy is some kind of a dude!"

"I don't believe it," Samuel said. "Woody's too hip. Even killing a sonuvabitch like Masters is nowhere. The pigs have got to be framin' Woody."

Hellman thought he saw an advantage. "That's why I went to

see Woody, that's why I came down to Lanston. I agree with you—Woody's being framed. But why Woody Silas, I asked myself. I thought there might be some link between Hilda's death and Woody's arrest. If I could find out what it was, I might be able to blow the frame, get Woody out." Hellman looked around; no eyes met his. He went on quickly. "If Hilda was deliberately killed I can put it all together. If I knew about that killing, I might be able to find out why W. W. Masters was shot."

"You tryin' to set Woody up!" Samuel said.

"No," Hellman said. "No. I don't think he did it. But other people do. They want him to be brought to trial and found guilty. Somewhere in all of this there must be a sensible explanation, some connection . . ."

"There's a connection," Samuel said. "There's always a connection when black folks find trouble."

"McClung says none of his people fired the first shots. His man, Bandifer, believes maybe an IIA agent fired first and that he killed Hilda Mann. A man named Flood."

"Could be," Samuel said. "There were three of them there that day."

None of them spoke and in the deep blackness Hellman felt less apprehensive. He sat down on the edge of the porch and lit a cigarette. He offered the pack around; no one accepted it. Hellman waited but no one said anything. In those silent moments, his fear was transformed into annoyance, resentment. He swore.

"You people talk a good game," he bit off. "Woody Silas, all of you. But you don't say anything. You're mad but you don't do anything. You won't help."

"Like how?" Samuel said.

"Woody said Hilda was shot in the back, murdered."

"That's the truth of it."

"Why? Why should she matter to anybody except her friends, her family? Why, for example, should she matter to an agent of W. W. Masters?"

Samuel answered presently. "Hilda was a good gal, smart and good lookin', both. She was into the Movement, only she liked to think that whites were a lot more decent than they are. She put down talk of violence.

"You see, mistuh, around here, everybody fishes and swims, the water bein' so close. Hilda, she loved the Gulf and she had bought her a little old outboard engine and she fixed it up and hung it on a beat-up dingy and kept it together with spit and prayer. Hilda, she liked nighttime fishin'. On this one night, she went out and made her catch and came back in, tied up in her usual place in the finger of the bay and started on home. That's when they jumped her."

"Jumped her?"

"Three of the mothers. College students. *White* college students. Drinkin' twelve-year old whiskey and hidin' in the dark looking to dip themselves into some black pussy. That's when Hilda come along. Hilda was no ass-swingin' chippie, you see. She was okay. Hip, but okay. Not even nineteen years old that night, pretty and soft, and she liked to sing when she was alone. Those white bastards took ahold of Hilda and held her down and took turns on her. They kept her till mornin', puttin' it to her, till they hurt her insides pretty good.

"Hilda, she recognized one of them boys. Fred F. Calvin, was his name." Samuel was breathing hard, After a while, he went on. "Old Hilda, soon as she could walk, she went downtown to see Sheriff McClung. She told him the way Fred F. Calvin and them other boys done her."

"What did McClung do?" Hellman asked.

"Nothin' is whut he did. Just nothin'. McClung, he says to Hilda, whyn't you forget about it? Ain't no way to prove nothin'. 'Sides, jes a few good ole boys havin' fun, gettin' some nigger nooky. Hilda, she weren't havin' any and she wanted to bring rape charges against Fred F. Calvin and those two John Does. That's when McClung tells her how it is. How Fred F. Calvin is goin' to be a big man in the state one day, how well-*situated* he is. McClung tells her to go on home and think on it, and change her mind. But Hilda didn't change her mind. That sister of mine was mad and she jes' stormed around mutterin' and thinkin' hard. Next day she went back downtown and told McClung she wanted to charge Fred F. Calvin.

"That same day, Woody Silas come to town. He was into vote registration and boycotts and like that. Woody was nonviolent then . . . Every day he went around rappin' with folks and every afternoon he was holdin' meetin's in this shack and organizin'. Hilda, she started droppin' by, listenin'. Soon she started helpin' any ways she could. Folks got to know that she was at the shack every afternoon. Even the white folks knew, cause Lanston is too small for secrets. And one day McClung came out there with his deputies and the IIA people and they put a bullet into Hilda's back . . ."

Hellman tried to order his thoughts. *If* Herman Flood had deliberately shot down Hilda Mann, and if he had done so on orders from W. W. Masters, there had to be a reason. No one had supplied it yet. Was Fred F. Calvin the link?

"What was Fred Calvin to Masters?" he asked.

"Nothin'," came the quick, sullen response.

"Then why would Masters want Hilda shot?" he persisted.

"That one's easy," Samuel said. "Fred F. Calvin is the favorite nephew of Senator Leland Fitch Abernathy."

In his room in Lanston House, Hellman was stretched out on the bed wearing only his jockey shorts, staring into the dark, struggling to assimilate what he had learned. It all seemed to fit: Woody Silas' description of Hilda Mann's death, McClung's version of the shooting, the presence of agent Flood and his men to instigate and lead the raid that would silence Hilda Mann, end her role as a troublemaker and so protect the bright future of Leland Abernathy's nephew.

And there was the excuse given for the raid—an arms cache. A suspected arms cache; that had been the reason for the raid on Woody Silas' apartment, the reason Hellman had used to convince Joe Capolino to make that raid; also done to help Senator Abernathy. All of them were in the same poison bag: McClung,

Herman Flood, Masters, *and* himself. All of them for hire to Leland Abernathy.

Hellman was never quite sure when he fell asleep, never sure of that precise moment when his thoughts faded into fantasy and finally into dream fragments that wouldn't be remembered. The sleep was unrestful, marred by interior confusion, by wild flashes of color and jarring sounds, by a physical dislocation. There was a long moment of rising panic until Hellman was able to comprehend what was happening; he was no longer asleep. The glaring light, the heavy hands, and rasping voices were not part of any dream. Ardis McClung loomed over him.

"Now, boy!" McClung grunted. "You shouldn't've done it, comin' roun' makin' like the Senator approved and all."

"What is this?" Hellman managed.

He felt himself being dragged out of the bed, mauled by the big hands of Deputy Bandifer. Hellman struggled. Laughing, Bandifer slammed Hellman back into the wall. A stabbing pain lanced into his chest.

McClung moved closer. "Boy, where your good sense? Comin' down here and stirrin' up my niggers! Should've known better. You ain't so smart. Guess you figured I was too dumb to check on your story. That kind of mistake costs a man."

Bandifer shook Hellman, drove him into the wall a second time. He gasped, waited for the pain to pass. He dropped his head, then without warning threw a looping right hand toward the tall deputy's face.

Banidfer moved without haste, catching Hellman's fist in his open hand, fingers closing tightly, squeezing. Hellman groaned and his knees buckled.

Chuckling softly, McClung stepped forward. Bandifer released Hellman and moved away. Hellman lifted his chin.

"There are laws—" he began.

McClung's chin hung almost to his thick chest. "Don't appreciate bein' held in low esteem, mister. Not flatterin' to a man."

His big fist swung in a low tight arc, went crashing into Hellman's groin. He moaned and bent double. McClung struck again, this time catching Hellman in the lower back. He went sprawling to the floor, pain exploding into his lower torso, eyes tearing, unable to make a sound.

McClung kicked him. "Get the Jew bastard out of my sight! Ever you show your ugly pocked face 'roun' here again, you'd best give your soul to Jesus cause your ass'll belong to me . . ."

XXI

SEVEN JAMES COOLEYS were listed in the Queens telephone directory. Malone began calling and on his sixth attempt found the
man he wanted. James Cooley's mother answered the phone in a
faint Irish brogue. Yes, James was a fireman. Yes, he had known
Marie Craig, may God bless her and keep her in Eternity with
Him forever, amen. No, James was not at home. He was at the
firehouse in the East Bronx. Malone asked for the address and
went there.

The neighborhood had been a slum forty years before and
had been unimproved since. The Jews and the Irish had moved
out and now only black faces were seen in the streets. A trio of
husky white men in work shirts stood in front of the firehouse,
hatless, arms folded in a kind of outpost defiance. They watched
with wary interest as Malone approached. They waited for him
to speak first.

"You've got a man named James Cooley here?"

The firemen looked at each other. The oldest of the three cleared
his throat, as if about to make a speech. "What's he done?"

Malone kept himself from smiling. He flashed his Agency
identification. "Is Cooley here?" he said.

"I'll fetch James, mister," one of the men said. He disappeared
inside the station. He returned shortly with an open-faced man of
thirty with thin brown hair, the seeds of sleep in the corners of
his eyes.

"I'm James Cooley. You want to talk to me?"

Malone showed his ID again. Cooley seemed impressed.

"What's it about, Mr. Malone?" he said, reading the name on the card.

"Privately," Malone said.

Cooley put his hand on Malone's elbow, guided him over to the curb, speaking in an exaggeratedly confidential manner. "That's a good idea with those fellas around. I have to work with 'em, y'see, but they're a bad lot not to be trusted. Ethnic inferiors, y'might say. Polacks and Eyetalians and all." He laughed cheerfully at the jeers of the other men. "They're really a very fine bunch of men," Cooley said to Malone. "That's a way of jokin' we have is all. Though I don't mind sayin' that I'd rather be a Irishman than any other."

"Why?"

"Well, Malone's an Irish name, isn't it? You are an Irishman yourself, aren't you?"

Malone considered his answer. "My grandfather was a Dubliner."

"Well, then, y'know the kind of people we are." Cooley glanced along the street and frowned. He made an inclusive gesture. "They hate us, y'see, the blacks I mean. Want to drive us out and take over things."

"That bothers you, a black takeover?"

"There's reason, man, I tell you. Look what's happened in Gary and Newark with black mayors and whatever. Cops are being shot from ambush and firemen attacked. It ain't right."

"You feel pretty strongly about this, Cooley?"

"Well, sure. Don't you?"

"Strong enough to do something about it?"

"What's that supposed to mean?"

"Perhaps you've already done something."

Cooley's regular features squeezed together. "What are you talking about, mister?"

"Let's talk about Senator Reese," Malone said softly, watching the other man.

Cooley took a backward step. "What's going on? What's this all about?"

"Cooley, this is official. Talk here or down at the bureau. Make it easy on yourself."

Cooley sighed and made a half-turn in the direction of the firehouse. "What're you asking me?"

"About Senator Reese?"

"Reese," Cooley said, voice gone flat and weary. "If Reese runs he won't get my vote, and none of my friends'. He's too quick to give in to them. The blacks, I mean. The radicals. All the talk about revolution. I'm against that. I mean, things are good for people. They should be content. I'm not one of those who claims blacks have it as good as whites. They don't. But all this trouble! It takes time to put things right."

"Do you own a gun, Cooley?"

"What would I do with a gun?"

"Talk about Marie Craig," Malone said without emphasis.

Cooley went pale and his lips came together. "Ah, Jesus! You don't leave nothin' alone, do you? I loved that girl, wanted to marry her. But she couldn't see me. Couldn't see livin' in Queens and bein' a fireman's wife. She wanted fun, she always wanted to have a good time. But it isn't like that. Life isn't just havin' fun. She found out . . . ."

"Why did she kill herself?"

Cooley flushed. "That's a terrible lie, Malone!" His voice climbed erratically. "Whatever she did, Marie would never've taken her God-given life. Not Marie." He ended weakly.

Malone kept his eyes fastened on the fireman. "Marie was on drugs, Cooley."

"No! I won't believe it. What did you come around for, to louse up the reputation of a decent girl? Is that the way you people spend your time?"

"Marie used LSD," Malone said deliberately. "People on acid do weird things."

"She was a good, Catholic girl. She liked a good time, but that doesn't mean she did all those terrible things. She was a fine girl, Malone, and would've made me a fine wife."

"She jumped out of Martin Williams' window."

"No! No, not Marie. Not her. Oh, sweet Jesus, I wish I knew

2 1 6

what happened. I won't believe she did that to herself. I won't."

"Would you believe she was murdered?"

Cooley's eyes went wide. "Yes. I believe *that*!"

"That someone pushed her out of that apartment?"

"Yes, yes. All this talk of drugs and sex that the papers were full of. All lies. Marie wasn't that way. Those people in Washington, they're the sick ones. When she wouldn't go along with their ideas they got rid of her. Someone pushed her out of the window."

"And you'd like to revenge yourself on the man who did it?"

"Yes, *yes*."

"Maybe you've already tried, Cooley, with a rifle?"

"What?" His mouth opened and closed. "What are you talking about? I've got no rifle, I told you."

"Marie worked for Reese. You blame him for her death, don't you?"

"No . . ."

"Did you decide to kill him, Cooley?"

"No, no, I told you." Cooley hung his head. "It's not me you should be talkin' to. It's Mike."

"Who?"

"Mike Craig, her father. Mike, who's got the book and lives with it and his memory of Marie. Mike who worries everybody."

"What book?"

"There was a diary that Marie kept. It was with her things. He found it and lets no one see it. Not even Marie's mother. Mike reads that book all the time and talks to himself and even when he goes off in the woods he carries it with him."

"The woods?"

"Mike has always been a hunter."

Malone waited for Cooley to go on.

"He's got all kinds of guns, if it's guns you're lookin' for. Mike was a fireman, too, y'see, and a real hero more than once. Hard inside and out, but he loved Marie. I'll tell you this, if y'want to find someone who hates Reese, Mike Craig is your man. I myself heard him blame Reese for Marie's death. Once I told him that was dangerous talk and Mike never mentioned it again. But if you know the man, you know he's never changed his mind. He's that kind." Cooley paused and wet his lips. "It's crazy, isn't it, thinkin' that Marie was involved with a man as big and important as Charles Reese. It is crazy, isn't it, Malone?"

"Does Mike Craig hate Senator Reese enough to want to kill him?"

A startled look came into Cooley's eyes. "Oh, no, no. He might *say* things but he doesn't mean them. A man like Mike, he might kill animals, all right, but not another man. Not as long as he was in his right mind."

"And what is his mind like now?"

Cooley's tongue appeared in the corner of his mouth. "I wouldn't want to mislead you—Mike's not exactly himself."

Malone looked through the other man as if he weren't there. It was too late to start guessing. Too many pressures were building, too many unseen forces for him to take risks. Mike Craig was a man who wanted Charles Reese dead, he had a motive—real or imagined—and a gun, the ability to get the job done.

"Where is he?" Malone said.

XXII

HELLMAN WENT to a doctor who assured him that nothing was broken or permanently impaired. The purple-yellow bruise on his lower back represented only ruptured blood vessels and his ribs were not fractured; since no blood had shown up in his urine it was assumed that no damage had been done to his kidneys. Convinced at last that he would survive, Hellman spent a great deal of time by himself, soaking his tender flesh in a hot tub, trying to make sense out of what was happening.

On the afternoon of the day he returned to New York, he received a note in the mail canceling a paid television appearance he was to have made the following week. Next, a pair of radio interviews were called off. A change in format was the excuse offered in both instances.

The following day a letter arrived from Hillary Smithson informing Hellman that the publisher had decided not to go ahead with the book. According to Smithson, by the time the book was written and published the subject would be dated. Hellman promptly phoned Smithson and insisted that he fulfill the demands of their verbal agreement. Smithson pointed out that there had been no witnesses to their meeting, no record kept of their conversation. He went on to inform Hellman that there was no reason to believe that he could deliver a suitable and publishable manuscript.

"You didn't feel that way a few days ago," Hellman said without thinking. "Abernathy's not going to like this!"

Smithson began to laugh, a high, gasping sound of delight. And in that moment Hellman understood that all this was happening *because* of Leland Abernathy, because the Senator had become disenchanted with him, had set forces in work to damage him. As if to underscore his own weakness and Abernathy's strength, his booking agent phoned the next morning with the news that a series of lectures he was to give at five Catholic girls' colleges in the area had been canceled without explanation.

The pain had shifted from Hellman's flesh to his pocketbook and he did what he always did whenever he was hurt or afraid—he went after a woman. He called Joanna Cook, but she refused to see him, saying she saw no point in prolonging a relationship that was clearly transient.

Angry now and frustrated, he phoned a redheaded girl who checked hats in a bar on First Avenue. She told him he could come over and when he arrived at her apartment, he found the door unlocked and the redhead waiting in bed. He applied himself to her with furious diligence and when they were finished she remarked that he was among the top ten lovers she had had. When she persisted in talking, he got dressed and went home, unhappy with himself.

Later in the day, he called Joanna Cook again and this time she listened to him, agreed to have dinner with him.

"But that's *it*," she warned. "Dinner and I take a cab home by myself."

He agreed, not really believing her, certain that she would change her mind when they were together. But he was wrong. After dinner, she suggested they go for a walk. They wandered uptown to Eighty-sixth Street, turned east until they came to Carl Schurz Park. They took up positions along side each other and looked down at the East River, careful not to touch.

Hellman leaned on the iron guard rail and winced, allowed a small sound to seep out of his mouth. Not quite a complaint; a contrived utterance to indicate the aches and pains he suffered in those areas where Ardis McClung had savaged him.

Joanna gave no sign that she had heard. Or if she had, that she cared.

Hellman had told her about his experiences in Lanson, exaggerating his beating only modestly. She had listened, responding infrequently, and he knew that she was displeased by his continued effort to connect Woody Silas with the killing of W. W. Masters. He made up his mind to make her understand.

"I want you to know," he declared, "that I'm very angry."

She made no response.

"Not at you," he added.

She looked up into his face, as if trying to penetrate the swarthy facade.

"This whole thing, Hilda Mann's death. I see now that it was a deliberate murder. And Masters probably passed the word, at Senator Abernathy's request, that put it in motion. Herman Flood was the hand on the trigger—or at least put one of his minion's hands on it."

"Woody Silas said as much."

"I had to find out for myself. I'm stubborn, okay. I admit I was wrong about Silas. I acted badly, got greedy, and dumped on what was left of my principles. But that's past now. I am going to get to the truth of this mess, expose the real criminals. The IIA, Masters, Abernathy."

"Hellman," she said, "if you're putting me on—."

"I mean it."

She glanced at him in profile. The low thrust of his face, the way his dark hair curled behind his ears, along his neck. She wanted to touch him, to be with him again, to let his heavy masculinity fill her up again. She looked across the river to the neon lights of Queens.

"Hellman, you talk pretty damned good."

"I've been doing a lot of thinking since I got back. Every step in this case has brought me up short. Nothing but dead ends. At the same time, there's always a new slant, new involvements, as if everybody is linked with everybody else. Conspiratorial ripples spreading out from a Masters in the middle."

"What are you trying to say?"

"I don't know. Just reaching and not getting hold of anything. My mistake was to begin with preconceived notions and try to make the facts fit them. The result is I'm left with a lot of loose ends and nowhere to go." He turned his back to the river, elbows on the railing.

"Help me, Joanna. There was an article you mentioned—I should see it. What was the name of the magazine?"

"I don't remember."

She said it easily with no suggestion of guile. But he didn't believe her. "Joanna," he said, considering his words, "I am not going to stop."

"I know," she said, voice subdued.

"You still don't trust me?"

"How can I? You're out to make a killing. If it isn't Silas, you'll get somebody else. Anybody helpless, whoever can't fight back."

"What the hell are you talking about! This is murder!"

"I can't help you."

He could hear the clenched emotion in her voice, as if invisible knots, tightly strung, were strangling her with pain. She seemed to be choking on some painful secret. He cautioned himself to proceed with care, not to build an insurmountable wall between himself and Joanna. His mind drifted back to that night in her bedroom and he tried to hear again what she had said about homosexuals in authoritarian groups, about their need for a strong figure to admire and emulate, their need, perhaps, for a W. W. Masters.

But she hadn't said that; the conclusion was his own. She had spoken about the article in . . . what was it? . . . an academic journal . . .

"*Journal of Pragmatic Psychiatry,*" he said in a solemn voice, masking the triumph he felt. "That's a mouthful. Do you always read such exotic publications?"

She avoided his eyes.

"Come on," he urged lightly. "You're so uptight. Trying so hard to keep me outside. Let me in, Joanna. You might as well, you know. Like it or not, I'm into this case all the way, no matter who gets hurt. I meant it about being angry. I am going to turn over the rocks and take a look at what comes crawling out. With or without you, Joanna."

"What do you expect me to say?"

"You know something—something that puts you inside. Share it with me, Joanna."

"Oh, dammit!" she said in a small voice. "I never wanted it to go this far. You're no damned good, Hellman."

He touched her cheek with the back of his hand. She shivered, pressed against him, felt an unaccustomed weakness.

"I had a brother—" she whispered, and stopped. Hellman waited for her to continue. "His name was Paul. We grew up together, just us two, in foster homes, and with relatives that didn't want us. My parents died in an auto accident. Paul and me, against everybody else. You don't know what it's like never to be hugged, never to be told that somebody loves you and thinks you do something well. Paul became my life, Hellman. I was his sister and also his mother."

"Tell me about Paul."

She began to speak in a detached manner. "Paul was a lawyer in the civil rights division of the Justice Department. Working in Washington. I would go there often to visit him and I met many people through him. Political people. Because of those contacts, I was able to establish myself as a writer with a political beat."

"What about Paul?"

She shrugged. "He was an excellent lawyer. He cared about his work and about the people he was trying to help. Paul wasn't like you, Hellman. Not tough. Not aggressive. He didn't know how to squeeze life. He wasn't strong. Maybe that was my fault. Maybe I mothered him too much when we were growing up. But he was all I had and I was all he had. I wanted to do for him, protect him. He was a sweet boy, generous, a gentle face. A good young man . . ." She tossed her hair as if making up her mind, went on. "In the line of his work, Paul was called upon to make a report on school integration in towns with under twenty-five thousand population. He made an extensive survey and turned in his report. His superiors complimented him on the work and he was very happy. He phoned to tell me the good news and we arranged to meet in New York for a weekend and celebrate. He autographed a copy of the report for me. I still have it."

"What happened then?"

She said the words without expression. "W. W. Masters heard about the report. He didn't read it, of course. Masters never read anything in its entirety; his staff people did the reading for him, fed him predigested synopses. He invited Paul to visit him."

"And?"

"And . . . Masters began to seek Paul out."

Hellman held himself very still, anxious for her to go on.

"There was so much I didn't know until later, until after Paul was dead and Harvey told me about it."

"Harvey?"

"Harvey Bass. Paul's friend; he wanted me to know the true story."

"What is the true story?"

"W. W. Masters seduced my baby brother and when he was finished with him, turned on Paul, harassed him, tortured and threatened him, made life impossible for him. Paul was shifted to less important work, transferred again and again. He was hauled out of the field to be confronted by some agent of the IIA who questioned his patriotism, virtually accused him of being in the employ of a foreign government. He was accused of cheating on his income taxes, of having a secret source of income. There were anonymous phone calls at all hours of the day and night, insults, threats. Paul was convinced that his mail was being opened and read. He became afraid, afraid of being alone, of going anywhere, always afraid."

"What happened?"

She looked at him. "One day Paul just had enough, I suppose. He killed himself."

Hellman stayed with Joanna that night. They slept together, touching each other all during the night, but not making love. Once Hellman woke, instantly alert, mind returning to what Joanna had told him about her brother. Somehow it was all just a bit too easy and convenient, a myth of homosexual existence given life by a grieving sister—the innocent youth seduced, then badly treated. As for Masters' homosexuality, doubtful information had been submitted by Harvey Bass, an admitted homosexual and hardly a disinterested witness. At best Bass had been repeating what Paul Cook had told him, very possibly distorting it with each telling. Even more likely, the entire story was a fabrication, invented by Paul to make himself appear important in the eyes of a homosexual friend. He must have been a weak and lonely man, desperately trying to make a place for himself, even if that place existed only in his own fantasies. Hellman glanced over at Joanna; she *needed* to believe Harvey Bass's story. He did not.

In the morning, Hellman felt uneasy, guilty, almost, as if something had been left undone. When he left Joanna's apartment, he walked aimlessly, trying to make up his mind. Finally he hailed a taxi and told the driver to take him to the Public Library at Forty-second Street.

He discovered what he was looking for in the card files under the title "The Family Extended; Authoritarianism and the Homosexual." The author was Sidney Karl, M.D., M.S., PH.D. It took only a few minutes for Hellman to obtain the issue of the *Journal of Pragmatic Psychiatry* he wanted.

Hellman began to read, making notes as he went along. Soon his normally swift tempo slowed; the article was too technical, and he was forced to reread some passages a second time. There was still much that puzzled him when he finished and he considered rereading the article, but decided against it.

He looked around and saw that no one was watching him. Moving with practiced skill, he quietly tore Sidney Karl's article from the magazine, folded the pages into his jacket pocket. He returned the magazine to the librarian, thanked her, and left.

On Forty-second Street, he found a phone booth and located a Sidney Karl in the directory; he dialed. A man came on, his voice curiously soft.

"Hello—."

"Dr. Karl," Hellman began.

"This is Dr. Karl."

"The same Dr. Karl who wrote "The Family Extended" in the *Journal of Pragmatic Psychiatry?*"

"That's right," Karl replied, pride and caution in his voice.

"My name is Hellman, doctor. I'm in the midst of an involved and sensitive investigation. I've read your article, doctor, and I'm sure that we can be of assistance to each other."

There was a smile in Karl's voice now. "Ah! And tell me how you are going to help me, Mr. Hellman."

Hellman recognized his mistake; he'd underestimated the other man. He manufactured a short laugh, properly sheepish. "That's one for you, doctor. Let's leave it at this, I can use your help."

"I'm a practicing psychiatrist, Mr. Hellman. Are you in need of treatment?"

"There are times when I wonder. But that's not why I called. I'd like to talk to you, doctor."

Karl hesitated and Hellman imagined him glancing at his appointment book. "I'm afraid my schedule is full."

"Doctor, I don't mean to get dramatic, but this is a question of some national importance."

"Mr. Hellman, I'm sure you believe that, but—"

"I'm serious. Very serious. I'm talking about murder by assassination. Give me an hour and I'll explain. I'll be glad to pay your fee, whatever it is."

For a long moment, static was all Hellman could hear. He waited. "A recent assassination?" Karl said at last.

"Yes."

"Well, I think I might squeeze some free time between two and three this afternoon, if that is suitable . . ."

"I'll be there," Hellman said, and hung up.

Sidney Karl's office occupied the entire first floor of an old town house in the Murray Hill section. There was an aged mustiness in the foyer and a thin mist of accumulated dust rose up from the carpeting as Hellman walked toward the tall door alongside the staircase. The upper panel was a single pane of translucent glass. A neatly lettered sign taped to the glass instructed visitors to ring the bell and walk in. Hellman did so.

Inside, a cluttered sprawl. A large room with intricate molding on the high ceiling and a wood-burning fireplace, the main feature of one wall. There were magazines scattered about as if recently glanced through and found wanting. Hellman settled into a worn Victorian love seat that smelled of cleaning fluid and a clinging perfume.

Masculine voices could be heard in some other portion of the apartment in a conspiratorial murmuring. He strained to listen, but the words were an unintelligible jumble. Then, silence. Moments later, Sidney Karl materialized out of a dark hallway. He was a tautly constructed man with a shoulder slump that made him seem shorter than he was. His face was pinched and his long nose turned toward Hellman with the dipping rhythm of a divining rod at work. He nodded and spoke in a thin tenor voice.

"We'll talk in my office," he said, and disappeared back down the hallway. Hellman went after him, past four closed doors, the light dim and eerie, until he found himself in a medium-sized room. Here the walls were lined with books, and an old refectory table served as a desk; it was piled high with books and papers and a tape recorder in a worn leather case. Heavy cotton curtains covered the window, excluding all daylight. A green leather couch with a Mexican blanket across the cushioned head of it stood nearby; and an ancient French provincial needlepoint chair.

"Sit there," Karl said, going behind the desk.

Hellman obeyed, aware suddenly that this seemed a room of presences, of secrets and sad voices, of haunting memories and human pain. He looked at Sidney Karl.

The psychiatrist rearranged a stack of books on the desk so that he had a clear view of Hellman and began to speak, each word coming out as if by accident.

"On the telephone, Mr. Hellman, you used some very interesting language. You spoke of murder. Of assassination. You mentioned something that was of national importance. It was a ploy, yes. To arouse my curiosity. It worked, as you see. You are here."

"I meant what I said, doctor."

Karl frowned. "Then you should be talking to the police, should you not? Murder is, after all, their province."

"The police are involved, locally and nationally."

"You are not a policeman?"

"I've been cooperating with the authorities, local and Federal."

"I'm a naturalized citizen, Hellman. A man lives in other places, he values the advantages of this country very much. Very much. If I can do something for this country, I would be pleased. But how . . . ?"

Hellman started to make a joke, a flip remark, thought better of it. Sidney Karl was a sober man and meant every word he said. Hellman looked into his eyes. "I appreciate your sentiment, doctor. I won't waste your time. I am working on the murder of W. W. Masters. Along with millions of other Americans, I want to learn the truth."

"Ah, the always elusive truth. Well, Hellman, after you dig out this mother lode? What then?"

Hellman scrutinized the man behind the desk. He had the notion that Karl was toying with him, playing his own private game. Hellman had no idea what that game might be and he dared not take any chances. "I'll carry the truth to the people," he said.

"You'll publish?"

"An article, a book. It depends."

"I understand. Publish or perish. It is not too different in the scientific field and among academics."

Hellman forced back an angry remark. He arranged a smile on his wide mouth. "There are a number of theories about why Mr. Masters was killed. Every citizen seems to have his own."

"You think so?"

"Don't you, doctor?"

"It is so easy to theorize, to guess."

"I'd be interested in your theory, or your guess, doctor."

"I am a cautious man. In areas outside my professional expertise, I speculate infrequently."

"It's your professional expertise I'm after, Dr. Karl. I read your article in the *Journal of Pragmatic Psychiatry*."

"I commend you, Hellman. It takes a man who is either very

interested or very stubborn to wade through that swamp of academic prose style."

"I was interested and I am stubborn." When Karl said nothing, Hellman went on. "According to the article, you've worked extensively with homosexuals. You've even managed to cure some of them."

"Cure! The word is yours, Hellman. Occasionally men come to me, saying they wish to be straight, as the expression goes. Such men, if they are sincere and singular of purpose, may possibly attain their desire. They are able to live reasonably well-adjusted heterosexual lives."

"Reasonably?"

"As reasonable as most people one meets at a New York cocktail party, I would say."

Impatience insinuated itself along the network of nerves in Hellman's body. A harsh edge came into his voice. "In your article, you said that certain occupations and professions attract homosexuals."

"I did write that. I believe it's true. Many people require an extremely well-ordered existence. There are times when the structure by which such persons live is concealed and they appear to be nonconformists, free souls, swingers, you might say. But they are not. Other people live so that the structure and the discipline are highly visible."

"Such as the military?" Hellman prodded.

"The military, yes. And the police. Rigid religious groupings. These allow men to deposit their faith and their devotion without question. Duty becomes the *raison d'être* in their lives. Once he has surrendered to such a system, a person is relieved of all the anxiety of making his own choices, he no longer has to think for himself—which is why such a life attracts him in the first place . . ."

Hellman interrupted. "Then anyone who questioned the system might be a threat, might have to be done away with."

Karl contemplated his manicured fingernails. "Yes. This would be the supreme human value in a sense—freedom of choice."

"But always within the hierarchal structure?"

"Exactly, Hellman. Let me go on. To pursue a military career, for example, is to surrender much of one's humanity. Life becomes less valuable than duty and the good soldier does not seriously question his duty. He accepts his role and obeys, no matter how vague or irrational an order may be . . ."

"You spoke of freedom of choice?"

"The *appearance* of choice might be more accurate. Our subject may believe he is making a choice when in fact he frequently acts with an intuitive awareness of what is expected of him in a crisis situation."

"Like Pavlov's dogs?"

"Something along those lines," Karl conceded.

"I can understand men acting that way in wartime."

"At any time. Let the pressure be severe enough and reactions will be similar. However, let me caution you, there is a point where a man either withdraws or a sort of a psychological safety switch is tripped whereby he may forget all that he has done and so is able to continue operating within the system."

"How convenient!"

Karl smiled reluctantly. "All of us make accommodations to reality, accommodations that allow us to continue to exist with our conscious principles reasonably intact, isn't it so, Hellman?"

Hellman chose not to consider the question.

Karl continued. "This is a fascinating subject, I find. For a man to succeed in an authoritarian subculture he need only fulfill expectations. He is often able to bury in his psyche some terrifying need or desire and he may commit crimes against nature and at the same time not recognize them as such." Karl lifted his hunched shoulders and laughed mirthlessly. "A human being is a fascinating creature, Hellman. To discover each man's *truth* is to embark on an exploratory journey to challenge Magellan. Or the fascinating Conan Doyle . . ."

"To get to the substance of your article, doctor, is every man who enlists in a controlled system essentially a homosexual?"

"Not at all. The heterosexually active male might do the same job for the same psychological reasons, though the manifestations would be different. There is also the asexual man. His life style

2 3 0

generally demands a high degree of what he would describe as purity. His sexual energy is directed into other areas. Work may be his sole interest. If he were a soldier, he'd be completely devoted to country, to duty, to his superiors."

Hellman tried to match this with what he already knew. "You must have a number of such cases, doctor."

Karl made a head gesture that directed Hellman's attention to the rear wall. "In those file cabinets are the transcripts, tape recordings, the complete histories of my patients, as well as the many subjects I've interviewed for my research projects. These concepts, Hellman, as outlined in my article, are based on my practice and research. The kind of man we're speaking about—having surrendered himself, he is content. He has no doubts, no questions. He performs with confidence. Such a man has an adolescent adoration for strength, for power. He requires some representation of a father image in every aspect of his life. The implication, even if not direct, is sexual."

"Homosexual?"

"Frequently homosexual. Authoritative faith, Hellman, can be very reassuring. Supportive. Life becomes simple. Consider—the Manichean heresy saw the world dualistically, placed everything into the camp of good or of evil. Thus God and country become one and people are either good or bad. If one is on the side of the Goodies, Hellman, the True Believers, as Eric Hoffer calls them, then every action, no matter how extreme, is justified and just!"

An idea shook Hellman. "Given such a man, devoted to some philosophy, some ideal, to someone. Suppose he discovered that it was all a waste, a trick, that he'd been betrayed?"

"The safety switch would be automatically tripped in most cases."

"And if not?"

Karl shrugged. "Man has been known to destroy what he most loves, especially if something turns that love to hatred."

Hellman's impatience returned and he grew brusque. "Let's talk about W. W. Masters, specifically the Internal Investigative Agency."

"My article dealt in generalities, Hellman."

"You did discuss the IIA at some length. I've heard some speculation about Masters, that he was a homosexual . . ."

Karl assessed Hellman, spoke without urgency. "You told me you were trying to discover who killed Mr. Masters."

"First the motive, doctor, then the killer. For a while, I believed the motive might lie in the political area. Now I'm not so sure."

"So you came to my article and thought you saw there another angle, is that it? Not a very scientific approach."

"Science was never my subject, doctor. But when I get an idea in my head, I can worry it to death." Hellman decided to force the issue. "If Masters was gay, could he have been killed by one of his lovers for some real or fancied rejection?"

"Given such circumstances, the answer must be yes. But the supposition is entirely your own."

Hellman thought about Paul Cook. "I've been told that Masters had an affair with a young government attorney. When Masters ended the relationship, the attorney committed suicide. Now in your article, you refer to interviews with IIA agents——."

Karl cut Hellman short. "No, no. I wrote that I was interviewed *by* representatives of the Agency. The nature of my research had been brought to Mr. Masters' attention and he wrote to me expressing the thought that I might be able to devise a system of interviews whereby undesirables would be excluded from the Agency training program. With that in mind, I did meet with an agent."

Disappointment spread through Hellman. If what Karl said was true, then it was not likely that Joanna's vision of W. W. Masters as a predatory homosexual preying on innocent young government employees was accurate. Apparently grief or her brother's friend had misled her; she believed what she wanted to believe.

"I'd like to talk to that agent, doctor, the one who interviewed you."

"Impossible. Information given me in a session is as privileged as that in my files."

Hellman turned back on himself, convinced he was very close to something vital but unable to isolate it. He wondered: those bland metal file drawers across the room—did they hold what he was looking for? His mind went back to Lanston, to his conversation with McClung, with Samuel Mann, and further back to Woody Silas. All of them had talked about Herman Flood, putting him on the gun that had killed Hilda Mann. If Flood had killed once *for* Masters, he might have committed other crimes as well. All in the name of duty. And it could have become too much for Flood; the safety switch refused to work any more . . .

"Isn't it true, doctor, that IIA agents are men anxious to please their superiors?"

"Oh, that's true enough."

"And how would you describe Masters?"

"I assume he falls into the same general pattern as any other authoritarian figure."

"Come on, doctor," Hellman said tersely. "Take a small chance. What's your *opinion*?"

Karl thought before he spoke. "For some he was a sort of contemporary godhead. He *was* the Agency, its head and its body."

"Would an agent want to make himself part of that body?"

"That's perceptive of you, Hellman. Yes, to become incorporated into the body of the larger organism so that all are one and the same, without beginning or end. The system is strength and goodness, life itself."

"Under those circumstances, a man might try to fulfill an order that was never actually issued?"

"Possibly. A hint might do it, a suggestion."

"Would you describe these agents as programmed, doctor, performing even when they believed what they were doing was wrong?"

"You are more certain than I am, Hellman."

Hellman went over the conversation. Something had been left unsaid. Unasked. But what? He settled for a different approach.

"This agent you say you met with at Masters' request—is he a homosexual, doctor? Is he really a patient?"

"*Mister* Hellman. I will not discuss this with you in any way. You must understand that—."

"Does he have a tendency?" Hellman said, grinning.

2 3 3

Karl threw up his hands. "Let me explain something. A man might have an abiding interest in other men without being an active homosexual. The sexual act might be relatively unimportant to him. Some men are not very concerned with sex of any kind. Women are of only casual concern. Work is primary. It captures their imaginations, answers all of their needs."

Hellman decided to take a chance. "Let's talk about Herman Flood, doctor."

For a moment nothing showed on Karl's face. Then he laughed and stood up. "I'm afraid we've come to the end of the time . . ."

Hellman rose slowly. "It's possible that this man you're shielding is dangerous, a murderer. I intend to pursue this, to build a strong case."

"Unfortunately, I can be of no further assistance . . ."

"You've already helped, doctor. I think I know where to find the information I need."

Karl said nothing, escorting Hellman along the long hallway, ushering him out, and double-locking the glass-paneled door behind him.

XXIII

It was a street typical of many in Queens, split-level houses painted white or pale yellow, with two-car garages and sloping lawns, neatly tended.

Malone appreciated the tone and the style of the street; there was a carefully preserved attitude of order and concern. It was the kind of street, and Mike Craig's house was the kind of house, he had thought about living in after he retired from the Agency. It occurred to him that the men who lived here would also be men living on their pensions; cops and firemen, retired Army officers, captains and majors mostly, civil servants like himself. It might be a pleasant place to live. He went up to the front door of Mike Craig's house and rang the bell.

From deep inside, he could hear soft chimes, and approaching footsteps. A woman's voice spoke in the guarded aggressive accent of South Boston.

"Yes? What is it y'want?"

Malone said his name, asked to speak with Mike Craig.

After a moment, the woman replied. "What d'ya want him for?"

Malone said that he was from the IIA on official government business. The door swung open. Kathleen Craig was a gaunt woman, gray, braced for trouble. Her right cheek was swollen and discolored. She looked at Malone as if trying to make up her mind about him.

"From the IIA, y'said?"

He displayed his ID card.

She looked at it, then quickly away. "This time he's gone and done it, I suppose."

"Done what, Mrs. Craig?"

She stood aside and indicated that Malone was to go inside. The living room was a shambles. Furniture was broken and over-turned, lamps had been smashed, a mirror shattered. Kathleen Craig touched her bruised cheek. "Craig did it all," she said, almost proudly. Always did have a heavy hand when he got going."

"Where is Mr. Craig now?"

"He's not been himself for a long time, since Marie passed on. He was brought down by grief and torment and couldn't stand up to the strain no longer. The last few days have been something terrible. Him not able to sleep, drinking more than usual, speaking only about his revenge."

"Revenge against whom, Mrs. Craig?"

"There's no way to stop a man like Craig, y'see. I talked and talked to him and at the end tried to keep him here. But nobody could do it. Craig's a big man, y'see, powerful—what a muscular brute he was when I first laid eyes on him! He's been brooding for too long and I guess he had to go and do it."

"Do what, Mrs. Craig?"

"Marie never gave him much happiness. Nor me either, if y'want to know the truth. When she was a child it was different. She was always playing and laughing, jumping up into Craig's lap. I warned him he was spoiling her but he paid no attention. Said I was a jealous old lady and he'd take care of me at night, excuse me for saying so. What a bawdy man he was. Of course, Craig's seventy now.

"Poor Craig. He couldn't put up with Marie when she was grown. It wasn't *his* lap she wanted anymore. And that killed him, I think, more than anything. He wanted her to stay a sweet child and she wouldn't do that. When the news came that she was gone, I told him to let her go. Let her stay dead, I said. But Craig couldn't do that either. He drank and cursed and lived with whatever he remembered. You'd thought he was the one that carried and birthed her and that I had no part in any of it. It was plain to see, Craig's madness coming on, but nobody could do anything. Not nobody."

"Where is he?"

"He said this morning that he couldn't live with it anymore. That his belly was full. That's when he started smashing things. The lamps don't mean a thing to me, but my dear mother gave us the mirror when we was married."

"About Craig?"

"I tried to stop him and he knocked me around a bit. Then with me laying on the floor he took his rifle and left. It's a wonder a man can hit anything with a gun that big, but Craig's been hunting and fishing all his life. In his hands, that rifle's like a toy."

"Who is your husband after, Mrs. Craig?"

She tilted her head, eyes misting over. "Why, Senator Reese, of course . . ."

Hellman resented Sidney Karl. The interview had tantalized him, suggested directions that might be profitably followed but provided no concrete leads. He felt stymied and locked out. He struggled to make sense out of everything he'd learned, trying to isolate the single crucial fact. Nothing came.

His bitterness increased. He was being punished for failure; and the failure compounded. The cancellation of his lecture tour at the five Catholic colleges was a painful blow; lectures fees provided his basic income.

A wry thought came to mind; perhaps he should contact Cardinal McCoy again, seek diocesan intervention to restore those bookings. Perhaps he would call McCoy . . .

"Dig it, Cardinal, those bookings matter! That's bread, man. And face it, those chicks with the scrubbed look of future nuns ain't all that pure and holy—."

Abruptly Hellman grew sober. Not McCoy. Perez. Father Nestor Perez. He was the one to call. He was the one who made the call . . .

Father Perez lifted his olive face and squinted at Hellman as he advanced the length of the antechamber. "Mr. Hellman! How nice to see you again. What a surprise! His Eminence is unavailable, of course. He isn't even here today. There's an investiture of a new church on Staten Island. The project is dear to the Cardinal since it is in the parish where he himself was brought up. How thoughtless I am, do sit down, Mr. Hellman. The weather outside must be frightful, summer in New York. May I order some iced tea?"

"I came to see you, Father."

"How nice! In what way may I serve you?"

"I won't waste your time."

"Not at all, Mr. Hellman. One gets so few unexpected visitors."

Hellman recognized the quiet rebuke and chose to ignore it. He had deliberately not phoned for an appointment, anxious to give Perez no chance to refuse to see him. Nor to prepare himself.

"On the night of the Cardinal's birthday dinner, you made a call for Mr. Masters."

The dark face drew together. "Yes," he said tentatively.

"Who was the call to?"

"Oh, I don't have that information," he replied. "Mr. Masters mentioned no name and naturally I made no inquiry. He instructed me to deliver the message to whomever answered."

"What was the message?"

"Ah, shouldn't that remain unsaid, Mr. Hellman? After all, with Mr. Masters gone . . ."

"The man who killed Masters is still at large. That message may help find him."

Father Perez' soft eyes went wide. "Had I believed that I would surely have mentioned it to the police. But there was clearly no importance to it."

"You read the papers, Father, look at TV. People are demanding a solution. You may be part of that solution."

"Oh, dear."

"The message, Father?"

The priest hesitated. "Mr. Masters had such a lovely voice, so well-spoken . . ."

"The message, Father?"

"Yes. The message—. 'Be ready in thirty minutes. I depend on you.' Yes, that was it."

The words were an enigmatic stimulus to Hellman. There was

the element of authority in the message, of command. What did it mean and to whom was it delivered?

"What else?" he said.

"Nothing, I'm afraid. Having given me the message, Mr. Masters returned to the dais. I didn't see him again until the proceedings were over."

Hellman struggled to make sense out of it. Again he had the feeling that something was missing.

"What brought Masters and Senator Reese together when they left?" he said, reaching blindly. "You said you saw Masters?"

"Ah, yes. It gave me pleasure to watch him, a beautiful person. I seem to remember that Mr. Masters took the Senator's arm."

"And?"

"And they left, Mr. Hellman."

Disappointed, Hellman rose to leave, turning back at the tall double doors. "Did you make a note of the phone number, Father, the one Masters had you call?"

"I'm afraid not."

Hellman grunted unhappily, opened the door.

"But I do remember it, quite clearly."

When he left Father Perez, Hellman went looking for a public telephone. It took four tries before he found one that was operating. He dialed the number Perez had supplied. It rang three times and a female voice answered as if by rote: "Gerber, Little and Kinderman. May I help you?"

Hellman froze in place. He spoke the number into the phone.

"This is the number you called," the voice said. "Gerber, Little and Kinderman. To whom would you like to talk?"

"Theatrical accountants?" Hellman said, visualizing the gilt letters on the glass entrance door.

"That is correct. May I help you?"

Hellman hung up, mind racing. Masters had contacted the office from which the fatal shot had been fired, calling the gunman. Why? All at once pieces began to move into place and Hellman thought he understood everything. But he had to be sure.

Malone sat in a glass-enclosed cubicle not far from Herman Flood's office. He sat behind a metal desk, the same kind of desk Flood would be sitting behind, the same kind of desk Masters had used; the Director had insisted that all agents' offices be furnished identically. Malone stared at the telephone and willed it to ring, to announce that the police of New York City or Connecticut or Washington, D.C., had located Mike Craig.

Malone wondered if Craig would resist. If he should use that rifle of his, he would be shot and killed. Perhaps that would be best; Masters' death could be laid to Craig, to faulty aim brought on by old age and rage. That would wind it up neatly.

Malone felt sorry for Craig. The old man was undoubtedly too addled to understand that a man of Reese's position and character, of such personal integrity, would never allow himself to become involved with a girl like Marie Craig. Williams and Marie—that pairing made sense.

A girl appeared in the open doorway. Like all Agency secretaries, she was pleasant-faced, modestly dressed and blended into the office just as the gray metal desk did.

"There's someone to see you, Mr. Malone. A Mr. Hellman."

Hellman, Malone remembered with distaste. A friend of Captain Capolino. He had been present when Malone had visited Roy Brewster.

"Send him in."

The secretary went away and returned shortly with Hellman. Malone invited him to sit down, examining his visitor.

"Thanks for seeing me," Hellman began.

"On the phone, you said it was important."

"As you know, Malone, I've been investigating the death of Masters."

Malone held his eyes steady, waited. Hellman shifted in his chair.

"I think I've got something. That's why I came to you. I think I can help."

"The Agency appreciates assistance from any citizen."

Hellman hesitated. Malone made him uneasy, made him feel *watched,* as if under a microscope. Still, there was no one else.

Not now. "On the night he died, Masters made a telephone call."

Malone disapproved of Hellman's appearance. The pebbled cheeks were in need of a shave and his collar was open, the tie yanked to one side; and his socks curled around his ankles displaying an expanse of hairy leg. No agent of the IIA ever appeared in public that way.

"An agent must be properly turned out. Well-groomed and clean. A man is what he appears to be and what he appears to be is what he often is."

Malone held himself straight and stiff. "How did you find that out?" he said, issuing the words one at a time.

"Well, he didn't actually make the call," Hellman said. "He wanted to make it. He left the dais but all the booths were occupied. There was a priest, and he offered to make the call for Masters."

Why not a priest? Malone asked himself wryly. Where one found a cardinal there also would be found any number of priests. To make a call for W. W. Masters would clearly be an honor.

"Hellman, did you come up here to tell me Masters made a call to someone? It doesn't add much to the case."

Hellman grinned. "That's true. But there's more. More and interesting. The call was to the office of Gerber, Little and Kinderman."

Malone blinked once, mind turning swiftly. "Do you know who answered the phone?"

"No," Hellman said, slumping in his seat.

"Then you don't have much. If we knew who was in that office when the shot was fired—." Malone stopped talking. He berated himself for not finding out about the call himself. He should have interviewed Cardinal McCoy personally, talked to the priests who were with him that night; or had one of the agents working for him do it. Not that it would have made any difference, the call was apparently a dead end. Still, it came as a shock to realize that he'd been less than thorough and he wondered what other mistakes he'd made. Masters would not have approved.

"There's more to it than just the call," Hellman said.

"Such as?"

Hellman thought he detected an ironic edge in Malone's voice. Hellman realized that this intrusion was unwanted, that he had discovered information which neither the police nor the IIA had been able to come up with. Before contacting Malone, he had spoken to Capolino. He too had been defensive and resentful; and, like Malone, Capolino had been unwilling to lend importance to the call.

"The man on the rifle that night," Hellman said, "had to be accustomed to handling guns, an expert shot."

Malone looked at the telephone and thought about Mike Craig. He asked himself if Hellman had found out about Craig.

"Something interesting happened at the hotel that night," Hellman said. "Masters and Senator Reese left together. Masters seemed to be with Reese, wanted them to be seen together."

"What are you getting at?"

"Just this. Masters had ambitions to be President, was working toward that end."

Malone brought his eyes up to Hellman. "You're wrong. Mr. Masters was not a political person."

Hellman remembered his conversation with Leland Abernathy. "My information is correct. He was running for the office. Running quietly but very hard."

"No one who knew the Director will believe this."

"He was driven by ambition," Hellman said aggressively. "He dreamed up a wild scheme to put himself in the White House and at the same time make it appear he was beyond political interests."

"No," Malone said firmly, placing his palms on the edge of the desk. He brought his hands back to his lap, spoke evenly. "If what you say is true, that's no reason for anyone to kill him. He was an incredible man, the best of us all."

"He needed power so badly," Hellman went on, "he decided to get rid of the one man who might keep him from fulfilling his ambition—he already had made the necessary back-room arrangements, his connections with politically powerful men, with men who would support his campaign with large sums of money, with an army of workers."

2 4 2

"What does this have to do with the Director and Reese leaving the dinner at the same time?"

"Masters wasn't sure he would win the election if Senator Reese was his opponent. So he made certain arrangements, made sure that Reese left at the proper time, by the proper exit, in front of the hotel at the precise moment that the man with the rifle expected him . . ."

Malone leaned back in his chair, stared at Hellman.

"Masters had never put his reputation on the line, never put himself before the voters," Hellman rushed on. "He was afraid he might lose and he wasn't a man who could wait for power to come his way and Reese figured to be the favorite. Time was running out."

"You're saying Masters set Reese up to be killed?"

"Masters put a man into that office, somebody he knew and could depend on, a reliable finger on that trigger. At the right time, he signaled the gunman . . ."

"The phone call—."

Hellman nodded. "That alerted the man in the office—gave him the timing."

"You're forgetting—*Masters* was killed, not Reese."

"An error. A miss."

Malone considered Hellman's presentation. It was wild, full of flaws. "You've got a fine imagination," he said, making it sound like an insult. "But none of it will stand up, none of it can be proved."

Hellman grinned happily. "Maybe not, but it makes one hell of a story if I can put it together. A few more facts and I think I can. Nobody's done any better so far."

"You're wasting time."

"I'll try to do better this time."

"What do you mean?"

"Oh, I neglected to mention it, I guess. I've come up with two possibilities. Try the second one—you won't like it any better. Begin with the same motive, Masters' obsession with power. As before, he put a trusted man in that room with a rifle. As before, the telephone call was a signal for that man to shoot at *him* . . ."

"You're saying the Director arranged to have himself killed!"

"Not killed, Malone. Shot *at*. The difference is crucial. The idea was to *miss* and dramatically create a great uprising of public sympathy, to make Masters out to be the target of a conspiracy of the political Left, a Left that tends to support Reese. Now that would have been a perfect platform for Masters to campaign on! The ultimate public servant, a symbol of the struggle against radicalism and rebellion, against crime. The man would've been an easy winner. It was a mark of his guts and obsession, not so much that he could think of it but actually have the will to put it into operation."

"In that case, it was also a failure. Masters is dead. The same missed shot . . ."

"It could have happened," Hellman said, energy suddenly flagging. He'd been so confident earlier. Now, faced by Malone's imperturbable skepticism, he wasn't so sure.

"You suggested that the man selected by Masters was an expert with a rifle. Such a man wouldn't be likely to miss what he aimed at." It pleased Malone to be able to indicate the flaw in Hellman's case so easily. His dislike for the other man was increasing.

Hellman tried hard to recover. "No," he said, shaking his head. "He wouldn't miss the target. Not unless he *chose* to." Hellman reached for the idea that had eluded him all along. "Not unless Masters was the target! Yes! Masters was so much more than his public image. And much less. Did you know, Malone, that he was homosexual?"

Malone stood, leaning slightly, eyes glazed and still. "Don't bring that filth into this Agency."

"I can prove it," Hellman said, less confident than he sounded. "Besides, it's part of the motive."

Malone sat back finally.

Hellman felt relieved. "I think the guy on the gun was one of Masters' friends. Or he had been. One of his lovers."

Eyes holding on Hellman, Malone placed his hands flat on the metal desk. "Sixty seconds," he declared. "One minute to make your case."

The words came rushing out of Hellman. "The man who killed Masters killed *for* him earlier. At least once that I know about. Masters protected him that time, promoted him, gave him a choice assignment removed from the scene of the murder—"

Conditioned restraint kept Malone from exploding his rage. He wanted to hear everything, no matter how insane.

"Conjecture," he said. "Unless you can specify places, people . . ."

"Herman Flood," Hellman said, lowering his voice. "The man who heads this bureau. He was one of Masters' particular favorites. Flood shot and killed a girl named Hilda Mann on orders from Masters so that Masters could satisfy an obligation to Senator Leland Abernathy. I can prove Flood went to a small town in Alabama where he organized a raid on the headquarters of a black political group. I can prove that he shot without provocation, shot Hilda Mann in the back. I can prove that the reason given for the raid—a supposed arms cache—was only an excuse. There were no arms worth mentioning.

"I'm convinced that Flood was once Masters' lover and had been rejected. He carried around a deepening resentment. When Masters sent Flood into that office building with a rifle he hired his own murderer. Imagine it, Malone. Flood, jealous and bitter, waiting in that darkened office. He looks down and sees Masters and Reese on the steps of the hotel. He brings the rifle to bear. Whether to shoot Reese or just to miss Masters doesn't really matter. He's been angry for a long time. Now it takes over, his jealousy, his hatred of Masters for treating him badly. The rifle wavers, swings over to Masters. A shot. Masters goes down. Dead at the very moment he was beginning to anticipate his ultimate triumph!" Hellman looked at Malone.

The agent pushed himself erect. "Your minute's up."

Hellman stood up. "I came to you because this is your case. I was sure you wanted to get to the truth of it. I was wrong. You're part of the Agency and you've got to protect it, protect Masters, no matter how rotten he was."

Malone kept his voice soft, flat. "You're right in only one particular—it makes a good story. That's all it is—a story. There are some things you should know. First: the shooting of Hilda Mann occurred under severe pressure. In the line of duty. Those people were militants, radical extremists bent on making a revolution. The record shows that. And the girl was part of it. Shots were fired and the members of the raiding party responded. In their own defense. Professionals doing their jobs. There was no homicide. . . ."

"Flood fired the first shot!" Hellman said. "Hilda was running away when Flood shot her down."

"Wrong."

"People in Lanston will testify to it."

Malone shook his head. "Flood couldn't have shot that girl. He had been summoned to Washington two days earlier and assigned to the New York bureau. He was here when the raid took place."

"If that's true, who did kill Hilda Mann?"

Malone turned toward the window, his profile made unclear by the soft light. The interview, Hellman knew, was ended. He left without speaking.

XXIV

DOUBT MADE Hellman sluggish. Malone had shattered his case against Herman Flood. And for the first time he questioned his ability to collect and assess the fragments of information necessary to accomplish what he had set out to do. He cursed himself for being too believing.

Joanna's references to her brother, Woody Silas and Samuel Mann, McClung and Bandifer. He had believed so readily, accepted what each of them had said, had assumed too much. Assumed that Masters was in fact a homosexual, that Flood had actually been in Lanston, had shot Hilda, that Senator Abernathy had spoken the truth in describing Masters' ambition to be President.

Hellman had been looking ahead to the rewards of his investigation, to the acclaim that would be his, the money. Malone had ended all that. Flood had not killed Hilda, had not shot Masters, fitted none of Hellman's nice assumptions.

Needing some reassurance, he called Joanna Cook. The first ring was not completed when he hung up. All the weariness drained away, replaced by an electric urgency. Once again he had assumed too much. Herman Flood might be innocent of one crime and be guilty of another. Hellman remembered how Sidney Karl had abruptly ended the interview when Flood's name was mentioned. Initially, Flood may have come to Karl on official business, but his concern with the world of the homosexual was deeper than that, personal. If he was a covert homosexual . . .

Hellman's mind raced backward. All that he had been told about Masters amounted, as he'd realized before, to little more than rumor, gossip. In characterizing the Director as a homosexual, Joanna Cook was only repeating what she had been told by her brother's friend. And neither of them was a disinterested party. According to Sidney Karl, Masters sought a method to *exclude* sexual deviates from the Agency. Had he been able to identify any agents as homosexuals he would have fired them. Flood must have known this; as did any of his colleagues with the same sexual tastes. They had to realize that the IIA would not be a haven for them much longer, that Masters now posed a severe threat to their well-being. And realizing that, they decided to remove the Director. And the only way to do that was to kill him.

Hellman explored his reasoning again, trying to pick out the flaws. One item bothered him—the suicide of Paul Cook. Hellman packed an overnight bag, went out to LaGuardia Airport and boarded a shuttle flight to Washington. He would talk to Harvey Bass himself.

Harvey Bass was easy to locate; he was the only one by that name listed in the telephone directory. Hellman called and identified himself, said he wanted to talk about Paul Cook.

"I don't know anyone by that name," Bass said and hung up.

Hellman called back and nearly five minutes passed before Bass picked up the phone, responding in a sullen voice.

"Who are you?"

"Joanna Cook suggested I get in touch with you."

Bass said nothing and Hellman was afraid he was going to hang up again. He began to talk quickly. "Harvey, you can trust me. I don't intend to make trouble for you. But it's important that I see you, talk to you."

"I don't see why—"

"More and more homosexuals are coming out into the open," Hellman said toughly. "But you're not one of them, Bass. You don't sound very brave to me. Meet me somewhere, or I'll make a few phone calls. To the IIA, for example . . ."

"Why?" Bass said, voice growing tight. "I haven't done anything to you."

"Meet me. Pick a place."

There was a long silence and Hellman visualized Harvey Bass considering the situation, the risks involved. He wondered how Bass would decide?

"There's a bar," Bass said. "The Spotted Cat. I'll be there in twenty minutes."

"How will I know you?"

Bass laughed bitterly. "Ask for the ugly one. The one who looks like a truck driver." He slammed the phone down.

The Spotted Cat was located in the basement of an old town house in a quiet side street. Inside, psychedelic lights made seeing difficult and acid rock blasted out of concealed speakers. It was still early and only a few men were drinking.

The barman wiped the polished wood in front of Hellman. "What'll it be, luv?"

"I'm meeting Harvey Bass here."

"Oh, yes. He's sulking in the last booth on the right."

Hellman started back. "Send along a scotch on ice and another of whatever he's drinking."

Harvey Bass did look like a truck driver. Or a prizefighter. He was olive-complexioned, almost as dark as Hellman himself, with glowering black brows and a broken nose. There was a sullen, dissatisfied expression on his fleshy mouth and his deep eyes were flecked with red and watchful.

"I'm Hellman."

Bass said nothing.

Hellman sat down and grinned. "I'm glad to meet you too."

"I'm no hypocrite. Whoever you are, I'd like to break you in two."

Hellman leaned back and studied the other man. "From the look of you, you might be able to do it. But I didn't come to fight." The barman appeared, set the drinks in front of them and went away. "Tell me about Paul Cook."

"He's dead," Bass grunted. "There isn't anything else. Just life and death."

"Let's talk about his life."

"We worked together at Justice for a while. In the same department. Dammit, why am I talking to you?"

249

"Because you're not as tough as you look, Harvey. Because if you don't, I'll tell the IIA you've been shooting off your mouth about Masters being a fag. That should be reason enough!"

Bass folded his fingers into a lumpy fist. He glared at Hellman. Without warning, he smiled and his hand opened. He leaned back and spoke in a carefree voice. "Oh, what the hell! Ask me anything."

"Tell me about Paul Cook and Masters."

The dark eyes grew wary again. "There's nothing to tell."

"You're wasting my time, Harvey," Hellman drawled. "You and Paul were friends. You thought enough of him to seek out his sister and tell her about Paul and Masters. Now you're going to tell me the story, all of it."

Bass turned his face toward the wall. "You really don't know anything about it. *I* didn't go to her. *She* came after *me*. Paul must have mentioned my name to her. He always did talk too much. He had a big mouth. If he'd kept it shut more often he wouldn't be moldering in the grave right now."

"Joanna came to you?"

Bass shifted around to face Hellman. "How can I be sure that if I talk to you you won't expose me anyway?"

"Trust me, Harvey."

"Trust me, Harvey! Oh, that's very good. Let me tell you, I stopped trusting people when I discovered my mother was screwing my father and not me. Okay, okay, what do you want?"

"Tell me about Paul."

"He shoved his silly head into a gas oven and kept it there until he was thoroughly dead. End of story."

"Not a chance, Harvey. There's still W. W. Masters."

"Oh, God, I hate that man! What an unholy bitch! I'm glad somebody got him. I wish I had. He was no different than I am, a screaming faggot, a closet queen. Only he had power, real power, and he used it against us, against his own kind. What kind of a bastard would do that!"

"You're sure?"

"That Masters was gay! Oh, God, you better believe it!" The

heavy brows pulled down, masking off his eyes. "Paul could've vouched for it. Paul and I *were* friends. Just friends. We did things together and we talked. I knew about Masters from the first day they met. I warned him that it was a mistake. But he wouldn't listen. He loved it, being with somebody that important, I mean. I suppose most of us would—it's our arrested development, I suppose. Paul thought he had it made, that he could control Masters. The silly bastard."

"What happened?"

"Masters was too much for Paul. He overwhelmed him, made impossible demands, insisted he change his style of living. Paul was to be always available, to see nobody else. Masters would phone at odd hours, order Paul to meet him, or check to see whether or not he was at home."

"Do you think Paul might have been lying, that he wanted to make himself important by inventing an affair with Masters?"

"You must be kidding! Paul wouldn't lie to me. Anyway, I saw some of the evidence."

"What are you talking about?"

"Masters was a flake, a weirdo. He was into the S-M bag."

"S-M?"

"Sado-masochist. Masters got his jollies beating on pretty boys like Paul Cook. At first, he used one of those toy circus whips. Later it got really rough. One night he beat Paul with his cane. I saw the welts on Paul's back and his ribs were badly bruised."

"What happened next?"

"Paul's thinking was crazy. He talked about making Masters jealous, controlling him that way. He took up with Steve Houghton, a waiter in a ham-and-eggery. That's when it *really* got bad. Poor Steve, he never understood what happened. He was arrested for soliciting. He got out and was arrested again. One night he was mugged—by a couple of Masters' private specialists, I'm certain. He was beaten up pretty good and hospitalized.

"His first day out, or night, rather, he was jumped again and beaten again. Three days later his car was vandalized and a week later his apartment was burgled. Then he lost his job. That did it for Steve. He packed up and split. Last I heard he was living with an actor's agent above Sunset Strip, playing Queen of the Hill."

"What was Paul's reaction to all this?"

"He was really scared. Masters cut him off, of course. Simply stopped calling and wouldn't respond to Paul's calls. At Justice, Paul got a real shafting. He was given less and less meaningful work to do until finally he became the garbage man of the legal staff, getting all the junk jobs. They shifted him around without notice and criticized everything he did do."

"Did Masters explain this change of heart to Paul?"

"Now you're being funny, aren't you? Masters never gave reasons. Paul called him a couple of times at IIA headquarters, which was a mistake. He became obsessed with the idea of confronting Masters face to face. Paul was a switch-hitter, you see, and he went around beating his chest and saying *mea culpa* after every one of his little escapades. I suppose he wanted to clean out his system. Anyway, Masters was the wrong party to try it with. One night, very late, an IIA agent showed up at Paul's apartment."

"What was the agent's name?" Hellman said hopefully.

"I don't know. I don't think Paul knew."

"Did he describe him? Was he a blond man, heavy in the face and—?"

"Paul never said."

Disappointed, Hellman drank some scotch, told Bass to go on.

"A few days later, some vice squad fuzz picked Paul up. No charges were made and he was released."

"You're telling me the police pulled him off the street for no reason?"

Bass spoke with scorn in his heavy voice. "All of us oppressed minorities live with one foot in jail."

Hellman felt as if his circulation had slowed, his physical processes diminished. He believed what Harvey Bass was saying, but none of it seemed to bring the truth any closer. Abruptly, he corrected himself. He had verified Masters' relationship with Paul Cook, was convinced now of the Director's homosexuality. Masters and Paul Cook. Masters and Herman Flood. Perhaps the circle *was* closing. Or was it? And if so, with what significance?

"It was the obscene calls that finished Paul," Harvey Bass was saying. "Isn't that a stitch! You'd think a fag would love it, but it isn't that way at all. All that harassment, I guess Paul finally couldn't take it. He was not that strong, certainly not very brave, and when it got too bad he killed himself. That's what Masters wanted and he got his wish. He really was the murderer." He ended in an almost casual manner.

Hellman felt deflated, with no questions left to ask, with nothing to say. They finished their drinks in silence and Hellman paid the check. Together, they left the Spotted Cat. On the sidewalk, Hellman paused.

"I had to find out about Masters," he said.

Bass looked at him briefly. "I don't accept your apology. What difference could it make? Paul's dead, Masters is dead. It's all over."

"I hoped it might help me find the man who killed Masters."

"And has it?"

"Maybe. I wasn't sure about Masters before."

Bass grimaced. "And now you are?" Hellman nodded.

"When I heard Masters was dead, I laughed. I laughed and drank a toast in vintage champagne to whoever pulled the trigger. That man will always be a hero to me."

Hellman turned away just as a car pulled up to the curb. Three husky men stepped out. They reminded Hellman of Joe Capolino, the same thick bodies and the same cautious way of moving, the same baleful expression in their eyes.

"The two of you," one man said, showing a badge. "You're under arrest. Soliciting for immoral purposes. Get into the car . . ."

Harvey Bass began to laugh.

Hellman sat on the cold concrete floor and watched a fat cockroach hurry to freedom beneath the barred cell door. The creature seemed to know where it was going—unlike himself, Hellman thought.

The police had separated him from Harvey Bass soon after their arrival at this building, a holding station for prisoners. No one had spoken to them, even to tell them their rights. They hadn't been formally charged or allowed to call a lawyer. Hellman had been locked into this cell with only the cockroach for company. And now even he had found a way out.

Hellman tried not to consider the immediate predicament. Somehow he couldn't take it seriously, expected any moment to be released, to be told it was a mistake. He tried to recall Harvey Bass' words—"All of us oppressed minorities live with one foot in jail." But Hellman and Bass were not members of the same subculture, Hellman assured himself. Or were they? The trio of detectives who'd hauled them off the street had treated them alike.

Hellman put his mind to work, tried to hang it all together. Nothing happened. It was as if he had asked all the wrong questions, received the wrong answers. He went over everything, retracing his path from the beginning. At once a small, optimistic flame began to flicker and he strained to bring it up to full fire. Then it was there, filling his head, the way to answer all his questions, to find the answers he wanted, to discover who it was who had killed W. W. Masters.

The rattling of a key in the cell door made him look up. A guard motioned for him to come out. In the long, narrow receiving room, a sergeant returned his personal belongings. "You can go. Outside," the sergeant said.

Hellman obeyed. In front of the building, a long, gray Cadillac. A window rolled smoothly down and Sam Batsford's smiling face appeared. "Get in. I'll give you a lift."

Hellman climbed inside and the limousine eased into motion.

"Where are we going?" Hellman asked.

"The airport. You're on your way back to New York."

"You got me out?"

Batsford nodded, eyes on the road.

"Why?"

"Call it generosity of spirit."

"What took so long?"

Batsford threw a glance in his direction. "What do you mean?"

"You must've known the exact moment they took us there."

"You overestimate me."

"Then who tipped you?"

"Hellman, I'm disappointed. I never suspected you were a fag."

"You didn't answer my question."

"Officially, on police records, records which can easily be disseminated, should it become necessary, you are a homosexual." Batsford smiled thinly. "A thing like that could ruin a man, even one as apparently virile as you are."

"Abernathy again," Hellman said. "He's on my back since I went to Lanston. Well, I'm not so easily hassled. It might not be very hard to connect him and nephew Fred F. Calvin to Hilda Mann. Rape is a serious charge."

Batsford's long face drew down. "It's too bad that Hilda Mann is dead. But no charges were ever brought against that unfortunate young man . . ."

"Charges were brought!"

"No. Not officially. There is no record. Nor will there ever be. Believe me, Hellman. No one in Lanston will testify to what occurred. No one at all. If you think otherwise, then you're not as clever as I credit you with being." They drove without speaking for a few more minutes. "Didn't it occur to you, Hellman, that Harvey Bass would be under surveillance? He has been, for a long time. He's an unsavory young man. Certain people . . ."

"Abernathy."

"Don't be tiresome, Hellman, be smart. Let me say my speech. Certain nameless persons . . . are inclined to establish dossiers on certain other persons, as a protective device. Harvey Bass is linked closely with Paul Cook who was involved with Steve Houghton and so on and so on. Given the right set of circumstances, such information might prove useful."

"And now I'm linked to Bass?"

"Immutably. Some advice, Hellman—forget you ever went to Lanston. Forget also about Hilda Mann and about your meeting with Senator Abernathy. The Senator views it as a mistake in judgment on his part and is willing to forget it and allow you to do the same. The meeting never took place, in fact. My friends, Hellman, have close friends in various important sectors of public and private life. Mind your manners and you will never be bothered. Act up and you will inevitably discover that tonight's sojourn in the tank was only an hors d'oeuvre, a taste of what trouble can be."

Hellman spoke in a calm, quiet voice. "What about Harvey Bass? What's going to happen to him?"

"Your concern is commendable. Harvey will resign from his job in the morning and leave Washington without word to anyone. His friends will wonder about him, of course, but being the sort they are they will soon put him out of mind. Harvey will be done no injury, he will simply vanish and turn up elsewhere under another identity to begin a new life. No one expects you to do the same, Hellman, but your continued good behavior will be looked upon favorably."

Hellman said nothing; it was better that way.

XXV

MALONE MOVED through the darkness with neither stealth nor silence. He made his way through the woods behind Charles Reese's Connecticut home, taking pleasure in the resilient ground underfoot and in the fresh, green scent of pine.

Word came ten minutes after Hellman's departure—Mike Craig's car had been spotted by the State Police on a back road. By the time Malone made the helicopter trip from New York, the car had been found empty and out of gas only a few miles from the Reese estate. There was no trace of Craig. Malone had ordered a tight security net thrown up, then sent the troopers and local police into the woods after the retired fireman.

Malone listened to the curses of the police as they stumbled, bumped into trees in the dark. Their flashlight beams reached óut eerily in the night, criss-crossing, isolating each other. It would have been easy for a marksman to pick off one or two of them without being spotted. But Malone was convinced that Mike Craig would not kill a policeman; it would have been out of character.

Malone's foot caught on an exposed root and he almost went down. He righted himself and went on. He wanted the old fireman; by going after Charles Reese this way, Craig was proving his guilt. Any reasonable jury would agree.

Craig presented Malone with a chance to write finish to the case. His conviction would end the investigation for all time; he had the motive and the ability to kill and only his age had caused him to miss. It made sense; it would make sense to any other investigator, to the press; the American people would be calmed, understand that justice had been done, that murder committed in any cause had to be punished. Malone touched the pistol at his belt, loosened it in its holster. Craig was a dangerous man; his death would displease no one.

"Over here!" came the excited cry of a trooper. Booted feet went pounding through the woods. "Don't shoot!" someone shouted. "Hold your fire!"

Malone took his hand away from his gun and went toward the sounds, the dancing fingers of light. Troopers stood in a semi-circle around Mike Craig, flashlights trained on him. He sprawled against the base of a tree, a tall man with the big, rangy body of an athlete gone soft. His eyes were lidded and unseeing and spittle seeped from the corner of his mouth. A damp circle stained his khakis where he had lost control and his hands trembled uncontrollably.

"Pathetic old bastard," a trooper muttered. "Out of his head."

Another trooper picked up Mike Craig's rifle, pulled back the bolt. "Empty. The poor sonuvabitch didn't even load up."

Malone kneeled alongside Craig and went through his pockets. He found half a dozen catridges, a pipe and some tobacco, and a small book covered in green leather. Malone opened it: Marie Craig's diary. He stood up and looked around.

"Somebody see that the old man is taken home. No reason to make anything out of this, is there?"

The trooper in charge answered at once. "No reason at all . . ."

Charles Reese, in pajamas and a seersucker robe, ushered Malone into the library. It was a pleasant room, book-lined, with white rattan furniture. Lamps threw a soft, yellow light, lent an air of intimacy to the moment. When they were seated, Reese gazed at Malone with restrained interest.

"Sorry you had to come out at night this way, all for nothing."

"It might have been serious."

"Craig was a misguided old man. I'm sorry for him."

Malone displayed the green leather book. "Craig was carrying this," he said. "It's Marie's diary. Craig lived with the information in this book for a long time."

'You've read it, Malone?"

"Enough to know about you and Marie. Craig had a reason for wanting you dead."

Reese laughed easily. "Really, Malone. Let's not make this into a Victorian melodrama."

"You don't deny it?"

"Deny what?"

"That Marie Craig was your mistress."

"That word, Malone. That *is* old-fashioned."

"Marie Craig is dead because of you," Malone said, the words coming out in that deliberate style of his.

"Marie Craig is dead," Reese replied, with obvious distaste, "because she was a foolish girl with no self-control. Politics, I'm afraid, is well populated with her kind. Pretty secretaries and receptionists who are fascinated by power, drawn to it, to its practitioners. Power is very much what politics is about, Malone, and it is one hell of an aphrodisiac."

"The girl is dead and you don't care."

"Don't judge me, Malone. You're not equipped for the job. I don't feel guilt over Marie." Reese sighed, an expression of regret at the turn the conversation had taken. "Malone, Marie was beautiful, very young, sensual. I wanted her. It's that simple. I wanted her, I had to have her. Haven't you ever *had* to have someone, Malone? Even when you knew that she wasn't right for you, that it would be a mistake in the long run? Haven't you ever done something that was . . . well, irrational, uncontrollable?"

A suite of related images stuttered onto the screen of Malone's mind, brilliant images that caused him to shudder and turn away, close them off. Sounds of protest, of fear and despair, echoed in the depths of his skull.

"No," Reese went on, when Malone offered no reply. "Of course you never did. You're a rational man, with all your emotions firmly in check." The corners of his mouth lifted in an understanding smile. "You're very much like Masters, I think."

"An agent fulfills the demands of his job without thought of personal gratification."

"All men demand something of life. Some make the demand out of weakness, others out of strength. Let's leave the care of my soul to my confessor, shall we?" The ingratiating smile returned and as quickly went away. "You are a Catholic, aren't you, Malone?"

Malone tried to recall when he had last been inside a church. He had attended parochial schools, been an altar boy, gone to Mass regularly. Until abruptly it had all stopped being meaningful. All ceremonial shadow and pious bleatings of the priests who understood nothing of his life, of his requirements.

"There is no God," Malone heard himself say, and was shocked. He had never voiced that sentiment aloud before.

Reese lifted his brows in mild surprise, decided to drop the subject. "What are you going to do, Malone, reopen the case. Why? You'll only reopen the grief of those people who care about Marie."

"You lied, Senator."

Reese's face closed defensively. He stared at Malone for a long interval. "I could order you out of this house, Malone. I'm a Senator of the United States. But I'm not really angry with you, I discover. A little envious, perhaps, because you seem to be a man who doesn't know how to lie, doesn't know how to dissemble. Still, I don't envy you your inability to understand such a weakness in someone else. Yes, I lied. Most men do. How else can we survive?" The thin sound of complaint edged Reese's voice and Malone perceived the aristocratic face in misted outline; it appeared to be altered, yet a very familiar persona. For a blink of time he imagined he was again looking at W. W. Masters. He leaned forward, spoke harshly.

"Senator, how did Marie Craig die?"

"Exactly as Martin testified. Marie drank too much. And she used drugs. Oh, not that she was an addict; she wasn't. But she smoked pot, sometimes used speed, and LSD. On the night she died, she had dropped acid, not telling me until afterward. She was feeling very good, light and airy were the words she used. She began to talk about being a bird, about flying. Before I could stop her, she went out of the window of Martin's apartment. Afterward, Martin offered to take my place. Had I been another man, I would surely have faced the consequences. But I am Charles Reese, Malone, and I intend to become President of the United States . . ."

Malone arrived in New York at three in the morning. He padded through empty streets without purpose, making an effort to arrange all the elements into a coherent whole. His flesh drew tight to a point beyond pain and a silent scream oozed out of unmapped regions of memory . . .

"The Agency is life . . . is to be served . . . to serve . . ."

His eyes blinked without control and he braced himself against the hurt and the discomfort. A man did what was expected of him, fulfilling his oath . . .

"Liars betray the public trust . . . sensualists are weak and unfit . . . ambition betrays the just man . . ."

He pressed his palms against his trousers as if to scrub away a layer of dirt. Suddenly he felt weak, with no central source from which to extract direction and strength. Fear came and made him cold and he drifted through the city, unable to know where he would finally be set down.

"There is no one . . . no one else . . . no stain . . ."

His mind tipped and tilted, seeking a quiet place. He felt himself at the mercy of a storm that pelted him with its rising fury. Unable to locate himself in the black emptiness, he broke into a run . . .

XXVI

It HAD gone beyond profit or pride, beyond right or wrong. Hellman was obsessed, driven. He could see that with each step he'd taken in his bizarre search he had been enticed, coerced, kept in motion and off-base by forces operating for their own concealed reasons; or seduced by his own compulsive ambitions away from the truth. But no more; now he knew where to look.

It had begun to surface back in that police cell in Washington. Karl had talked of being interviewed by an IIA agent. When Hellman asked if the agent were really a patient, Karl professionally refused to discuss the possibility, but he didn't really deny it. And he did launch into a clinical explanation of sex and degrees of homosexual interest in men that hardly applied to an agent on official business.

Hellman wanted to know the identity of that agent, recalling how abruptly Karl had ended their interview at the mention of Herman Flood. He wanted to know what secrets rested in Karl's files. By the time his plane landed at LaGuardia, Hellman knew exactly what he was going to do.

He went directly to his apartment, trying to remember everything his father had taught him; and all of Capolino's refinements, picked up over the years. He put on a quiet, gray business suit with a navy-blue shirt and striped tie. His shoes were black bluchers with crepe soles; as silent and sure-footed as sneakers and not nearly so conspicuous.

Satisfied with his appearance, he went into the kitchen and from a storage drawer withdrew a soft plastic case. He spread it open on the table and chose three tools of varying sizes, a glass-cutter and a small suction cup attached to a short length of wood. He slipped them into his pockets and left.

He walked rapidly to the Murray Hill area. By the time he reached the town house, Hellman had become intensely aware of his own body and mind, had plotted every move he was going to make. He felt as if he were functioning at the outer limits of his abilities.

A quick glance up and down the street revealed no one. Hellman took the steps three at a time. In the small, dimly lit outer lobby, he worked swiftly, using a tool very much like a dentist's pick to open the spring lock. It gave him no trouble, catching almost at once, the door giving way under the steady pressure of his shoulder. He stepped inside.

He crossed the musty foyer to Sidney Karl's office. At a point no more than four inches from the lower left corner of the door frame, he attached the suction cup to the glass. Using the glass cutter, he scratched a square around it, then sliced deeply into the pane. Using the handle of the cutter, he tapped along the cut, worked the square out of the panel. He reached through the aperture and opened the Segal locks, went into the apartment. He closed the door and secured the glass square back in place with strips of Scotch tape.

When his eyes were accustomed to the dark, he went down the long hallway to Sidney Karl's private office. He closed the blinds and drew the drapes, turned on a lamp.

He began to search through the file cabinets but was unable to locate a listing for Herman Flood. He went through the drawers a second time and failed again. A rising anxiety gripped him and he wondered if he was wrong again. He fought against doubt, telling himself that Flood's name had to be somewhere in these files.

He read the labels on the front of each drawer. One was marked "Research" and he opened it, flipped through the folders. Midway along, he found what he was looking for, neatly lettered: "IIA." Hellman almost laughed aloud.

He emptied the folder onto the refectory table. A number of yellow legal pages were clipped together, all filled with what he took to be Karl's notes; and five tape cassettes.

Hellman tried to read the first page but was too impatient to decipher Karl's scrawl. He turned to the tapes. Surely they would tell him what he wanted to know.

He read the labels: "IIA Interview #1, #2, #3, #4, #5." Each one was dated, all prior to the Masters killing. Hellman snapped the first cassette into Karl's recorder, hesitated, finger on the starter button. Time mattered suddenly, time and information. He removed the cassette, replaced it with the one marked "#3." He started the machine, adjusted the volume, and hunched forward to listen. He recognized Karl's faintly accented speech . . .

"We begin once more. You understand, these time lapses are not a good thing. Continuity is vital to the therapeutic process . . ."

A second voice came on, distant and muffled. "Work comes first. You know that."

"Yes, yes. No demands are made here. It is my job to listen, perhaps to help." There was a static silence and Hellman grew restless. He turned up the volume. Karl spoke again. "Some days it is difficult to speak. That is all right, very natural."

The muffled voice said, "What help can you give?"

"I try."

"It's always been the other way around. Agents are supposed to help other people. Goddamn!" The volume indicator leaped wildly. "Sorry, doctor. Mr. Masters doesn't approve agents swearing."

"You have a right to be angry."

"A man should be able to control his emotions, his language."

"Always?"

"Mr. Masters has been very clear on that point. An agent without self-discipline is an agent disposed to error. A man should know what he's doing every second. Precision in all things . . ."

"Most people would find that very difficult."

"Most people cannot become agents."

"You're proud of your work?"

"A man should take pride in his work. That's one of the

problems in the world, a failure of pride in the things men do. The old-fashioned virtues—pride, courage, accomplishment, these are not respected anymore. There is nothing more rewarding than serving your country, working for a man like the Director—"

Again the silence, longer this time, and strangely ominous. Alone in Karl's office, his apprehension increasing, Hellman willed the voices to begin speaking again.

"Suppose we review," Karl said at last. "You came first to me on Agency business . . ."

"The Director is a meticulous man. He wants more information about your study. He recognizes the possibility of human error, wants to close the door firmly against . . . unqualified people."

"You mean homosexuals, don't you?"

"Those articles you wrote. They make the Agency look like a private club for them."

"Does the word offend you?"

"People read your articles and tend to believe the worst. It's the way they are. They make obscene jokes, they laugh."

Listening, Hellman thought he perceived a detached quality in the voice as if its owner were compartmentalized, with certain vital connections severed so that he had become a man out of touch with his source.

"The articles are technical in content and style," Karl said. "The *Journal* has a limited, professional readership. Also, the research was diversified; it included other male bondings—"

"Always the sordid implication. Can't you understand there is a brotherhood of real men? Men dedicated and together without being . . ."

"Without being homosexuals?"

"Without being . . . weaklings."

"Explain that to me."

The tape was silent and Hellman's anxiety grew. Then the voice spoke again. ". . . He was an aberration. When he discovered what he was he . . ."

"Who?"

"He took his own life . . . a coward."

"Why did this man kill himself?"

2 6 5

"He found out what he was . . ."

"A homosexual?" Karl asked. "What did you have to do with him?"

"Nothing." It came out reflexively. Then, more hesitantly. "There was an investigation. Routine . . . *he was in the government!*" The voice tightened. "He had to be removed. Masters gave orders."

"To do what?"

"Talk to him, Masters told me. See that he does no damage."

"This man, he knew who you were?"

"There was no reason for him to know. He should have left the government immediately, left Washington. He had every opportunity to protect himself, to do the right thing."

"What did he do?"

"He said that Mr. Masters was no different than he was, that all of us were the same, that his sickness was in all of us . . ."

Hellman stopped the machine. Paul Cook; everything that disembodied voice was saying referred to Joanna's dead brother. This was the agent Masters had sent to harass Paul, to drive him, finally, to suicide. He must have been a tortured man, carrying an awful guilt with a deeply painful, private knowledge of W. W. Masters, a knowledge he couldn't really handle. Hellman punched the starter button and the tape groaned to life.

"Let's discuss Masters," Karl was saying.

"The man was incredible," the agent replied.

"You see no hypocrisy in him? Wasn't he a creature of his own making, born of his own will and ambition? A myth, a self-made legend?"

"You don't know what you're talking about!"

"Isn't it so, that Masters used the Agency to achieve personal and political advantage?"

"No!"

"Were you upset at all by Masters' relationship with Paul Cook . . ."

"No!"

"Were you jealous? Did you want to destroy Paul Cook?"

"No! *Goddamn you . . .*"

2 6 6

There were loud noises on the tape, a heavy thump, and the sound of harsh breathing.

"Ah," Karl's voice said presently. "Just an inexpensive ashtray." Hellman thought he sounded nervous. "I try to discourage violence, especially in a man who is so expert at it. You move so swiftly. I consider myself very fortunate."

The voice was low and soft. "There was no reason for that. It shouldn't have been done."

"This time," Karl said, "you cannot deny that you were angry, very angry."

"And you were frightened, doctor, weren't you?"

A mocking edge had come into the voice on the tape. Hellman strained to match it with Herman Flood's voice. He recalled Flood's sardonic manner. He couldn't be sure. Damn it, voices on tape, without the physical presence of the speaker, were so tough to identify—even when you knew the speaker. . . .

"The ashtray missed my head by only an inch or so. Had it struck me, I could have been badly hurt."

"Most people are afraid of physical violence."

"One of the rewards of your work?"

"What do you mean?"

"That an agent, aware that fear exists in most people, uses that fear against them."

"The Agency never uses intimidation. Still, why not use a person's weakness against him? Every effective weapon must be enlisted in the struggle against . . ."

"Do you ever feel fear?"

"Agents are trained to use their bodies as a weapon . . . a defensive weapon. A good agent never thinks about his own welfare—he does what he must."

"And you *had* to throw that ashtray at me? Did you want to hurt me?"

"There's no reason to hurt anybody."

"Yet you have hurt people."

"No!" There was a short wait. When the voice spoke again it was strong. "Accidents occur in the line of duty. There is a war going on, a war most people don't know about. Every agent has taken an oath—"

"This business of hurting people," Karl interrupted. "It interests me."

"Violence fascinates most people, but they won't admit it."

"You did. At the start of our second interview you mentioned it, and our relationship was no longer the same. We became therapist and patient. Shall I play the tape for you?"

A sound—almost inaudible, despairing? Hellman wasn't sure.

"It was an accident. There was a report that black militants were planning an indiscriminate attack on white citizens. They had a supply of guns, ammunition, explosives. These things must be dealt with. Mr. Masters issued orders."

"What orders?"

"There was shooting, the girl ran out of the shack. At that distance, in the confusion, it was impossible to see who it was. She was hit . . ."

"You told another version last time," Karl said gently.

"I only know the truth."

"Let me play the tape for you . . ."

The agent was coughing. Hellman willed the tape to run faster. After a while the voice returned. "Masters said go to Lanston. Two men from the Mobile bureau were assigned to me. The girl was mixed up with armed insurrection, with revolution. She was a danger to security, you can see that. She was a leader, a demagogue . . ."

"Masters said that?"

"She had to be removed, can't you see? They were all given a chance to come out, to surrender. They refused. They *cursed* us, defied us. We represented legitimate authority, the *government*. Someone began to shoot."

"Who fired first?"

"The girl ran very well, I remember, very fast . . ."

"You shot her?"

"She was an enemy . . . She was *Masters'* enemy . . ."

"Masters never actually ordered you to kill her?"

268

"He wanted her removed," the voice insisted.

"But he didn't order her killed. No such order was ever given . . ."

"Every agent knows his job. Knows what is expected of him."

"You assumed Masters wanted the girl to be shot. And so you killed her. You must face this . . ."

"Dammit, Hellman! What are you doing here!"

Startled, Hellman looked up and saw Sidney Karl in the doorway, holding tight to a fireplace poker in his upraised right fist.

Hellman fought for control. Moving deliberately, he punched the off-key on the tape machine, leaned back in Karl's chair.

"Doctor," he said heavily. "You have got a problem!"

Karl, the poker raised menacingly, stepped further into his office. "A thief is what you are, Hellman! A burglar! To break into my office! What could you be thinking—?"

Anger dominated the fear in Hellman; he came up to his feet swiftly, leaning forward, tension in every line of his muscular body.

Karl stood his ground, the poker wavering in silent threat. "I'm not afraid of you. This is my office and you have no right to be here."

"Let's talk about rights, about your right to conceal a murderer."

The long face drew down mournfully. "I don't know what you mean."

Hellman came out from behind the desk, eyes fixed on Karl.

"Stay away!" Karl said, the poker coming up, holding his ground. "I'll use this if I have to."

Hellman took a forward step.

"Stop! I want you to know—I anticipated this, I called the police."

"The hell you did," Hellman said, but he wasn't sure.

"A neighbor reported a prowler, called me . . ."

Hellman smiled. "Doctor, the police would've been here first, at this hour of the morning. No, something else brought you. What was it?"

"I have nothing to say to you."

Hellman took a deep breath. "Who murdered Masters?" he said.

Karl's lips pressed together. "You have no right to be here. No right to invade my files. The information they contain is private, protected, it concerns my patients."

"Exactly! Your patient, that nameless agent-patient. Doctor, we are talking about a man who has killed at least once. We both know he murdered Hilda Mann. It was done *for* W. W. Masters, who did it *for* Senator Leland Abernathy . . ."

"I don't know—"

"Political favors, doctor. And I'm sure that it never became necessary for either Abernathy or Masters ever to use the word kill. They *knew*, each of them knew, what was wanted and they performed accordingly. Masters and Malone. Just a friendly little favor. Murder in the line of duty. And there's more, doctor—the matter of Paul Cook."

Karl, watching Hellman warily, lowered the poker. "You know about Paul Cook?"

"Not only from the tapes, doctor. There are other sources."

Karl shook his head. "Whatever you're trying to accomplish, your methods are offensive. You must go. I want you to go!"

Hellman took a forward step. "Make up your mind, Karl. You are going to talk to me."

Karl moved back, the poker swinging up. It was an ineffectual gesture. Hellman reached quickly and twisted and the poker came away in his hands. He tossed it aside. "Stick to fixing heads, doctor."

"I will not be intimidated."

Hellman spread his hands. "Doctor, please, talk to me. Do it the easy way. Must I listen to every inch of tape? Must I read your notes page by page? I know everything will be there. Please. Sooner or later this is going over to the police. That will mean serious trouble for you . . ."

"You will find no name mentioned anywhere, nor will you get one from me. There is nothing you can do that will force me to divulge—"

"The man on the tape," Hellman said. "He is obviously deeply disturbed, sick, desperate to approve of himself. What a shock it must have been for him to discover his entire life was a fraud, that he'd wasted himself on a false god, and a false church. His self-hatred must have been monumental, doctor."

"There is some truth . . ."

Hellman pointed to the tape machine. "That man killed W. W. Masters!"

"*I* don't know that."

"Doctor, here is a man who held close to his manhood the way a child hangs onto a favorite doll. A man so vulnerable, so threatened, that he carefully erected special defenses around himself, structuring every detail of his existence. Someone gets beyond those defenses, wounds him critically."

"Perhaps you should be the psychiatrist," Karl said, looking away. "Obviously, I overestimated your good sense and ability to understand our *general* conversation."

"Masters seemed like the perfect man," Hellman went on, ignoring him. "Your patient—and sooner or later you'll have to stop protecting him—must have tried to turn himself into a reflection of Masters, until the mirror broke and he saw only his betrayed innocence."

"All supposition."

"More than that, and you know it, doctor. Masters had to be killed, from your patient's point of view. Senator Reese's presence that night, it confused the issue. It made us all look for political motives. But that man killed because he finally came to understand that he had been betrayed by Masters and by Masters' system, by all those Boy Scout rules he had lived by."

"Few of us so-called normal people can exist for long without illusions," Karl said. "Tonight, when I spoke to this man—"

"What?"

"He came to see me, at my home. He was extremely agitated, almost incoherent."

"You saw him tonight?"

"No more than half an hour ago."

"Where is he now?" Hellman shouted.

"Oh, please. I will not be shouted at. This is all so difficult for me."

"You let him get away."

"What do you expect of me? This is a violent person. He carries a gun."

"Where did he go?"

"I don't know. Hellman, I'm sorry. Maybe you could have stopped him. I couldn't. He came and woke me, talked and then went away. It may be unprofessional, but I admit it to you, when he left I was glad."

"Did he indicate where he was going?"

"In no way."

"The man is a killer. He may do it again."

Karl shook his head. "That's why I came here at this hour. He seemed out of control . . . I tried to administer medication but he refused. To go back to sleep was impossible so I decided to study my notes, listen to the tapes. In that way, I thought I might find a way to help him, to anticipate him . . ."

"Did he talk about anyone in particular?"

"Only Masters."

"Always Masters."

"This time was different. This time he showed antagonism toward the man, the first time I heard him do so. He called him a hypocrite . . . and then mentioned Senator Reese . . ."

Hellman was sure now. "What else?"

"I was frightened. In all these years, he is the first patient who actually frightened me . . ."

"Did he threaten you?"

"He said, 'There is no one else. No one to save us, no one to remove the corruption.' "

"Did he talk about killing again?"

"He never used the word, still . . . I had the impression he wanted to say more, was trying to explain himself, perhaps to me, perhaps to himself. But no words came. And after a moment or so he walked out of my office."

Hellman got up. "He's going to do it again."

"How can you be sure?"

"He killed Masters. That was supposed to make the world right, purify it and avenge himself. But this is a man who needs someone to follow, someone to look up to. With Masters gone, he looked for another leader, someone to transfer his loyalties to. He found Senator Reese. And I don't need to tell you inevitably Reese didn't measure up either."

Hellman's strength seemed to leave his body. This time he knew he was right; there was no mistake. Everything he had ever wanted was going to come real for him now. And in his triumph he could feel nothing at all.

He knew what was going to happen, knew what he had to do. He reached for the telephone and dialed the police. . . .

XXVII

SECONDS TICKED away inexorably inside Malone's head. Timing had become crucial.

He drove slowly, finding a parking space under a street lamp in a side street near Tenth Avenue, secure in the shadows cast. There was a sense of *déjà vu,* of having done all this before.

Hands moving with practiced skill, he drew a false mustache from a plastic case on the seat alongside. He spit on the adhesive, moistened his upper lip, and fastened it into place. He studied himself in the rearview mirror. The brooding face of a Western gunfighter stared back at him, solemn and dangerous.

He got out of the car and took the guitar case out of the trunk, strode up the street, pacing himself deliberately. The route had already been plotted . . .

When?

Wild images swooped through his brain, searing ecstasy. There was much to remember; and things he had to forget. This was a most important assignment, *the* most important . . .

"The job you're on, Peter, is the one that matters . . ."

The Director's voice sounded cheerful inside Malone's head and he was glad. He wanted always to please Mr. Masters.

For what we are about to do, oh, Lord, we thank thee . . .

The words jarred Malone and he cautioned himself to concentrate, to be alert, aware of what was going on around him. *"Function at the peak of your powers always, Peter."* Masters had caused him to be better than he was, had taught him everything he knew until they thought as one, reacted as one. Distance had never really separated them and Malone was sure that he understood and was understood by the Director in the absence of spoken words.

The sound level grew louder as Malone came into the midtown area, the streets crowded with people and cars. No one paid any attention to him, a gray man in a gray suit, indistinguishable from anyone else. There was no way they could know he was *their* agent, doing their work, protecting their lives.

He checked his watch as he approached the building. Right on schedule. The watchman would be making his first inspection tour of the night; at this moment, he was on the fourth floor, seeing that lights were extinguished and doors were locked. Without haste or hesitation, Malone went up to the entrance and using the master key he had prepared himself, unlocked the doors as he had done before . . .

Before!

He struggled to recall and a dim vision faded into view. It flickered, then held steady. He saw Masters, that elegantly evil face so smug in the conviction that he was beyond the laws that governed lesser men, believing that he could escape judgment, escape punishment.

But Malone would not allow that to happen. He would do something about it. Had done so already, he corrected silently. He had looked down along the barrel of his rifle, squeezing inexorably on the trigger, waiting for that explosion to erupt . . .

The Director was dead; Malone had killed him. Or had he?

He could take no chances; he had to be sure. Masters had so very shrewdly insinuated himself under Malone's skin, into the marrow of his being, and he still existed there. Thinking became increasingly difficult; and Malone closed off his brain as he stepped inside the building lobby, locking the doors behind him.

On the emergency stairs, he climbed carefully, making no unnecessary noise. *Walk softly, swiftly* . . . He moved confidently in the darkness, was thoroughly prepared, able to run this course during the day without notice.

Yes, that accounted for the familiarity . . .

On the second floor, he turned a corner, stopped at a door that read:

Malone reached in his pocket and withdrew a second key; this one identified by a dot of red polish. He opened the door and went inside.

Soon his eyes grew accustomed to the darkened office. He picked his way into an adjoining room, past some metal desks. Now, he commanded himself, prepare as before . . .

Before . . .

A flush of triumph. Everything had gone so well the last time, each step thoroughly planned and rehearsed, executed with precision. He had remained cool, nerves controlled, his aim unimpaired. A single shot had destroyed Masters for all time

He hadn't wanted to kill even as he knew that he must. He had tried to stop himself, knowing that he could not be stopped. *It had to be done.* . . . There was no other way.

He almost smiled. Masters would have approved of the way he had dealt with this assignment, solving all problems as they arose, perceiving obstacles and finding ways to bypass them. He had been proud to accept the case as his own. Masters would have approved; he had fulfilled the highest demands made by the Agency on an agent, operating at maximum efficiency as he sought the assassin, who it now seemed was . . .

Remembering was not good. It diverted a man from what had to be done, made him question his commitment, confused him. He didn't want to remember, would close off the past as he had before . . .

Before . . .

He went to the window and made a brief assessment of the street below. Almost reluctantly, as if the effort tired his arms, he raised the window. He considered the result, then pulled down the old green shade until the glass was masked off. He rolled a typist's chair over, sat down, and lifted the guitar case onto his lap.

The ticking inside his head grew louder while he waited for the time to be right. He heard people laughing and he grew angry; this was a serious affair.

Betrayal had to be punished. Corruption wiped out. Threats to the nation had to be eliminated. Malone's body tensed into a spasm and he opened the guitar case. All the parts were secure. Working deliberately, he peeled away the tape, wiped each part with a clean, dry cloth. He fitted the barrel into the stock, inserted the trigger mechanism and locked it all together.

The solid weight of the rifle, so cool and reassuring, so smooth and powerful. He sighted down on the hotel steps and squeezed the trigger. *Clunk.* A satisfying response. He leaned the weapon against the wall and listened to the night sounds, heard again the terrible ringing.

Who called?

That unknown voice. Tinged with mockery, with danger, cunning and smug. The voice of a priest.

He sat straighter. A priest. All of them sounded that way, all the Brothers at the Academy of the Sacred Blood. Sly, cruel men, so quick to ridicule, to punish. So ready to hit.

A renewal of disappointment took hold of him and a clouded uncertainty. Serrated echoes prodded the lining of his memory and he braced himself against them, struggled to concentrate on what had to be done.

Must do . . .

Arrangements had been made. "Give me a number where you can be reached," Masters had told him. "I'll give you thirty minutes notice. Bring the car to the hotel. I hate to be kept waiting."

All that was behind, the memories buried where they could do no damage, leaving his mind clear and alert, prepared to act. *"Don't look backward, Peter. Always ahead, toward the future . . ."* And always before he had been able to obey. Only now was the past escaping out of the dark portions of his brain into the light. He fought against the memory.

Increased activity in the street drew his eyes into focus. Soon it would be over and they would all be safe again. Sweat broke on Malone's wrist and he changed the position of his watch. The target was late.

Why?

Kneeling now, peering through the window opening. All the

people oblivious to the plots against them, blind to the dangers. How naive they were! How trusting! Even as he had come to trust Charles Reese, to look to him for guidance. But the Senator too had failed him, deceived him. Charles Reese had wasted himself on Marie Craig, had fouled himself . . .

The world had to recognize the truth . . .

The rifle was in Malone's hands, the barrel pressed against his mouth, the steel so smooth and cool. With no lost motion a cartridge was inserted into the chamber, the bolt shot, the butt snapped up, the rifle brought to bear on the steps of the hotel.

The street sounds grew louder, painful, a closing scream in the night that might have been the wail of a siren. The wood-warmth of the stock brought comfort to his cheek. No more to be used in behalf of evil . . .

"Evil must be rooted out and punished . . ."

Masters' words. Malone had lived by them, would continue to live by them. Malone focused on the present. The past contained only disappointment and pain. Sweat gleamed on his brow, his eyes blurred. Coming out of the hotel—two men.

Squint, strain, be *sure*. Yes, no mistake there. Masters and Reese, arm in arm, laughing and talking as if everything were all right.

The rifle came down, wavered, refused to hold on the target. The watch on his wrist was heavy and oppressive. It was put aside.

This time his left elbow was planted on his knee in the accepted form, the rifle steady, a man ready and able to do the correct thing. A single shot had been enough last time . . .

What?

That elegant face swam into view, balanced delicately on the front sight of the rifle. The face of betrayal, of treachery. A face that had to be removed.

Sirens were screaming louder, coming closer, but the man on the rifle didn't hear. There was a procedure to be followed. Lungs filled with air, a slight exhalation, and the rifle was held on line.

The trigger squeezed . . .

THIS BOOK WAS DESIGNED BY IRVING PERKINS,
THE TYPE FACE USED IS TIMES ROMAN
AND THE BOOKS WERE COMPOSED, PRINTED AND BOUND BY
THE BOOK PRESS, BRATTLEBORO, VERMONT